PRAISE FOR CRA

"Craig Wallwork has a strong and steady voice, well deserving your time and attention" Dan Fante, author of Chump Change.

"Tune your ear to Craig Wallwork's prose and you'll soon make a fascinating discovery: he's really funny. And he's a damned fine writer." Mark SaFranko, author of Lounge Lizard.

"Craig Wallwork's The Sound of Loneliness has a few things in common with the agonized work of Thomas Bernhard, where the pain of ailment sometimes crosses the threshold of pleasure, and the reader is revolted and riveted at the same time. I enjoyed my time in Wallwork's pages." Kyle Minor, author of In the Devil's Territory

"Wallwork is a hugely creative thinker. An emerging talent who won't take long to reach the limelight." Nigel Bird, author of Dirty old Town.

"If Etgar Keret had grown up in northern England instead of Israel, he might've turned out to be Craig Wallwork, but Wallwork hits harder and more often, both with the humor and insight." Lit Pub

"Craig Wallwork's writing is adventurous and comical, and joyfully anarchic. His work is always compelling and exciting to read." 3AM Magazine.

"Like a Grindhouse version of Grimm's Fairy Tales, Wallwork's fiction is smart, innovative, and a hell of a lot of fun." - Carlton Mellick III.

"Only a writer of Wallwork's talent can create such a viscerally encompassing experience that leaves you with literal nightmares. Gory Hole isn't just a trip down a rabbit's hole, but a gory plunge." - Peter Tieryas Liu, author of Bald New World.

BAD PEOPLE

Craig Wallwork

Copyright

ISBN 9781657186675

Underbelly Books

To my parents, for keeping me safe.

PROLOGUE

The young man was unconscious when they pulled him out of the car. Lip busted, chin and neck bloodstained. Before the chloroform wore off, the two men would need to bind his ankles and wrists with rope, gag his mouth with a strip of cloth. If they didn't, and there was a struggle, they'd have to kill him. Slade, the taller and much skinner of the two men, didn't want that, not right away. Slade wanted the young man to understand how he was going to die. He wanted to see the fear in his eyes before they closed for the final time.

Slade cut the car engine, turned off the headlamps, and helped pull the young man out of the car. The old abandoned water works at Blackthorn Hill stood in the distance like a crouching demon, its windows like eyes, black and infinite. The wind coming off the moorland sounded like its breath, and Slade thought he could hear it say to him, *Bring the boy to me. Bring me another sacrifice.* A fine white dust collected along the young man's hands as they dragged him through the filtration plant to the engine room. Discarded glass cut his skin, and against the chalky dust, blood seeped out of the cuts like poppies in a snowfield. In the recesses of crumbling brickwork, pigeons fluttered recklessly around the ceiling as Slade slammed the door behind them. He watched as they settled on steel girders, allied in rows of over a dozen; an audience waiting to be entertained; a jury observing a sentence.

They placed him in the centre of the room. Slade looked down at the young man. He was in his late twenties, thin as a rail, but handsome. It was easy to see why those perverts wanted to sleep with him. When Slade pulled the car up on some back street in the city where only lonely men drive down, he knew the boy was the one. He saw innocence in his expression, a guilelessness that would be a real turn on for some. *You want to party*, the young man had asked when Slade wound down his window. *Sure*, he replied. *Get in*. They headed out of the city, along the long stretch of motorway that flanked the Yorkshire moorland, the same where Hindley and Brady buried all those children in the 1960s. No names were given during the journey, so the young man referred to Slade as Sweetie, Darling, Babe. *You mind if I smoke, Sweetie?* he asked. Slade shrugged. The young man lit up and tendered what services he would offer, and for what price. Slade played along. He said he liked the young man's eyes. *They're pretty, like diamonds.* The young man smiled and placed his hand on Slade's thigh. *You've got nice eyes too*, he said. It was probably a line, but Slade drank in the compliment, thirsty for it. By the time they reached the A road outside the small village of Stormer Hill, the young man had smoked two cigarettes. They passed a lay-by and the offer of a blowjob was tendered. Slade said he was shy. *It's my first time.* The young man believed him. The car took a sharp left about a mile down the road, taking them along a dirt path cut into the moorland. The young man wanted to know where they were going. *It's a secret*, Slade kept telling him. *I'm shy. I can't do this where people might see.* Slade saw from the corner of his eye the young man squinting, as if trying to get some idea of where he was. It was dark on that moorland, the kind of dark where nothing exists beyond the windscreen but ten feet of road, pale as corpse skin. Moths threw themselves at the headlamps. Gravel struck the underbelly of the car. The young man told Slade to stop. *Take me back to the city. You can keep your money.* There was no 'Sweetie' this time, no 'Darling'. Only fear. *I said take me back to the city!* The young man unbuckled his belt and reached for the door. Keeping one hand on the wheel, Slade struck the young man's jaw with his fist. His head struck the passenger window with a dull thud. *You're not going back to the city*, Slade said. *You're not going anywhere, ever again.* The young man whimpered and pressed his hand against his lip. *I'm sorry,* he said. *Just take me back, please. I won't say anything.* Slade looked into his rearview mirror. The shape of a man slowly rose up from the backseat. *Be quiet*, Slade said to the young man. *He's here.* The young man's voice splintered into a million pieces. *Who?* he asked. Slade turned and looked toward the backseat. *The Ragman.* The young man didn't have time to turn. There was a brief struggle when the rag was placed over his mouth and nose. Shoes kicked the glove compartment, cracking the plastic in two. But the Ragman was strong. The Ragman didn't let go until the young man had passed out.

Slade removed the young man's clothes and replaced them with a Beatles t-shirt and denims. They were a perfect fit. Slade knew they would be. Ropes had now been secured; the gag put in place and tightened. Light came from a handheld electric lamp, powered by a diesel generator that hummed somewhere in the darkness. The young man lay on the floor sleeping like a child. Slade stood over him, waiting, biding his time until the chloroform wore off. When he finally opened his eyes, the young man began to thrash like a fish hooked from a river. *He's ready*, said Slade. The Ragman emerged from the shadows, in his hand a small tattooist's gun. *Get him up*, he said. Slade lifted up the young man, held him tight. He pulled up his sleeve, and positioned the lamp close to the skin. The young man's eyes widened as the gun came to life, buzzing like hummingbird wings. The gag muffled the young man's scream. *Shush now*, Slade said. *This ain't nothing compared to what's coming next.* The Ragman pressed the gun's tiny row of needles into the skin, scoring it as easily as a rake through soft sand. Ink bled into the flesh, marking it forever. Every now and then, the Ragman wiped a small white cloth over the ink and checked his work. If instructed to do so, Slade positioned the light closer to avoid the Ragman ruining the tattoo. *Be quiet now. You take your pain,* Slade said. He held the light closer and watched the words, *Hell's Gateway*, manifest into the young man's raw skin. When he was finished, the Ragman stepped back. It was now Slade's turn. He produced a paring knife from his belt and grabbed the young man's index finger. *Call me Sweetie*, he said. *Call me Darling.* The young man was crying into the gag, snot and tears soaking into the fabric. Slade pushed the edge of the blade through the flesh. The young man whipped his hips from side to side, and a sound comparable to a whale's haunting cry filled the room. Slade looked down. Blood seeped up like oil around the cut, coating the blade red. He put his full weight on the knife until the bone broke in two with a loud snap. *Call me Babe*, said Slade. *Call me, Honey.* The young man sobbed. The young man called out to God. But no one was listening, save for the pigeons. The final act required something larger than a knife. Something noisier than a tattoo gun. Slade walked to the other side of the room and retrieved a cordless sander. Placing it close to the young man's face, he revved it like a chainsaw. *Be still*, he said. *I don't want to fuck this up.* The rough kiss of sandpaper removed the first layer of skin within seconds. A minute later, it had reached muscle. The young man passed out shortly after it began to sand down his cheekbone.

The lengths Slade went to to achieve the required disfigurement were great and measured. When exactly the young man died was uncertain, but he was saved from ever seeing what had happened to him. That pleasure was reserved for the Ragman, and the many pigeons sat staring from up on high.

CHAPTER 1

The 5th of July, 2011
TUESDAY

The car fought against whipping rains as it snaked along the back roads of the quiet little village of Stormer Hill. Tires churned the earth. Mud decorated the car's doors in an arching pattern, comparable to blood splatter when a major artery is severed.

"It's been pissing down like this for five days," said Detective Constable Tom Nolan.

Alex Palmer watched Nolan wrestle with the car's steering wheel with curiosity. In profile, Nolan's face appeared pinched and drawn out, as if the end of a very powerful vacuum cleaner had at one time been placed on the tip of his nose, the lasting effects being a long, pointed nose and slight overbite. A thick moustache canopied his top lip, protecting teeth the color of cockleshells. Palmer estimated Nolan was a little over six feet. The collar of his shirt gripped his neck with the purpose of a noose, and the navy suit he wore was ill-fitted, as if tailored for a refrigerator and not a human. The rings around the eyes suggested that the detective was dedicated to his job, though not because he loved it, but because he didn't have much to return home for. Palmer returned to the road ahead. Condensation framed the car's windscreen, making it difficult to see well.

"We don't have many writers come by here," said Nolan. "Don't get many people come by here, if truth be told. Stormer Hill isn't what they call worthy of the attention."

Before taking the train from London, Palmer had found the village of Stormer Hill on an old ordnance survey map. The contours resembled the outline of a human heart. This, he assumed, was why the Local Authority had afforded it two anterior routes leading in and out; one to the surrounding village of Barkisland, and the other to Soyland, both considered catchment areas long steeped in agriculture. Before moving to London, Palmer had spent a little time in the quintessential chocolate box village of East Bergholt, so he knew what small towns were like; people were close, some near incestuous. The men drank in the same alehouses. The women solicited scandal from each other and gossiped in the playground. They attended the same church and ended up being buried in its grounds. Many were fearful of the outside and had a kind of psychological apprehension to life beyond the boundaries of what they knew and had grown comfortable with. In Stormer Hill, Alex Palmer was an outsider. He would smell different, sound different. Even if he was downwind and didn't open his mouth, there would still be something about him the locals wouldn't like. But if he had gathered anything since arriving, it was that Stormer Hill was still raw-skinned, and any questions he asked concerning the missing children would sting like salt.

"My DS tells me you're going to use the case of the Cook girl as a basis for your new novel," Nolan said, realigning the car. "That right?"

Palmer kept his eyes on the landscape. "Fact finding at the moment," he offered.

"Grist for the mill?" Nolan asked.

"Something like that."

Nolan turned the car onto a road marked with a dead end sign.

"What else did your sergeant say?" asked Palmer, curious to know what instructions had been given to Nolan.

"To offer support and answer any questions you may have about the case."

"And what did he *really* say?"

"Shit rolls downhill."

Nolan brought the car to a stop just outside a small wooden gate. Police tape rattle-snaked in the wind. A notice nailed to the gate's transom read: *Appeal for Witnesses. Missing Girl Sarah Cook.* A phone number underlined a photo of a girl holding a teddy bear. She was wholesome looking; strawberry blond hair and round-face.

Grabbing a pack of Benson and Hedges from the glove compartment, Nolan turned and said. "We walk from here."

Palmer had read about the girl while researching for a new book. He had been able to glean that nine-year-old Sarah Cook had gone missing from a clough known locally as Hanging Lee on the afternoon of January 13th, 2011. Sarah had slipped down a staircase while searching for her older brother, Jonathan, aged fifteen. When Jonathan found Sarah, she had twisted her ankle and could hardly walk. He tried to carry his sister back up the staircase, but didn't have the strength so left to get help. When he returned with two of his friends, Sarah had gone. It was stated the duration of this lasted only four minutes. The mother, Elizabeth Cook, following Jonathan's return home, rushed to Hanging Lee, but after searching the immediate area without finding Sarah, called the police.

The timeline—from when Sarah Cook fell to the call coming in on 999—was twenty-three minutes.

The Cooks lived off the approach to Hanging Lee in a honey-colored cottage with window baskets and solar-powered lights in the shape of owls, details Palmer later found when he searched YouTube and saw news footage of Elizabeth being driven back to her home by plain-clothed police officers. The senior investigating officer allocated to the case was Detective Inspector Coonan. A Google image search presented a man in his early fifties with skin the color of tripe in moonlight. Palmer also found footage of a press conference where Coonan gave an appeal for witnesses. His words were well-rehearsed and delivered with the right amount of humility. Had the reporter's flash photography not lit him up with the pallor of a ghost, you would believe him to be more human than most officers of a similar rank.

Palmer recognized the photograph on the gate leading into Hanging Lee as the same one released by the Cook family. It had been taken at Stormer Hill Primary School a couple of weeks before Sarah went missing. A further trawl led Palmer to an article where Amanda Clews, the head teacher at the school, used adjectives such as kind, honest and polite to describe Sarah. In this same article, Palmer discovered Sarah Cook played ukulele in a county band, took French lessons in her dinner hour, and adorned her walls with posters of kittens and a popular boy band. On Saturday mornings, she applied herself to swimming lessons at the municipal pool in the nearby town of Sowerby Bridge. During Sunday Service she listened patiently to sermons delivered by Reverend Karen Kelly in the local Methodist Church. There were no issues at home. She was not dependent on medicine or undergoing treatment for any complaint or affliction. Sarah Cook was bright, healthy and above all else, loved.

What surprised Palmer the most about her disappearance was that Sarah Cook girl wasn't the first child to go missing in the village. Over the span of four years, three other children had vanished from the area. No bodies were ever discovered. No evidence or witnesses had been found. What dovetailed each case together was the place they had last been seen: Hanging Lee. Palmer spent days searching archived news reports, both regional and national, and discovered the first child was Lucy Guffey, aged seven. She was last seen riding her bike along the approach to Hanging Lee. The second was George Levy, aged five. George had vanished from Hanging Lee with his mother merely a few feet away.

This wasn't coincidence.

***

For all his counsel on appropriate attire before setting off, Nolan entered Hanging Lee wearing just his suit. As the rain came down like stair rods, calling to mind the sound of bacon frying in a pan as it landed on Palmer's waterproof coat, Nolan looked soaked to the bone. The two men continued along a path flanked by hornbeams and the common ash tree. Old sweet wrappers and cans of lager peppered the route.

"The council try and keep this place clean," Nolan said. "But not a week goes by without a group of teenagers coming in here telling ghost stories, or trying to contact the dead with Ouija boards."

"They think the children are dead?" asked Palmer.

"They just want stories, Mr. Palmer. That's all."

"I guess I'm no different," Palmer replied.

Nolan appeared to consult the ground for way to answer, his steps slowing as though reflection proved too demanding while walking. He then gathered his pace, choosing to walk a few feet ahead of Palmer like some over-sized monk internally conversing with God. Palmer gazed at yellow ribbons tied around tree trunks, hearts fashioned from red felt suspended from branches. Some were bleached by the sun and threadbare, others more vibrant. The names of the missing children had been stitched in the centre of each one. They were the flickering flame of the votive candle, the poppy wreaths and the headstones; they were ways of remembering those who were no longer around. Maybe the teenagers were onto something.

The path opened up to a staircase that led down to the gully, the same one Sarah had slipped on. Palmer took his time, not wanting to risk a similar injury. When they reached the bottom, Palmer came to a clearing where anaconda-sized roots traversed a ground cushioned by aged pine needles. Nolan stopped and looked over to Palmer.

"This is where she was taken," he said.

Scots pines hid all four horizons, their bark fissured with age.

It's a good place for an abduction, Palmer thought. *Sheltered and quiet.*

The ground blushed in shades of brown and reds. On the trunk of one tree was a photograph of Sarah Cook. The same bloated teddy bear Sarah held in the photograph lay at the roots. Alex Palmer circled the copse as he watched the detective try to light a cigarette. Nolan cupped his hands to shelter the flame but the wind buckled it.

Putting the cigarette back in his coat pocket, Nolan asked, "Heard you were a cop at the MET."

Palmer ran his fingers along the bark of a tree the color of rotting orange rind.

"You and the Superintendent used to be friends down there. I hear that right?"

"Superintendent Roberts and I were probationary students back in 93," Palmer finally said. "We worked the same division for a few years. He owed me a favour."

"We figured as much," Nolan said.

Palmer knelt down and assembled brown pine needles in his hand. They smelled loamy, like an open grave. Something in the distance unbalanced the air and Palmer leisurely craned his head toward the noise. Leaves shifted and the fracture of twig rang out like the sound of pool balls being struck. He looked over to a nearby bush and saw a girl standing there, pale as the pages from his books. She was wearing a school uniform, her hair drenched and clinging to her face. Slowly, and deliberately, she raised her hand and pointed directly at him. Rain fell into his eyes, blurring his vision. Palmer stood up and moved toward the girl, his steps slow and forced as though under water, struggling against some mysterious and invisible current. The closer he got the more unclear his view of the girl became, until finally her face was nothing more than a smudge of pale skin.

"You okay?" Nolan asked.

Palmer stopped and blinked. When he opened his eyes, the girl had gone.

"You see something?"

Palmer turned to him. Nolan was staring at the bush too.

"It's nothing," Palmer replied. "Thought I heard something."

"You get paid more writing about crime than helping solve it?" asked Nolan, directing his attention back to Palmer.

"What can you tell me about the day Sarah Cook disappeared?"

"Probably no more than what you've read in the papers," he replied.

Palmer addressed the detective with a formality colder than the rain, "Let's assume I've not read any."

"Should we get off on the wrong foot here," Nolan said, "you better know that I was given certain instructions."

"Them being?" asked Palmer.

"Seeing how this is an ongoing investigation, I was told to be courteous but not too obliging. The thing I'm struggling with right now is why you wanted to visit this place. Surely you can get what you need from the reports on the Internet. Maybe you can help me with that."

Palmer shifted his weight before replying, "I'm just a writer trying to find a story, Detective."

"You might find a story here, Mr. Palmer, but for many who live in this village, this is far from fiction. You should remember that while you're here."

"I will," Palmer replied.

Nolan popped the collars of jacket to protect his neck. Palmer surveyed the scene and allowed time to lag as he listened to the percussion of nature. The pop of raindrops striking leaves, the delicate dance of birds seeking shelter under bush and shrub. Hanging Lee was pleasant and calming, but he knew evil hid in beauty. *If only the trees could speak*, he thought.

Knuckling his eye, Nolan asked, "You mind if we go someplace warmer? There isn't much else to see here but squirrel shit."

Palmer tendered a look of penitence toward Hanging Lee before adjusting his expression for Nolan.

"Where did you have in mind?" he asked.

CHAPTER 2

TUESDAY

The Old Swan public house was nestled within the centre of the village. A barman with a gnome-like face greeted the two men cordially at the bar. Nolan introduced Palmer as a visitor from London, and with the exception of ordering two large cappuccinos, nothing else was said. This was intentional, Palmer assumed. Nolan probably didn't like the fact he was babysitting some outsider, least of all one wishing to nose his way into the lives of people still struggling with loss. This was confirmed when he ushered Palmer to a quiet table in the snug, out of earshot of anyone. The fireplace had been lit. Palmer still felt cold following the walk through Hanging Lee and spent a moment exhibiting his palms to the flames. Nolan removed his suit jacket and hung it on a nearby peg before sitting. It had been quiet on the journey to the pub. Had potholes not jolted the two men closer, or the slick runs pushed the occasional expletive from Nolan's lips, they would have remained paralyzed by their indifference toward each other. Only now, in a neutral place, did Palmer feel comfortable asking more about the circumstances surrounding Cook's disappearance.

Settling into the seat opposite Nolan, he asked, "What can you tell me about Jonathan Cook?"

Nolan thumbed a few grains of sugar left on the table and said, "Fifteen years old. Plays cricket for the local valley. Saw him once hit five boundaries in twenty-seven balls. Boy’s got an arm like a cannon."

"Not strong enough to lift his sister, though," Palmer said.

"One thing hitting a ball, it's another carrying a person up thirty steps."

Palmer remained unruffled by the change in Nolan's tone.

"The mother, Elizabeth, did she know that Sarah and Jonathan were playing in the clough?" he asked.

"Jonathan had gone out with friends. Liz believed Sarah was in her room watching a movie."

Palmer missed a beat before stating, "Thought I read that they were playing together."

"Liz is a good woman," replied Nolan. "Not a chance in Hell she would have let those kids play in the clough with its history."

"So how did Jonathan and Sarah both end up there?"

Nolan relaxed into his chair and said, "Jonathan biked over to Hanging Lee with a few of his friends around 11 AM. They'd been told not to go in without an adult present, but I guess they wanted to see who was brave enough to enter alone. From what we understand, Jonathan never told his sister what he was planning on doing. He knew she'd tell their mother and that would have put an end to it all."

"So why follow him?" Palmer asked.

"We had a Family Liaison officer assigned to the Cook house," Nolan continued. "She was able to get Jonathan to talk a little more. He'd gone into Sarah's room before he left and made a point of telling her what time he would be back. Maybe he wasn't in the habit of announcing his exits so gravely. Maybe something in the way he said it spooked her. Whatever it was, it caused Sarah to leave the house and follow him."

Palmer glanced toward the bar. The distraction of hearing milk being steamed halted the conversation for a moment. He turned back to Nolan and asked, "So Sarah went there to stop him?"

"That's what Miles Rommel and Ethan Leech told us."

"Who are they?"

"Jonathan's friends. They live on the Stones estate close the Cook home. They've been running around with Jonathan since they could piss standing up. Miles and Ethan were at the gate when Sarah arrived, all panic-stricken. She told them to go in and get her brother. Miles tried to reassure her Jonathan wasn't in any harm, but Sarah had heard all the stories about Hanging Lee. She was worried. Are you going to write any of this down?"

Picking up on the way he'd been marshalled away from the barman, Palmer replied, "I'm trying to make this as informal as possible, Detective. Figure writing in a pad might draw attention."

Nolan nodded.

"Did the boys see what happened in the clough?" Palmer asked.

"No. They stayed at the gate."

"They let Sarah go in alone?"

"They tried to stop her, but she was adamant. Jonathan heard Sarah calling out his name, and then saw her at the top of the gully. It had been raining and the steps were slippery leading down there. She started to make her way, only she tripped and fell a few steps from the bottom. Jonathan said she landed awkwardly and twisted her ankle. He tried to help her back up, but Sarah wasn't the most petite of girls. He called out for Miles and Ethan, but they were still at the gate and couldn't hear him. He needed their help. Jonathan left her three or four minutes, and when all the boys returned she was gone."

There was a weight to that last word that left the conversation hanging until Palmer asked, "And Sarah, what was she like?"

Nolan held Palmer's stare enough for it to feel uncomfortable before he replied, "I've reviewed the statements and school reports, and listened to enough people in the village to know that girl better than most, but a piece of paper will never tell you the little details that make a person human. Now I'm okay with that. I've spent too long chasing ghosts in that damn clough to be haunted by Sarah Cook too. All I know for sure, what happened to her and those other children was the work of something evil."

The statement had all the sensation of being prodded in the throat with a broom handle. Palmer changed the subject.

"Okay, what can you tell me about the scene?"

"Scene of Crime Officers couldn't find anything," Nolan continued. "The clough gets a lot of heavy footfall due to it being a regular for dog walkers and runners. Trying to lift footprints is like trying to pull a contact lens out of a barrel of jellyfish."

"No other lines of enquiry?"

"House to house gave us nothing. We were able to get the Force helicopter to do a shout out a few hours after Sarah went missing. Once the village heard, well, you can imagine. A dozen or so took it upon themselves to start searching Hanging Lee. Our search team advisor is a guy called Bob Wood. He managed to stop them from potentially ruining any evidence. His team spent three days down there and brought nothing back but neck cricks and backache. There was one potential lead. A service station CCTV showed a white van entering its forecourt close to the time of disappearance, but the guy turned out to have witnesses who vouched for his whereabouts."

The barman arrived with the two coffees and placed them on the table. He pointed to a porcelain holder that contained sachets of white and brown sugar before leaving the men alone. Nolan added three sachets into the cup and stirred it with the spoon.

Palmer asked, "How's the brother doing?"

Tapping his spoon on the rim of the cup, Nolan said, "Finding comfort in the apostles, and what he doesn't get from them he gets from counseling."

Nolan took a few sips from the cup and placed it down delicately.

"Tell me something, Mr. Palmer; why did you leave the cops to become a writer?"

Palmer measured the question and said, "Less chance of getting hurt behind a desk."

"You miss it?"

"Being a cop? Can't say I do."

Palmer watched as the lines knitted across Nolan's brow began to ease. The detective rolled his shoulder, releasing a snapping sound that married well with the wood burning in the fireplace. Then, similar to those with the powers of tasseography, Nolan conferred momentarily with the dregs of coffee lacing the inside of his cup.

"You know this book you're writing won't bring those children back to their parents," he said.

"Never thought it would."

"Some folk around here will look at what you're doing as profiting from the dead."

"I don't write books to hurt people, Detective." Palmer said. "I am sorry for what has happened to all the families involved. Superintendent Roberts speaks highly of you and the officers tasked with locating the children. I'm not here to find fault with anyone else's efforts, and I'm certainly not here to make enemies."

Nolan looked up from the cup. "I read about what happened to you, down south. Figure you more than anyone should know that not all wounds are visible. Maybe you should think about that while you're here."

Palmer's skin suddenly chilled, and from behind him came a voice, low and haunting.

Live with it, said the voice. *Live with it.*

He turned back to Nolan.

"Did you hear that?" he asked.

Nolan paused, brow buckled and eyes narrowing.

"Heard what?"

"Nothing. Must have rain water in my ears."

Nolan finished his coffee, placed the cup down and stood up to leave.

"I have a stack of jobs that need processing back the station," he said. "If you need me, you have my card."

"Yellow ribbons," Palmer said.

"What's that?" asked Nolan, grabbing his suit jacket from the peg.

"You talk like the children will never be found," Palmer replied. "If the parents believed that, why did they tie yellow ribbons or messages to the branches? They think they're coming back."

Nolan placed his jacket on and said, "As an ex-police officer, I'm sure you dealt with your fair share of missings. This isn't London, Mr. Palmer. It was out of character for these kids and things escalated fast. We did all we could. The chance of finding any of those children after the first forty-eight hours was going to be low. Seventy-two hours and the likelihood of abduction seemed the more viable conclusion. I've not given up hope, Mr. Palmer. I'm just preparing myself for the day we dig up the bones of those children and I have to knock on their parents' door."

He pulled five pounds out of his wallet and left it on the table.

"That'll cover the cost of the coffees."

Before he left the snug he turned back to Palmer and asked, "You still think of Christie Purlow?"

A deep, resonating ache stirred behind Palmer's chest.

"Every day," he replied.

"Then you know what it's like to be chased by ghosts too. If you want to witness the meaning of hope, go to Hanging Lee tomorrow night at 8 PM."

Nolan buttoned his jacket and left the room. Palmer watched from the window as the detective trundled toward his car. His spine was curved, shoulders hunched. Whether this was the affect of the rain or the consequence of Stormer Hill's sad and mysterious history, Palmer couldn't quite figure out. But he knew all too well how the past can shape people, both physically and mentally. The second thing Palmer saw in that moment was a small school girl that looked to be waving at him from the opposite side of the car park. She had strawberry blond hair and round-face, and was holding a sodden teddy bear.

CHAPTER 3

1996, London

The 999 call came in as a domestic disturbance. The informant had contacted the police after hearing glass smash and a woman screaming from a house on Fraser Road. Palmer radioed in that his partner, Christie Purlow, and he would attend. They hit the blues and twos in the livered vehicle and made their way toward Edmonton, a rough district of London known for gun crime and violence. It was dark. The siren summoned the attention of drunken teens, young couples leaving restaurants, and the disenchanted souls who carry their shadows like a ton weight around their necks. Christie radioed one of the police Communication officers to check the address for any previous warning markers. Shortly after getting the information back, Christie told Palmer there had been over half a dozen domestic abuse incidents reported over a two-year period between an Alison and Jason Legge. Other checks from the Comms operator revealed Jason had previous history of violence, affray, and taking a car without consent. Christie turned to Palmer and said, "He's probably using Alison as a punch bag."

"Probably," replied Palmer. "And I bet she'll tear our eyes out if we try to arrest him for it too."

Since being paired up together, Palmer had observed Christie with the same curiosity scientists have for mice in their labs. She was not like most of the other officers on their division. Christie Purlow was a slender, petite woman with short blond hair she kept neatly tied back in a bun while on duty. Her skin was never bronzed, her eyes—

though perfectly almond and bright—never profited from mascara. Occasionally, she painted her fingernails letterbox red, which she would then pick at in the patrol car, as if the act was reckless and silly. It seemed to Palmer that Christy did not want to appear feminine in any way, lest it be interpreted as a weakness. He made the mistake of testing this theory by suggesting he take the lead on public order offenses should they escalate into the physical. Shortly after this statement, Christie tore him a new arsehole. She made it clear that if he ever treated her differently for being a woman, he would be the one in need of police assistance, and in all probability a proctologist too to help remove the end of her boot. After that, Palmer never questioned her grit, nor did he presume she was not up for whatever came her way. So when the patrol car pulled up outside a brandy-colored brick town house, its living room window punched through, Palmer hung back so Christie could be the officer in charge.

The door was ajar. There was no screaming from the other side. Things had presumably calmed down since the call came in.

Christie shouted through the gap, "This is police!"

Nothing came back.

"Maybe we should wait for back up?" suggested Palmer. "The guy does have previous."

"Further patrols won't get here for at least ten minutes," Christie said. "I don't want to be the one explaining to the Sarge that while Alison was getting the shit kicked out of her, we were stood outside waiting for back up. And I'm guessing you don't want to either."

"And give you the satisfaction of seeing me squirm, no thanks."

"I'll go round back, in case he makes a run for it. We'll take it slow, yeah?"

"Slow," Palmer agreed.

Christie smiled and added, "Like a sloth."

She then turned and made her way around the side of thc building, leaving Palmer to enter through the front door. The first thing Palmer noticed was how quiet it was. Sometimes it was better when there was screaming, at least then you knew where people were. But silence, that was like shadow; things hid within it, dangerous things. Christie had been gone only a few seconds and already Palmer could feel the adrenaline kicking in. His Kevlar jacket was getting tighter around his chest, and breath more pronounced. Against Christie's counsel, Palmer called for further patrols to attend, and was told by Comms, as per Christie's prediction, that they would be at least ten minutes. Palmer was about to radio Christie that they should wait when suddenly a dull sound, like something heavy had been dropped, came from the house.

He pushed open the door and called out, "This is police! I'm coming in!"

An empty hallway lined with framed photographs led toward the kitchen. He shouted up for Christie using his lapel radio and asked if she had seen anything. Static.

"Fuck, Christie, where are you?" he said.

Another dull thud shook the ceiling above him. Palmer extended his baton, moved hesitantly toward the bottom of the staircase and waited before declaring who he was and his reasons for being there. He heard a faint gurgling sound coming from somewhere on the landing, like that of bath water draining through a plughole. Palmer ascended the steps slowly. Stairs moaned under the pressure of his boots. His knees sang as they suffered under the weight of his uniform and all he carried on it. As the landing came into his view, he found Alison Legge laid flat on the floor, naked from the waist down. Her white satin blouse was stained red around the collar. She was still alive, scratching frantically at an open wound on her neck. The language she used was unique only to the dying, a primitive, alien noise that had no form but to evoked terror and worry in those listening. Palmer ran over and placed his hand on the cut, blood pulsed from between his fingers as he applied pressure.

"Hold on," he said.

Using his spare hand he activated his radio and requested an ambulance and back up. He articulated Alison's condition in short, hurried sentences to the operator. By then his own voice sounded choked, as if a hand had gripped tight his throat.

"Hold on," he said."The ambulance is coming. Just hold on, okay."

He attempted to contact Christie again, but the radio tendered another bleak and unnerving hiss.

Alison Legge never got to see the paramedic's face. She did not hear the extent of her injuries, which were many and brutal. She died in Alex Palmer's hands moments after he finished trying to contact Christie Purlow. It would never be reported in his statement, but when Palmer saw life fade from Alison's eyes, he stroked her forehead and said that he was sorry. He never knew why he tendered that apology, but never regretted it either.

The shock of seeing Alison Legge die left him hollow, weak and unsteady. By the time he arrived back downstairs in the hallway, Palmer was surprised, contrary to his own evaluation, that he hadn't been sick. He entered the living room area; an overturned table, a porcelain vase lay on the floor in a hundred different pieces, many shaped like shark teeth. There were framed photographs of Alison with a man on the walls. He assumed this to be Jason Legge. In Palmer's experience, photographs rarely portrayed the dangers and evil found in a person. He had seen many on the Police National Computer, and weighed against the brutal and senseless crimes they had each undertaken, their faces were much less serious and important. A camera had a way of removing the subtleties that made a person unapproachable and unsafe. He could stare for hours at a photograph of a criminal without ever averting his eyes. From their two-dimensional prisons, they were simple and compliant. But looking at the photographs of Legge gave him a chill. The man was a giant with eyes that sparkled with menace and depravity. His stare followed him around the room, and though it was probably a trick of the light, Palmer was sure he saw Jason Legge's smile wane as their eyes met.

Palmer made his way to the kitchen. He hoped to find a back door and Christie guarding it. Instead, as he entered the hallway, he was met by Jason Legge. The man was completely naked. An intricate mosaic of tattoos traversed his arms and legs, winding like choking vines on a tree trunk. A single light hung above head, casting shadows under his eyes so they looked like holes punched in the snow. Pressed against his chest, and with her hands hooked upon his forearm, Christie stood in front of him shaking, her face wet with tears. Palmer didn't have time to register the handgun against her head, but he remembered clearly Legge's face turn into a novelty devil's mask as it was sprayed with Christie's blood. She fell to the floor, doll-like. Palmer screamed her name so loud it tore his throat. The instinct to run over and take down Jason Legge was great, but Palmer never got that chance. Legge raised the gun and turned it upon himself. Before pressing the trigger, he smiled and said, "Live with it."

CHAPTER 4

WEDNESDAY

Palmer awoke with the image of Jason Legge lingering in his mind. He reached for his mobile phone to check the time: 2.33 AM. The cottage he was renting in Stormer Hill was off the main drag, tucked away on private farmland. The owners were an elderly couple called Bill and Linda Moffet. They lived in a small stone-built farmhouse on the same land, and save for when Bill greeted him to hand over the keys, he never saw or heard from either of them. Palmer liked that. He wanted the peace and quiet. The wind and gentle tapping of rain on the windowpane had replaced the sounds of vehicles and ambulance sirens common in London. The jeering of drunks and the screeching of car wheels had been swapped for the bleating of sheep and the plaintive, drawn out whine of their lambs that sounded like children crying. He turned on the bedside lamp, hoping the new light would purge his mind of that night Christie Purlow died, but from somewhere in the shadows he heard Legge's voice whispering to him again. *Live with it. Live with it.*

The stairs led directly into the kitchen. Palmer flipped the light switch and went to a small cupboard above the work surface. Placed beside a box of Paxil for his anxiety were three blister packs containing Diazepam. Palmer snapped one out and downed it with a swig of milk before going over to the patio doors. Light from the kitchen revealed a small decking area. Bill was a keen gardener and kept the place well groomed. Borders were filled with Rudbeckia, lavender and phlox. A small table and two chairs overlooked this modest haven and Palmer promised to himself that if the rain kept off long enough, he would sit outside one night and look at the stars. He was about to return to his bed when something in the garden caught his eye. At the edge of the lawn, partly obscured by shadows, was a pair of men's boots. He blinked, assuming it was nothing more than an apparition like the Cook girl outside The Old Swan pub, something brought on by broken sleep and too much time reviewing the history of Stormer Hill. But as Palmer surveyed the area, he noticed the boots shift a little before withdrawing back into the shadows. Someone was watching him. He knocked on the glass.

"Hey! This is private property!"

He tried the handle to the patio door but it was locked. There was no key nearby so he ran out the front door and circled round the back. The night air was cool and fresh. When he arrived in the garden it was quiet and still. He didn't like silence. Bad things live in the shadows and silence.

He called out, "Is anyone there?"

The wind complained in Palmer's ear. He grew acutely aware of how vulnerable he was. He had no weapon to protect him. He wasn't even wearing shoes. With the Valium yet to take hold, Palmer returned back to the cottage with a hurried step and locked all its doors. He crawled back into bed and measured every creek of floorboard, and every yawn from heating pipes below him, with the same uneasiness of a mouse sheltering from a bird of prey. And as his attention centered on the ambient noises in the cottage, he began to think every part of that damn house was conspiring against him. Wth the light still on, he closed his eyes. Night did not smother the sounds. Palmer had to wait another hour in the company of the conspiring voices in his head before he finally drifted back to sleep.

***

The next morning he telephoned Juliet Klein, his agent. It was 6.24 AM.

"Everything okay, Alex?" she asked.

Her voice was annoyingly lively for that time in the morning. Palmer lowered his in contrast.

"Thought I'd check in and see how things were," he said.

"Are you bored already?" she asked.

"Is it that obvious? The detective assigned to help me is carrying more chips than a casino. I get the feeling he doesn't like me, or my reasons for being there."

Palmer heard the tapping sound of fingers on a keyboard.

"You working?" he asked.

"I've got a manuscript I need to get to Hutchinson by 8 AM. They've been on my back for days now."

"Maybe I should call back later."

"Don't be silly," she said. "You still think there's a story in Stormer Hill?"

Palmer scoffed, "Is it always about book sales with you?"

"I wouldn't be doing my job if I didn't ask. Besides, we're paying for this trip."

"Regarding that; can you at least find me a place that has Wi-Fi next time?"

"No Wi-Fi?" she asked, the concept sounding as incredulous as a boat without an oar.

"And the central heating is on the blink too."

"Sounds very Dickensian."

"I'll be surprised if I make it a week without fungal poisoning or rickets."

"The cottage didn't look that old on the Internet," Juliet said.

"Everything is old in the country."

"I'm sure you've aged while you've been there too."

"Don't make this personal," he said. "You know I'm sensitive toward the way I look."

Palmer was in his mid-forties, but kept himself lean and healthy. His parents were Scottish, but he had a Scandinavian look about him. He kept his dark-blond hair short to mask any gray around the temples, something he had noticed appear in the last few years. His eyes were glacial, wolf-like, and he was acutely aware that their coldness left some people with the impression he was just as unfeeling. Women would say they foreshadowed a danger or unpredictability, which they found attractive. For that reason, his bed was rarely unoccupied.

"So, what are going to do?" asked Juliet.

"I'll age gracefully, and if that doesn't work I'll have a chemical face peel."

"No, I mean about the book."

Palmer sighed.

"I'll stay a few more days. Have a chat with some of the locals."

"Do they have a library there?" Juliet asked.

"Unsure."

"I'll have a look online once I've got this manuscript sent out. If there is one, I'll get in touch and organize a signing."

"Whoring me out again?" he asked. "You know I hate those things."

"You'll have to suck it up, Alex," Juliet said. "A small signing with the locals might avoid you getting lynched. I suggest you play it down though. Tell them you're not there to pull the scab off. It's just research, no names or places will ever be used. If anyone has anything they want to share about the missing girl, they'll tell you. I'll send over a few dozen copies of your last book. Give them out, signed. It'll show you're a good person. You're more likely to charm them in a library with a free book than you are knocking on doors."

Palmer rubbed his chin and said, "You should work for the government."

"I'm just looking out for my client, that's all."

"Because you care about me?"

Juliet paused, and then replied, "Because you make me so much money, Alex. I'll let you know the time and day of the signing. Until then, try not to ruffle too many feathers. Is there anything else you need from me?"

"Can you send me an electric blanket?"

"It's July."

"Yeah," he said. "But it feels as cold as winter here."

CHAPTER 5

WEDNESDAY

Gram Slade woke to the sound of his alarm: 6.30 AM. Hung on the door of his wardrobe was his uniform; navy blue shirt and trousers. Under his bed a pair of polished steel-toecap boots waited to be occupied. The heels showed a little wear, a consequence of a foot condition where both his feet faced inwards. Gram's mother used to describe the birth defect as pigeon toe, and used to tell him that when the stork delivered him to her door, the bird was so taken by his beauty it left a piece of itself with him. Whether it was true or not, Gram always liked that story. It helped make him understand why he was different than other people, and why sometimes they would pick on him. It made him feel special.

Gram dressed into his uniform and then went downstairs to the kitchen. He sat alone at the breakfast nook eating cornflakes from a bowl and glanced towards the clock on the wall. 7.08 AM. He finished his glass of milk and washed his bowl and glass in the sink. His mother had prepared a packed lunch of two tuna sandwiches, a cheese stick, apple and fruit drink. Before leaving for work he crept upstairs to her bedroom. A small portable television at the end of the bed played news reports: A suicide bombing in Kabul. Fifteen reported dead. Colors danced around the walls and lit his mother's face in shades of gray and blue. Incense skulked across the floor like a rolling mist. Gram turned off the TV, kissed his mother gently on the cheek, and whispered, "Momma, your boy is going to work."

She didn't wake.

The bus route took Gram from his home on Nall Street all the way to the village of Stormer Hill. He greeted the driver cordially, and though he knew his name was Hank, he never used it, choosing instead to call him sir. Hank Bentley was in his early fifties, a large man whose waistline didn't profit from sitting down all day ferrying the populace of Stormer Hill to the boundaries of Barkisland and Soyland. His face had a reddish complexion, and when he smiled his cheeks looked like crab apples, polished and rounded by both indulgence and happiness.

"You winning there, Gram?" he asked.

"Yes, sir," replied Gram, handing over the fare.

"It's Beatles today, right?"

"Yes, sir. Today is Wednesday."

Gram listened to only two bands; Queen, and The Beatles. He would alternate between the two daily, beginning the process on the Monday, and continuing through until Sunday. Rarely did this routine change, and had become the stuff of superstition.

"Which album?" asked Hank.

"The White one."

Hank considered it briefly and nodded his head, "That's a good one, for sure. But for me, I like their earlier stuff. Twist and Shout. Love Me Do."

"I have all their albums"

"That's right, Gram," Hank said. "You have all their albums. And Queen too, right?"

Gram overstated a nod of head and moved to the seat behind the driver's pit. Placing his backpack on the spare seat next to him, he inserted his iPod earphones and began humming to Blackbird and Dear Prudence as the bus weaved through the quiet narrow lanes. Occasionally, Gram would remove the headphones and listen as passengers spoke cordially of petty issues in thc scats behind him, of a two penny rise in milk price, or rogue heifers that always stray from local farmland and caused traffic congestion.

Gram gazed out of the window at the tiny stone cottages, marvelling at the backcloth of sprawling moorland peppered with cotton grass and heather. As Hank directed the bus through the village of Stormer Hill, Gram saw the old Toll House that he heard had been claimed by a family of jewellers dealing in antiquities. Gram pondered on how much money he would need to buy his mother a necklace from there. Lots, he assumed, but he would try and save the money. His Momma deserved something nice. Passing through the centre, he reflected wistfully on the stone memorial in the form of a solider that marked the lives lost in the both wars. He saw a Pete Owen fill vehicles from his modest garage forecourt and trees flanking the roads that were more verdant than any others he had seen. The daffodils in March were more yellow in Stormer Hill, the brick and marshalite buildings of the old Conservative Club and Parish Council offices, more majestic and imposing. From the Hell he had come from, Stormer Hill felt like Heaven, and Gram prayed every morning that he and his mother could stay there until their final days, safe and at ease. And for the first time in his life, Gram had been offered employment in a place where the people showed him both civility and tolerance. It was a place Gram loved, and as the bus pulled up to the single story building, Gram read aloud the sign that marked its entrance, like he did every morning.

"Stormer Hill Primary School."

CHAPTER 6

WEDNESDAY

Rain clouds gathered in the sky like herds of elephants. A fine drizzle fell, varnishing the grass in the paddock and veiling Bill and Linda's farmhouse in a mist that added a sense of mystery and eeriness. Alex Palmer approached the old building and noticed its walls tinged green with moss, the roof sagged and window frames showed signs of rot. Two cars were randomly positioned on the driveway, as if abandoned in haste; a Defender in military green, the other an old Saab. Palmer knocked on the farmhouse door and a minute later Bill arrived.

"Everything okay, Mr. Palmer?" he asked.

"I'm out of firewood," Palmer said, wiping rain from his eyes. "It said in the welcome pack I could buy more from you."

"Sure, sure. Let me get my coat."

The old man reached behind the door and pulled out a waxed jacket. Putting it on, he led Palmer around the back of the farmhouse to a small wooden shed.

"You feeling the cold?" asked Bill.

"I'm what you call a Southern Jessie. That said, I think there may be a problem with the central heating."

"The heating not coming on, Mr. Palmer?" he asked entering the shed.

"It comes on, but some of the radiators are cold to the touch."

Bill grappled with a few bags. Palmer could tell he was struggling. *Probably arthritis*, he thought. The damp air wouldn't have helped. Bill was wiry with slapped cheeks and sunken eyes. Palmer estimated him in his late sixties, and as it is with the elderly, there is always the obligation to help. Palmer offered his services, but Bill ignored him.

Shouting from the back of the shed, "I'll come over later and bleed them! Probably just trapped air!"

Bill came out of the shed holding a bag of dry wood, his breathing more noticeable.

"If it's no problem," Palmer said, grabbing the bag.

"No problem at all, Mr. Palmer."

Palmer handed him ten pounds.

"Sorry, I've got nothing smaller."

Bill checked his pockets and replied, "Left my wallet in the kitchen. Come back to the house. It'll only take a minute."

"It's fine," replied Palmer. "Drop the change off when you come to look at the radiator."

"I'll forget," he said. "Best you come back to the house."

Palmer followed Bill back to the farmhouse. While they were walking he entertained his own curiosity toward last night's visitor in the garden.

"You weren't by any chance out late last night?" Palmer asked.

"Late, you say?" Bill scratched his forehead. "Went out around nine-ish to shut the front gates."

"Thinking more around 2.30 AM."

"Not me, Mr. Palmer. Someone been trespassing?"

"Hard to tell," Palmer replied. "I thought I saw someone in the garden last night. Could have just been the light."

Bill opened the door to the farmhouse and ushered Palmer in. The porch led to a small room that had a couple of armchairs beside a fireplace. A few bookshelves suffered under the strain of various hardbacks. In the centre of the room a large rustic table covered with newspapers and old rags acted as a roof for a gray Irish wolfhound lay sleeping underneath.

"That there is Eli," Bill said pointing under the table before walking into the kitchen.

Palmer crouched down and inspected the dog. It was two shades of gray, similar to the skies over Stormer Hill. Mud stained its fur around the paws and belly. Its ribs were visible beneath the pelt, but it had been well looked after.

"Strange name for a dog," said Palmer, stroking its belly.

"No good with names," replied Bill walking back into the room. "There's a graveyard down near Spinner's Hollow. Let him off the leash one day and the first gravestone he pissed on I promised I'd name him after the person buried there. Elijah Durrant. I was just thankful it wasn't a woman."

Bill removed five pounds from his wallet and handed it over to Palmer.

"That person you saw last night, maybe one of your fans?" Bill asked.

Palmer had considered this. Last year a woman in her late forties waited all day outside the communal entrance to his apartment block in London. A shock of white hair framed her face like gauze. It was raining and the caftan that enrobed her body looked to have gained the weight of a small elephant. She asked if he would be kind enough to sign her books. He'd always been careful not to release any information about where he lived, so he asked the lady how she knew his address. The question irked her. She began screaming at him, calling him a liar and a cheat. He tried to calm her down but she was getting worse. He went back to his apartment and rang the police. Palmer later found out from a responding officer that the woman's name was Sandra Prendergast. Records showed Prendergast had mental health issues so the cops were lenient, providing he didn't want to make a formal complaint. Palmer didn't, but the next day he was leaving the apartment to go for run when he found her waiting outside again. This time she didn't have any books. She wanted to talk about Palmer's fictional detective, Max Brooke. He indulged her briefly before making an excuse to go back inside. Prendergast remained outside for over three hours, looking up at his window until Palmer had no alternative but to phone the police again. When the police escorted her home, they told Palmer they found shelves packed with his books, all different editions. In the centre of the bookshelf was a framed old painting of Palmer that Prendergast had rendered to the canvas from memory alone. She wasn't the first. Palmer received weird letters from all over the country, sometimes from both men and women. Some said they loved him; others were going to kill him if he ever stopped writing those Max Brooke novels. These people were mostly harmless. They were lonely, and they had nothing in their lives but the worlds and characters Palmer had made for them. He could not condemn them for loving him, just as the clergy cannot condemn those that attend church. Palmer was their God, and if he had to put up with the odd screwball from time to time, then so be it.

"It's unlikely to be a fan," replied Palmer. "I haven't told anyone I'm here, except for my agent, you and Linda, and West Yorkshire police."

"Then it was probably just a fox," replied Bill, stroking his chin. "We used to have chickens roaming the garden outside the cottage. Two of them. You see how high those hedges were in the garden?"

Palmer nodded.

Bill pulled a chair from the table and sat down. Stretching out his back, he said, "We let them grow hoping it'd keep the chickens safe. Did okay for a spell too, but then a fox found a way in. Tore them to strips. So I bought a couple more, built a fence around the coop, and locked them in every day like prisoners. But that fox, it got a taste for blood. Came by a few days later and dug under the fence. Dragged one of the chickens into the middle of the lawn and had its fill. Took me the best part of an hour to clean up the mess. Didn't have the heart to tell the wife, you understand. She liked those chickens. Named each one. Mable and Abel. Do no good for her to know what happened."

"Which one died?" asked Palmer. "Mabel or Abel?"

"Dammed if I know. Chickens all the same to me."

"So you bought another one," said Palmer, pre-empt the ending. "And replaced it so Linda wouldn't find out, right?"

Bill's face pruned.

"No," he said, solemnly. "I went back to the coop and snapped the other one's neck."

Palmer waited for an explanation, but Bill became more preoccupied with rearranging the newspapers on the table.

"Didn't you think killing the fox was a better idea?" asked Palmer.

"Kill the fox?" Bill asked, looking up. "Why would I go and do that? Fox just wanted to eat. Probably trying to feed its young. You can't blame something for trying to survive, Mr. Palmer. It was my job to protect the chickens and I failed."

"Guess so," Palmer said.

Bill returned to his feet and walked toward the door.

"I'm sure you're busy. I don't want to be taking any more of your time."

Palmer thanked Bill for the wood and added, "I don't think it was a fox I saw last night, Bill."

"Maybe you're right," Bill said, opening the front door. He looked up at the sky briefly before adding, "This rain doesn't seem to be letting up any, does it? If you need more logs, you let me know, Mr. Palmer. Me and Eli will pop up after dinner to look at that heating."

And with that, Bill closed the door.

CHAPTER 7

WEDNESDAY

Halderdale City Council was opposed to all forms of unlawful or unfair discrimination. That Gram Slade had no previous employment before moving to Stormer Hill in the spring of 2006, and that his IQ was between fifty and sixty did not discourage them from considering him for the position of cleaner at the village Primary School. Before the position was offered, a Disclosure and Barring Service check was undertaken, which revealed no previous convictions for him or his mother, Zerelda, nor was Gram on the sexual offenders list. Training was given, and a few months later he successfully passed his probationary period under the supervision of Stella, a seasoned cleaner at the school. Gram was now a workingman, doing the morning and after school shift. He had a regular wage and colleagues who never questioned the burn marks on his hands, or why he walked funny. They never asked what happened in his hometown or why some days he was not his usual happy self. For the first time in his life, the staff at Stormer Hill Primary School accepted Gram for who he was. Gram was happy, and probably would have remained that way had the children not gone missing. Hearing the news about them made him sad. He couldn't look at Lucy Guffey, George Levy and Sarah Cook's lockers anymore, or their paintings that still adorned the school walls, because doing so would only add to the grief he was already carrying for each of them. He had wept when each had gone missing, and when talk came around to abduction, he had asked the same question everyone else asked; why? Why did they take such beautiful children? Gram was, to all that knew him, a sensitive and caring person, which is why everyone at the school, even the children, loved him.

Gram entered the playground using the side entrance closest to the staff car park. The air was spoiled by a dank smell that reminded him of a cellar. The rain, he assumed. It had been coming down for days now, soaking everything, from the great trees flanking the football field, to the benches where the children sat at lunch breaks. Doors had swollen. A thin film of moss coated the decking beside the playground. Even Gram's bones were cold that morning, as if the rain had gotten into them too. He headed toward the main entrance to the school, passing the small wooden shelter where parents congregated before collecting their children. Gram could hear the rain hitting its canopy from nearly fifty feet away. It kept everything under the shelter was dry; the concrete, the two small benches and large plastic bin shaped like a penguin. And today, something else. Gram squinted. He assumed it was clothing. Maybe one of the children had left their coat. It happened a lot. He'd need to collect it and put in the box labelled, Lost and Found, just in case a parent came looking for it. But as he drew closer Gram noticed blood trailing to the object. He looked over to the school; the lights were on, the classrooms empty. He turned back and approached the shelter cautiously. Blood pooled in the shape of a rose under the canopy of the shelter. That was when Gram saw it. In the centre of the shelter, lay on its side, was a piglet. Its eyes were oil-black. Its stomach cut from neck to groin. The pale pink skin had been folded back to reveal the fingers of its ribcage. In the cavity of its stomach lay a red felt heart taken from one of the trees in Hanging Lee. Crudely tattooed above the pig's loin were the words, The Devil's Ass is Hell's Gateway. Gram placed his hand over his nose and mouth, not because the flesh stank, but becausc he was fear-stricken.

After Lucy Guffey went missing, Gram had found a piglet hanging from a tree branch in the school grounds. Its belly had been cut open and its guts removed too, just like the one before him. He thought it might have been kids messing about, playing sick little tricks. There were no tattoos then. No black eyes. He cut the animal down and disposed of the remains before it caused anyone upset. Everything was okay for a while, but after George Levy's disappearance, Gram saw another pig hung by its neck from the goal posts at the back of the school. This one had a tattoo. It said one word, *Brethren.* Gram didn't know what that word meant, and thought it was bad word. He never wanted anyone, least of all the kind folk of Stormer Hill to ever feel bad. So like before, Gram removed the carcass and spoke of it to no one. Now, he would have to do the same.

Gram gathered himself and walked briskly to the main entrance door. He pressed the small bell and waved to the CCTV camera. A few seconds later the locks disengaged. He entered the small supplies office, picked up a hard brush and filled a bucket with soapy water and bleach. He put a refuse bag in his pocket and returned to the animal. Placing a pair of latex gloves on his hands, he put the remains of the piglet in the bag. It was heavy and the flesh was hard like cardboard. Gram then went to work on removing the blood from the concrete. He brushed hard, producing pinkish foam that framed the spot where the pig had been splayed. Gram's arms ached. His cheeks flushed as the brush ebbed and flowed. His eyes quickly searched out the school gate to make sure any parents hadn't turned up early, alternating between whipping his head around to the school to see if Stella was watching him. She wasn't.

She must be in the main hall, Gram thought.

Once he had brushed away as much blood as possible, Gram placed the bag containing the pig in the outside refuge bins and then walked back to the supplies room. Stella was there collecting paper towels for the toilets.

She looked at Gram and asked, "You look like you've run a marathon."

Stella reminded Gram of women he had seen in old photographs of the Beatles. Her hair was cut into a bob, the color similar to scrambled egg. Her eyelids shimmered in shades of blue, her lips coated in a pale pink. Lines cracked around her eyes and tiny veins the shape of spider legs crawled along her nose. Gram sometimes wondered what Stella would look like without any makeup. He imagined she would look better, but he would never tell her this. Like the pig, some things were best left unspoken in case it hurt another person.

Gram removed his coat and put it into the locker with the St Pepper's sticker on it.

"Bus was late," he said closing the locker door. "Had to run to get here."

He was about to leave when Stella said, "You've been cleaning the floors?"

Gram looked down at the wet spots on his knee. When she spoke again, Stella's words were softer.

"If the bus is ever late, Gram, you don't need to run. Just take your time. Don't want you hurting yourself now, do we?"

Gram remained fixed on the floor and said, "No, ma'am."

"How long have we known each other, Gram?"

He stopped rocking for a moment and said, "Years?"

"High time you stopped calling me, ma'am, don't you think?"

"But it good to show respect."

"It is, but friends call each other by their first names too. We're friends, wouldn't you say?"

Gram looked up to see her smile.

"You are my friend," Gram replied.

"And friends, they talk to each other and share whatever is worrying them. I know if I had a problem, I could talk to you, and you would listen, right?"

Gram nodded again.

"And I'd like to think you could talk to me. I'm not wrong for thinking that am I, Gram?"

"No. My Mamma says a problem shared is a problem halved."

"That's right. So, is there anything you want to tell me?"

There were lots of things Gram wanted to tell Stella. He wanted to tell her about the old shed in the family home back in Manchester, the one whose walls were pale green and silver with algal and liverworts, and how he liked to go there. Gram saw it as a sanctuary, a place to spend time alone without his mother worrying. It was the first place he considered his own, a little fortress like the one Superman had. It was Gram's special place, and no one could get to him there. Or so he thought. But those boys did. The memory came flooding back. He heard the shed hinges groaning as the door opened. He remembered the sunlight, blinding for a moment, and then blackness. The bag placed over his head smelled of potatoes and earth. He was told to be quiet, quiet as a mouse. Gram struggled, but the boys were strong. They told him that if he tried to escape, they would cut off his penis and feed it him. They bound his wrists with rope and then locked him in the shed.

We'll cut off your dick, Gram Slade. We'll make you a girl. A weak little girl!

Their boots against the door thumped with the same anger and impatience of bull's horns pushing to break through a rodeo gate.

You want to be a girl? A sissy little girl?

He soiled himself, cried and rocked with knees pressed against his chest until the boys got bored and left. Gram remained in the shed, sweating until finally the door opened. The bag was removed. Gram's eyes adjusted to the light to see who had saved him. There, with the sun behind its head, was the Ghost. It spoke to him quietly, the words unhurried and clear. He was told not to speak to anyone, not even his mother, about what had happened. The Ghost promised to deal with the boys. It would make them pay. For all the good in him, some part of Gram wanted those boys to suffer for what they did. He wanted the boys to hurt, and so he told the Ghost that his mother would never know. No one would know. That was his promise.

Gram figured Stella wouldn't believe him about the Ghost. No one would. She would laugh if he told her how it used to sit at the end of his bed, quietly observing him as he slept, face blurred by night, frame wiry like a man fashioned from twigs. She would scoff if he told her that after the big fire, the Ghost showed up at the hospital and said nasty things to him. How it blamed Gram for the fire that burnt down the family home. How it blamed Gram for nearly killing Zerelda Slade. And that until the day he died, he and the Ghost would be tethered like a reflection held in the mirror. Stella would never believe him because people say ghosts aren't real. But this one was. While his mother faced questioning from both the fire investigator and the loss adjuster from the insurance company, the Ghost would come visit Gram every night.

You burnt down the house, Gram. Naughty little piggy. You nearly killed your mother, too.

Gram never uttered a word about any of this. He was too scared. He didn't want his mother thinking he was a bad boy, or an ungrateful and stupid son. So he held it in. He buried the Ghost's words deep down where only he could hear them.

Gram looked at Stella. He knew telling her about the Ghost would do no good. And if he told her about the pigs, that would worry her, and Mrs. Clews, the head teacher. It might even get him into trouble because he never told them about the other two pigs he found. They may even fire him for keeping secrets, and if he lost his job, that would make his Momma sad. It would make Gram sad too because he loved his job, he loved the children. But what worried him more than anything, was that telling anyone about the pigs would make the Ghost angry.

"I got no problems," Gram finally said to Stella. "I got no worries."

Stella nodded and gave him a quick hug.

"You're a good man, Gram. I'm happy that you're my friend."

Gram kept his eyes on the floor and said, "And I'm happy you're my friend, Stella."

CHAPTER 8

WEDNESDAY

Alex Palmer received a text from Juliet saying that a courier would deliver thirty books the following morning to Stormer Hill library. The rest of the text read like a message from a wife who had substituted feigned laughter for honesty and eye rolls:

Don't try and make them understand you, Alex. I don't understand you, which is the only reason I like you. And avoid being funny and sarcastic. Adopt the demeanour of a completely different person and you'll be fine. Love, Juliet

The signing had been arranged for 4.30 PM. Juliet had spoken with Angela Kowal, the librarian who worked there. Hearing that Alex Palmer, a bestselling author, had chosen Stormer Hill to do a rare signing caused her to gush and stumbled excitedly over her thanks and platitudes. She had promised to email all members from the village to garner interest, and print out posters for local businesses to place in their windows. Palmer was about to text Juliet back, asking her where FedEx should deliver his pound of flesh, when he heard a knock at the door. He opened it to find Bill holding a large toolbox. Beside him was Eli. Rain had soaked into its fur making it look like a poster campaign for abused animals.

"You mind Eli joining me?" asked Bill, stamping his feet on the welcome mat.

"It's your place," Palmer said.

Bill tapped his leg. Eli shook off the deluge and entered the cottage.

In the living room, Palmer fastened a heavy knit cardigan around his body and asked, "Make you a brew?"

"All the same, Mr. Palmer, I'll have a look at the boiler and be on me way."

A door led off the main living area down to the cellar. Bill unfastened the latch and Eli followed him dutifully down the stone steps. Palmer followed too. The cellar had a musty, oily smell to it. Cobwebs hung like muslin drapes over two dirty windows. A few discarded items loitered in its four corners; a bottle of gas like those used for barbeques, an old lawn mower, and some non-descript plastic bags filled with planks of rotting wood. Palmer found Bill shining his torch at a nest of copper pipes hanging from beneath the boiler unit. Eli was already curled up beside his feet.

"Nothing too serious, I hope," said Palmer.

"Pressures dropped a bit," he replied. "Just need to isolate it before I can refill the system."

Bill began to turn a valve at the front of the boiler that caused a loud hiss. A needle set within a dial on the front of the unit began to rise slowly from red to green.

Kneeling down Palmer began to stroke Eli's head.

"People been talking about you," said Bill.

Palmer imagined all the houses in Stormer Hill connected by a system of short distance radios broadcasting every move made by outsiders entering the village.

"They said you've been up to Hanging Lee with Tom Nolan."

For such a well-connected grapevine, it's surprising these children ever went missing.

"You got an interest in that Cook girl?" asked Bill.

Palmer remembered what Juliet had said.

"The detective was just talking me through the case. You know I'm a writer?"

"Linda said as much."

"I'm writing something, nothing to do with what happened here, but it does involve missing children. Detective Nolan was walking me through the scene so I can add a degree of realism to my story."

"That's strange," Bill said.

"What is?" asked Palmer.

"You being an ex-cop," Bill replied, his attention still on the boiler's dial. "That's right, ain't it? You were a cop once?"

"Once," Palmer agreed.

Bill turned away from the boiler and asked, "Why does an ex-cop need another cop to explain what happens when a kiddy goes missing?"

Palmer stopped stroking Eli and stood up.

"None of my business, you understand," said Bill. "But people do like to talk. They say you're going to write about all those kids and make money."

"I'm not writing about Stormer Hill, Bill. It's also been a long time since I was police officer and I'm a little rusty on the procedures. Just wanted to make sure things haven't changed much."

"And you came all the way up from London to do that?" Billed asked, turning back to the boiler.

It sounded doubtful even to Palmer.

"I guess, the story of three missing children from one small village did interest me. But I can tell you now, I have no intention of using what happened here in my book."

Wiping his hands on an old rag, Bill said, "That's what I figured, but other folk may not be so understanding."

"I'll tread lightly, Bill."

Turning to face Palmer again, Bill said, "It's no skin off my nose, you understand? It's not like any of this is a secret now, is it. Those news vans were here for weeks. I bet you know about as much as anyone else. "

"True. But someone always has something to say. An opinion perhaps. A conjecture?"

"A what now?"

"A theory to why the children went missing."

Bill paused for a moment, as if considering something, and then added, "Oh yeah, they'll be plenty of those."

"How do you mean?"

"Ah nothing, it's just those kiddies probably didn't need much of a push to stray away from home."

"I'm not pushing here, Bill," Palmer replied.

Bill ran his hand across his nape, gave a quick glance to the Eli and said, "Maybe it's best I don't say anything else, Mr. Palmer. I don't want to be running my mouth off and it end up in some book."

"Anything you tell me is officially off the record, Bill," Palmer said.

Eli gave out a low sound of contentment, its hind leg twitching as if mimicking the act of starting a motorcycle. Bill noted it with a glance, and then returned back to Palmer.

"You know, people might consider us folk hayseed, but one thing we're not, and that's disloyal to those families."

"You wouldn't be. We're just two guys fixing a boiler and chewing the fat, that's all."

Bill's nose twitched as if a fly had landed on it. He scratched the point and turned back to the boiler.

Staring into the grid of copper piping, he said, "Well, that Levy kid; his mother used to mollycoddle him to an inch of his life. Hardly ever went out, and if he did she was always dancing from one foot to the other to make sure he didn't fall or graze his knee. I dare say he probably wanted a moment's freedom from his mother's watchful eye."

Palmer recalled the articles relating to George Levy's disappearance. The school had organized for the children to go around the village picking up litter as part of their environmental awareness month. Jane Levy, the mother, had volunteered with a few other parents to chaperon the children and make sure they were monitored at all times. They were instructed to remove any litter found on its boundaries, but not to go into the clough. George, and a couple a few of his classmates, was doing just that when he went missing. Jane Levy stated in an interview that she only took her eyes away from where George was working for a couple of minutes. A couple of minutes. An appeal for witnesses led by DI Coonan showed Jane sat next to the detective, her face stripped of makeup and emotion, her clothes chosen randomly and without care. She looked like someone had sucked the life out of her.

"If Jane Levy was so protective of her son, why'd she fail to see him disappear?" asked Palmer.

"She got distracted."

"How?" asked Palmer.

"Someone rang her phone. Least that's what I heard. She picked it up, and by the time she turned back, George had gone."

"Was any of this reported to the police?"

Bill turned from the boiler and said, "Sure. They even checked her bill, but couldn't figure out who had rung her. It was one of those pay as you go things."

"Did the person on the other end say anything?"

Bill placed the rag inside the toolbox and said, "Jane didn't hear anyone on the other end except for this god awful silence. I imagine that every time her house is quiet, that poor woman is reminded of that moment."

Bad things live in the shadows and silence.

"So George Levy strays because he feels suffocated, but what about Lucy Guffey?"

Bill checked the pressure gauge on the boiler and turned on the heating. There was click, followed by a noise similar to a roll of thunder.

"Lucy and her mother had a volatile relationship, you might say," Bill continued. "Folk in the village heard them on more than one occasion going at each other in the supermarket over something or nothing. Lucy had a way about her. Don't get me wrong, she's a good kid. Just, she liked to push her mother's buttons. We heard that Lucy and her mother had an argument before she went missing. It wouldn't have taken much for her to run out of the house, maybe strike up a conversation with someone. Seek a little sympathy, you know?"

"Doesn't explain Sarah Cook," Palmer said. "Sarah came from a good home. Her mother cared about her, her brother too. Unless I'm missing something else?"

Bill rubbed his ear before replying, "Guess you're right there, Mr. Palmer. Trouble with Stormer Hill is you hear so much tittle-tattle it's hard to know what to believe. Folk think they got it all figured out, but no one truly knows for sure. Be better all round if we get done with speculating among ourselves and let the police do their job."

Bill made a sound with his mouth that awoke Eli from his rest.

"Come on, lad," he said, patting his leg. "I'll check those radiators, Mr. Palmer, make sure the heat is coming through them."

The two men returned to the living room. Palmer felt the chill had finally abated from the room. Bill placed his hand on the belly of the radiator nearest the window.

"Should be fine now," he said. "Anything else I can do for you, Mr. Palmer?"

"You never mentioned the fathers."

"The fathers?" asked Bill. "That'll be because all the children lived with their mothers."

"They were single parents?"

"Thought you knew that?"

That seemed like a large piece of the jigsaw, and yet it was never mentioned in the articles. Either the media were instructed not to include it, or the police hadn't made the connection.

"I didn't." Palmer said.

"That detective babysitting you, he knew. Surprised he didn't mention it when you went into Hanging Lee."

"About that," said Palmer, trying to dust off the possibility Tom Nolan was holding back information. "The detective said I should go to Hanging Lee tonight at 8 PM. Do you know why?"

"The village comes together every three months to remember the children. Been doing it now since Lucy Guffey went missing. It's our way of showing support to the families. Reverend Karen Kenny will be overseeing the event. We sing a few hymns and light candles to help guide those poor souls home. Some folk hang hearts and messages in the trees. If you want, I can drop by and pick you up. Though if I was you, I'd stay back a ways. Keep your distance. Folk might not take kindly to seeing you there, all things considered."

Bill picked up his toolbox and Eli headed toward the door. Before crossing the threshold he turned back to Alex Palmer and asked, "Those novels of yours... they any good?"

"It's a question of taste."

The rain pelted Bill's cap.

"Guess the world's screwed up enough without reading about it too," he said.

"Can't argue with that, Bill."

Bill nodded slowly before tipping his cap. "I'll be seeing you, Mr. Palmer."

And with that Bill and Eli made their way back to the old farmhouse.

CHAPTER 9

WEDNESDAY

Gram paused in the vestibule and listened to the house. It was, as his mother would say, as quiet as a mouse. Even though he knew Zee was out attending the Between Friends Literary Book Club, as she did every Thursday evening, he stilled out for her.

"Momma! I'm back, Momma!"

No answer.

In the living room, Gram threw down his backpack, stretched out his back and took a deep breath. Zee's Dewberry oil lingered in the air, and was now joined by the detergent chemicals on his skin. The mix was sickly and Gram wished he hadn't needed to clean four extra classrooms, two sets of toilets, and buff the main hall's wooden floor.

There was the piglet too, with its black eyes and pomegranate flesh.

"Been a bad day," he said to himself.

Gram looked at the clock on the wall; Zee wouldn't be back for another hour. That hour would feel like five, maybe even ten hours today, because he wanted her back. She couldn't know about the pig, it would worry her, but she would fix him a potion to ease his worry, and if she asked what was causing the worry, he could make something up: *Momma, there's talk of people being laid off. I'm just worried about losing my job.* A lie. There weren't any redundancies to his knowledge, but his mother didn't need to know that. If he could just do enough to make it sound convincing, Zee would make a potion, hold him, and tell him everything would be okay. That's all he wanted right now; a mother's love.

Gram walked into the kitchen. A small glass cloche on the breakfast nook caught his attention. Inside was a lemon sponge cake with a note attached that read: *Eat Me.* He remembered the story of Alice and smiled. The message was his mother's way of reminding him that if he didn't eat he wouldn't grow. He lifted the cloche and breathed in the aroma of lemon zest and icing. He took a fork from the cutlery drawer, sunk it into the soft sponge, and was about to take a bite when the floorboard above him creaked. He looked up, holding his breath for a few seconds. The floorboard made another sound; something was moving up there. He followed the noise as it shifted. His appetite waned. His heart gathered rhythm. The room directly above the kitchen was his bedroom.

"Momma?!" he shouted to the ceiling. "That you?"

He knew it wasn't her. She was out with her friends, talking about books, books that he couldn't read very well. No, it was either someone burgling the house, or the Ghost. Right then, Gram hoped it was the burglar.

The curtains were drawn when he entered. He remembered opening them in the morning when he woke up, like he did every morning. But someone had shut them. Someone had wanted the room to be dark. But it wasn't completely dark. A splinter of light was able to squeeze through the gap where the two edges of the curtains didn't touch. Gram shut the bedroom door, but didn't flick the light switch. He sat at the edge of his bed allowing his eyes to adjust. Air struggled to pass through his nose, punctuating the silence like piston valves.

"I don't like you being here," Gram said to the vacant space before him.

He directed his stare to the corner of the room where the outline of a person emerged from the shadows. It was if a full sized mirror had been placed in the room and he was foolishly entertaining his own reflection. The figure had a similar build to Gram; its hair was cut the same way. But when the figure tilted its head to one side, like the same way dogs decipher strange sounds, Gram knew it wasn't a reflection. It was the Ghost.

"You leave me alone," he said.

The Ghost didn't respond.

"I took the pig away," Gram said.

"You shouldn't have done that," said the Ghost.

"People will get upset," Gram said. "I took the pig away."

The Ghost stepped forward, courting that fragile light to give shape to its face. Gram watched gloom shift from its hollowed cheeks and eyes, and then gather at the corners of a sinister smile.

"And how were the children today?" it asked. "You know how much I love to hear you speak about them."

"I'm not telling anymore. You did a bad thing. You killed a baby pig and you put it in the playground where the children play and that was bad."

The floorboard beneath Gram lifted slightly under his foot.

"You didn't mind me hurting those boys though, did you?"

Gram could smell the shed again. He could hear the boys chanting; *We'll cut off your dick, Gram Slade. We'll make you a girl. A weak little girl!*

"You pinky promised."

"I know," said the Ghost. "I don't talk about the boys, you don't talk about me, but we do talk about the children. Wasn't that the deal, Gram? Like you say, we pinky promised."

Gram nodded his head.

"So, how were the little piggies today?" it asked. "Did you watch them play?"

Gram said nothing.

"Did you smile at them as you mopped the floors? Did you talk to them, Gram? Did the little piggies smile at you? Oh, I bet they did. They like you, don't they? Poor little piggies."

Gram pressed his hands over his ears.

"Little piggies? Little piggies. Won't you come out to play?"

"Stop it," Gram said softly. "Stop it. Stop it."

The Ghost drew out its words as if singing a lullaby; "Little piggies. Little piggies."

Gram began to raise his voice, "Stop it! Stop it! STOP IT!"

There was silence. Gram lowered his hands and looked toward the shadow cloaking the Ghost. The figure there was still, and for a moment, Gram assumed the Ghost was getting ready to go back to where it lived, a place that would be both dark and scary. But the Ghost remained still, watching Gram. Then, without warning, it leaned into that splinter of light, its eyes black as coal, skin chalk-white.

"You're going to Hell, Gram Slade," it said.

Gram fell to his knees, crying. The Ghost knelt down beside him, finger lightly tracing over the burns on Gram's hands.

"Remember who you are," the Ghost said. "Remember where you came from. You owe me, Gram."

Gram kept his eyes tightly shut, rocking slightly as if in prayer.

"I'm sorry," he said. "I'll tell you. I'll tell about the children."

The absence of the Ghost's finger on his hand made Gram open his eyes. He looked around but the Ghost had gone. Gram brought his hands into the splinter of light and stared at the landscape of mottled skin that had once been licked by flames. Whatever happened to him, however old he got, Gram knew those scars would never fade. They would remind him every day of who he was, of his stupidity and weakness. They would remind him of the secrets he kept, and that he was the reason the Ghost existed.

CHAPTER 10

WEDNESDAY

The rains showed no sign of relenting. Townsfolk left their cars dressed in cagoules, and held tight to umbrellas as they meandered through the hollow way leading to the stairs where Sarah Cook had fallen. A breeze animated the limbs of trees along the route, stirring newly fixed hearts and messages skewered to their branches. Bill locked his Defender and him, Linda and Alex Palmer all headed into Hanging Lee. Palmer kept a slow and measured pace. He chose not to read the messages attached to the brushwood and trees. He did not wish to encourage eyes to linger upon him too much, or conjecture to escalate into suspicion. He had chosen clothes that were dark and non-descript, as if to camouflage himself against the woodland. He wanted to be invisible. A ghost.

Iron lanterns were positioned along the descent to the clough, casting the wooden steps in shades of saffron. In the centre of the clearing below, a horseshoe of people had gathered around the mouth of a galvanized garden incinerator that glowed pumpkin orange. They rubbed their hands and spoke in whispers, they allowed light from torches to dance across the foliage like spotlights in some tacky cabaret show. A cluster of well dressed people remained to one side rustling papers in their hands. Palmer assumed these were the choir, and he was thankful Bill had suggested he gain a vantage point far from the main arena of townsfolk, a place he could observe without having to feel the need to contribute, or sing. Bill had also told him to keep an eye on him and Linda, and to follow them once the vigil ends. Palmer searched them both out from the gathering crowds, and saw Bill stood with five other people who were all facing Linda. It was clear they were very popular in the village, and Palmer assumed that maybe Bill's suggestion to stay out of the way wasn't solely for his own benefit.

Palmer noted Linda look toward a portly woman moving through the crowd. Then slowly, the crowds hushed and everyone else's attention fell to the woman. She was dressed in black, hair the color of mushrooms and shaped similarly. Even from his vantage point, Palmer could see the dog collar around her neck. Reverend Karen Kenny. The townsfolk nodded their heads and smiled as Kenny passed them. She returned their gestures genially and leisurely. Taking her position aside the incinerator, Kenny cleared her throat and addressed the crowd as any member of the clergy would their congregation.

"Dear friends, tonight marks another three months without the return of our beloved children, Lucy, George and Sarah."

Palmer scanned the crowd as each child's name was mentioned. Emma Guffey shifted her weight but remained impassive, and Palmer concluded that her failure to reveal emotion was no different to a scar that cannot blush. The second woman to gain Palmer's attention was a small, bug-eyed woman who made a noise like a rusty hinge being drawn back when George's name was called out. He remembered her face from the videos he had seen when George had gone missing.

"Jane," he said under his breath.

Palmer watched as two women, one of which Palmer recognized as Amanda Clews, decorated Jane Levy's back with their arms. He then saw Elizabeth Cook standing beside the tree where Sarah's photograph had been pinned. She was slight in build, like a child herself. The caterwaul that came from her mouth when Sarah's name was said aloud resonated like gunshot around the clough. A man with a beard came rushing to her side, and he was joined then by a woman, and they both held Elizabeth Cook as best they could to stop her knees from buckling. Kenny paused, looked over at the grieving mother, and once given the nod from the bearded man, continued her sermon.

"Tonight we join together once again to light the lanterns that will help guide our children home," Karen Kenny said. "We write messages and pin them to the trees so that when they return they will not be met by darkness or loneliness, for each carries with it a message of love. And should the light we offer be weakened by the wind, or should the children not raise their heads to see the messages in the trees, they will not stray from their path or lose themselves in the clough, for walking beside them will be Jesus. He will guide them, as He has guided us all in times when we have lost our way. He provides hope when there is doubt, and He allows us to see when we are blinded by misery."

The townsfolk were listening, nodding, united in faith. It was a strange and hypnotic sight to witness. Palmer had never attended church for redemption or guidance. He refused to be present at Christie Purlow's funeral, blaming his absence on depression and anxiety. Had he a choice in the matter, he would have avoid the funerals of his parents too. His father, a cop who had reached the rank of Sergeant before retiring, enjoyed seven months of his pension before his heart gave out one morning. It was sudden, unexpected. Alex Palmer was nineteen when it happened. The following summer he enrolled as a police constable in the MET out of guilt, or respect, he could never quite decide. His mother took another eight years before she surrendered to a brief but agonizing fight against pancreatic cancer. When he found her in bed, stricken by death, he knelt beside her and poorly articulated a farewell. His voice quaked in that moment, the tone mysterious and flat. He then went and made a cup of tea. The truth was his mother's dead came as a great relief. She had been a burden those last few years, draining him of energy and money. Her death signalled the end of her demands and the guilt he felt whenever he visited. No more morphine induced ramblings. No more pretending to be a decent son. Following her funeral, Palmer avoided churches and religion at all costs, but often exploited the subject in his books. He knew the scriptures in the Holy Book could be easily misinterpreted and twisted by the deranged, and he used that to provide motive for the crimes his characters committed. Religion to him was no different than the way Agatha Christie uses the knife, or Raymond Chandler uses the gun; he made it a tool to kill. As for his own beliefs; he was a man driven by logic and commonsense. As a cop he had witnessed terrible and grizzly acts of murder and brutality that he had been left with no option but to discount the existence of a God. Babies suffocated in their beds by mothers, raped by fathers; children beaten to inch of their lives, the elderly bludgeoned to death and then sexually abused. If a God existed, Palmer concluded they must be as spineless and evil as the perpetrators of the crimes they witnessed, because had they been benevolent, they would have intervened. But God didn't. God allowed evil to rule here.

Karen Kenny cleared her throat; "When I seek peace in the midst of trail and tribulation, I am drawn to the Gospel of Matthew; in particular the Beatitudes given by Jesus during his Sermon on the Mount. They have been the scaffold that has supported me and my congregation for many years and I wish to share one with you all now."

Karen Kenny reached into her pocket and retrieved a small piece of paper. Struggling to see it in the dimness of dusk, one of the villagers, a man with the frame of a church bell, came over with his flashlight and shone it on the page.

"Last year I visited Stormer Hill Primary to thank the children for their contributions to the autumn harvest," Kenny continued. "While there, I spoke about the eight Beatitudes and asked what the children thought each one meant. Many of them felt uncomfortable articulating their understanding, and those that did were unsure and quiet. But when I asked what Jesus meant when he said, Blessed are they who mourn, for they shall be comforted, a little girl raised her hand slowly and said this to me; if we cry things will get better. I thought to myself, how true. Crying is a way of cleansing the body of grief. It allows us to rid ourselves of the pain we are undergoing. Sometimes, a good cry is as good as any medication. I spoke with this girl at the end of my visit and thanked her for contributing. Before leaving I asked her name. It was the same name I heard on the radio six months ago when she was taken from the village. I followed Sarah Cook's instruction and cried like many others here. Jesus may have intended the Beatitude to mean something else, but I preferred Sarah's explanation because a child knows how to see the world more easily than adults. They tell us what we fail to see, and in Sarah's interpretation I found comfort."

Kenny lowered the paper and addressed the crowd, her voice becoming dourer, "Sarah, George and Lucy would not wish us to slake the anger that burns in our hearts. They would not wish us to hate the evil that has robbed the village of their laughter. They would not want us to take vengeance. They would want us to seek comfort in each other, and in God. That we have gathered together again, united in our support for Elizabeth, Emma and Jane, shows God that we have not given up hope of our children returning. We must never allow time to overshadow faith. I now call upon Detective Constable Tom Nolan who will light the final lantern and bring to a close tonight's remembrance."

A cluster of people separated. From the divide trundled DC Nolan. He was dressed in a charcoal gray overcoat, hair flattened and parted like a choirboy. Kenny folded her notes and placed them back in her pocket. The man who assisted her earlier retrieved an iron lantern and handed it to her. She disengaged a small latch on one of its doors, and Nolan furnished its belly with a single flame submitted from a match. He closed the door and Kenny handed the lantern to him. He held it like a newborn, supporting its weight at both ends. As he withdrew himself into the gathering of people, he glanced over to Palmer. The light from the lantern turned Nolan's skin jaundice. Palmer smiled, but he knew it probably looked strained and was undetectable from the distanced. Nolan then addressed the people, calling upon each one to join hands and sing, Great is Thy Faithfulness. Palmer felt that he might have misjudged the man. It was evident he shared the grief of Stormer Hill. Maybe he really did care.

When everyone had retired their singing voices and relaxed from their positions, a few took the time to seek Nolan out and offer words of thanks. He held the lantern aloft, and with his spare hand accepted their handshakes and pats on the arm. The people of Stormer Hill then encircled Elizabeth Cook, Jane Levy and Emma Guffey, many crossing the threshold of personal space to embrace them. The display was too much for Elizabeth and she sobbed on the shoulder of a silver-haired woman.

"Crying will make it better," said Palmer, quietly.

When Kenny relieved Nolan of the lantern, Palmer considered approaching the detective, but was saved the task when Bill rejoined him.

"You want a lift back?" Bill asked. Palmer nodded and was about to set off toward the staircase when Bill added, "You get anything from tonight?"

Palmer thought for a moment before he spoke. He didn't want to tell Bill he thought a lot of what the reverend had said was spiritual bunkum. He didn't want to articulate the only thing capable of bringing those children back was good old fashioned detective work, and that Stormer Hill's hope of lifting the dark veil that had ascended upon it was now in the hands of Tom Nolan, not God.

Instead, he smiled amiably and said, "The human spirit is a humbling thing to observe."

"That'll be faith you're seeing," said Bill. "Nothing more."

A long line of people began ascending the steps in single file. Soon its full length was occupied. Palmer, Bill and Linda waited in line, and as Palmer gave one final look to the scene, he observed a tall man as thin as a broom handle standing next to a tree, a hood framing his gaunt face. It was the face of a ghost.

CHAPTER 11

WEDNESDAY

Slade followed the perimeter of Hanging Lee down toward a row of tiny houses along Gog Lane. His pace was slow. The moon cast a net of silver light that lit up the clough, making it look magical and enchanted. He navigated roots belonging to the common sycamore and birch without faltering. He hopped over ditches forged by the tireless rains. He did not carry anything on him. No bag or torch, not even a watch. He wanted to make himself as light as possible should he need to run. The only addition to what he was wearing was a folding knife made of beech wood and carbon steel. The blade stretched out to a length of 9cm. Due to its size the knife could be easily concealed without attracting attention, small enough so he could present it at the last moment. He crouched between two Hawthorn bushes, gazing toward a cottage fenced with dry stone. Of the four windows he could see, one revealed a kitchen. A woman with laundered skin and hair the color of hickory stood at a sink running water into a small cup. Slade knew her name was Kristen Taylor. Slade then looked toward the living room. The glow from a television and small table lamp presented a modest room; brown couch, armchair, a scattering of photographs pinned to the wall, coffee table. The upper floor had two windows identical in size to the bottom set. One window glowed in a warm yellow hue. A pattern of tiny flowers decorated the curtains. It was a child's room belonging to a girl named Amy Taylor, and she was sleeping peacefully inside. Slade knew that Amy was ten years old. He had seen her at the school and had spoken with her many times. She was wholesome looking with long brown hair and round face. A birthmark stained her neck the color of red wine, and she once told Slade that she liked winter the best because in winter she could wear roll neck sweaters, scarves and coats that would hide the birthmark. Sometimes her friends would ask if the birthmark hurt, or if it ever faded in the bath or when she swam in the municipal pool. Slade would listen and tell her that the birthmark was pretty. It reminded him of a rose, something delicate, just like her. Whenever they saw each other in school, Slade would smile and ask how his little rose was doing, and Amy would smile back and said that she was fine. One evening, Slade was finishing buffering the floor in the main hall when he saw Amy leave the toilet. Her eyes were red. He asked her what was wrong, and at first she didn't want to say, but Slade was a good listener. He made sure of that. He gave all his attention to every child when they spoke to him. The children liked him for this. Some would pick daisies from the back field and fashion bracelets for him to wear. Others would smile and wave from afar. No one had a bad word to say about Slade, not even the teachers or parents. He was a good man, a kind man. Amy told him why she was upset. It was the anniversary of her father's death. Slade asked how her father died and Amy said he was a soldier and he went to Afghanistan and never came back. Amy was five years old when her mother got the phone call. Her memories of her father mostly came second hand from her mother. Amy was told that his name was Paul and he could fill a door arch. He liked watching football, and though he claimed his favourite movie was Die Hard, it was really The Goonies. He whistled when he shaved, ironed his underwear and could fix pretty much anything broken. Amy could not remember any of these details. The only memory she had of her father came from the summer before he left for Afghanistan. He had spent the week constructing a small swing in the garden. She told Slade how she remembered sawdust on his boots, and when she looked up to him, the sun behind his head made his face hazy and dark. What she knows of his face now, his blue eyes and strong jaw, Amy later got from photographs her mother keeps around the house. But what she remembered that day was being pushed on the rope swing, and his laughter. When Slade asked what it sounded like, Amy replied earnestly, "Like summer."

The swing's seat was now swollen and bloated with age. Damp split the grain. The rope was frayed where Amy's hands had gripped it so many times, the frame tarnished with lichen and moss. It was a lonely, abandoned structure that offered no joy but to serve as a wooden tombstone in a graveyard of vague memories. And as Slade settled upon its seat, his feet setting into motion a slight rhythm, he watched Kristen retire to the living room. Slade suppressed a laugh bubbling up from his stomach. He held his gloved hand to his mouth, holding it in. Then, when he felt the urge had passed, he spoke softly into the night.

"Little pig, little pig, let me in," he said. "Let me in.

CHAPTER 12

WEDNESDAY

Tom Nolan removed his coat and hung it on a wooden peg next to his front door. He picked up letters from the doormat and shuffled them with the dexterity of a croupier before dropping them into a waste paper bin in the hall. The living room was decorated in shades of bachelor. An impression left in an armchair facing a flat screen television indicated it was the only seat occupied. The walls were simple and ignored, save for one, which Nolan used to explore his theories on the missing children. In the centre of this wall, and framed by press cuttings dating back to the first missing, was an ordinance survey map of Stormer Hill. Red string held by pushpins marked the areas where the children had vanished, as well as areas of note, creating a complex matrix of pentagons and trapezoid shapes. Manic scrawls in marker pen also emphasized boundaries and possible exit and entry routes in the village, all explored and all resulting in negative results. Photographs of footprints taken by SOCO overlapped artist's impressions of possible suspects, none of which yielded any possible culprit, and running below the map were family photographs of the children and Missing Posters that at one time had been stapled to lampposts in the village, their faces frozen in a moment of life that would have felt immeasurable to them. Over time, yellow and pink Post It Notes had fallen from their position on the wall, covering the floor like plucked feathers belonging to an origami bird, the writing small and indecipherable, as if written in haste or under poor lighting. And finally, running along the skirting, and probably the most important addition, was a handwritten time line of events, dating back four years ago when Lucy Guffey went missing. Nolan stood before the wall again, examining every detail if it was a piece of art hung in a London gallery.

Addressing the photograph of Sarah Cook, he asked aloud, "Where did you go?"

He poured himself a measure of bourbon in a tumbler and installed himself in the armchair. His fingers searched out the top button on his shirt, then the knot of his tie. He did not recline, choosing to remain perched on the seat as it gave him the best view of the floor. There, his shoes touched the edges of paperwork, some piled in stacks of twenty or so pages. Each child had its own row. The first belonged to Lucy Guffey, then George Levy and the one nearest his feet was Sarah Cook's. Statements, Computer Aided Dispatch records, scene logs, SOCO reports, Community Impact Assessment, Intel, anything related to the cases had been photocopied and brought to his home. Nolan took a drink and then picked up a précis based on statements given by family members and friends, and read over it for the hundredth time.

Emma Guffey's husband, Andrew, had left two years after Lucy was born and was now working in Dubai as a foreman on a construction site. George Levy had been conceived by artificial insemination using a sperm donor after Jane Levy had her ovaries removed due to cysts in 1998. Elizabeth Cook's husband, Dale, lost a long battle with bowel cancer 12 months ago. So far only four factors united Guffey, Levy and Cook. The children all attended Stormer Hill Primary School, none had any health issues that required medication, and as the précis showed, they all came from single parent families with the mother being the primary caregiver. Nolan placed the sheet in a manila folder and searched the rest of the paperwork for something else. The final link that tethered each case was geography. Nolan found the PolSA report typed up by Bob Wood following Sarah Cook's disappearance. The Place Last Seen was documented as Hanging Lee. The hypothesis to what may have happened to Cook was widely accepted as abduction. Wood had given initial search perimeters within the boundary of Hanging Lee and to each of its entrance and exit points; one main point of entry and exit at the north end of the clough, and an exit/entry point on the east side at Barrow Lane that led onto Edgerton Road. The perimeter of Hanging Lee had been compromised at various sections, more visibly at the area closest to Cog Lane. Seven cottages lined Cog Lane. Their gardens backed onto Hanging Lee and were fenced using sheep wire suspended between wooden stakes. The height of each fence was documented as three feet, making it scalable for any adult with very little effort. Nolan searched for the pocket notebook entries taken by the local constables during house-to-house enquiries. Kristen Taylor was the only person on Cog Lane with a CCTV camera. The camera was not installed on the exterior wall but mounted on the windowsill of a spare room that overlooked the back garden. When questioned about this, Kristen had informed the officer she had bought the camera for peace of mind, but couldn't afford to have the work done to get it fixed to the exterior wall. However, to anyone looking at the property, the camera was obscured by the window pane, and concealed by dark curtains. Nolan had already checked the footage at the Taylor home the day after Sarah Cook went missing but the results were negative.

"If only it had recorded something," he said to himself.

A copy of the Trace Investigate Eliminate strategy had been sent to Nolan after DI Mark Coonan had tasked him with the job of speaking with the residents of Cog Lane shortly after Sarah Cook went missing. It stated that the residents be implicated or eliminated from the Cook enquiry by the following mythology: 1. Obtain physical description. 2. Photo (with consent). 3. Statement (MG 11) of accounts and alibis. 4. DNA for comparison with recovered profiles (with consent). 5. Offenders with previous convictions with a similar MO seen in the area. 6. Persons in the area of Hanging Lee between the times of the abduction. The "area" was defined as anywhere within the boundary of Hanging Lee and its surrounding residential area.

Each person on Cog Lane was questioned and subsequently removed from further enquires when their location at the time of the abduction was verified by witnesses, which Nolan conducted himself.

Nolan stood up and circled the paperwork like it was a scene of a murder. His back ached, his neck too. He finished the tumbler and poured himself another.

"There's got to be something I'm not seeing," he said to himself. He approached the wall again.

The day Sarah disappeared Bob Wood had an extended line of search officers with whistles that walked the open areas of Hanging Lee in attempt to gain a response should the girl still be there. There was the belief in the very early stages that she could have been dumped. If the abductor got spooked when Elizabeth arrived, or Sarah had struggled enough, they may have left her in the undergrowth. Nolan closed his eyes for a moment and imagined he was back within Hanging Lee. He heard each note issued from the officer's whistles. He could smell the loam and rotting leaves beneath his feet. From memory, Nolan had sketched the position of every tree and knew every shade of moss and lichen that cloaked them. And yet, he could not find one piece of evidence that would lead him to the abductor. He opened his eyes.

"Fuck!" he said.

He approached the wall and slammed his hand against it.

"Fuck you!"

His anger abated as quickly as it arrived. He lent his forehead on the map of Stormer Hill and closed his eyes again. The tumbler in his hand tilted. A little bourbon fell to the floor with a splash. On hearing this, Nolan opened his eyes and lifted the glass. That sound resonated in his mind for a second. He titled the glass again and allowed a little to drip off the lip and onto the floor. It sounded like water running off a tap. Or rain. It sounded like rain.

"The day Sarah went missing... It was raining," he said.

Nolan returned to the paperwork and scrambled to find the Scene of Crime Officer's statement. He was kneeling now, the tumbler placed on the floor beside him. He began tossing pages left and right, muttering to himself.

"Footprints. There must have been footprints."

He found the two-page document and read aloud the first line.

"The disappearance of Sarah Cook followed heavy rainfall.... Yes, but what about the footprints?"

His eyes scanned the page quickly for the results. SOCO had found over thirty different footprint impressions around the area. Using dental stone they had made casts and submitted each to the lab. Those matching Jonathan, Sarah and Elizabeth Cook were ruled out, as were the impressions of Miles Rommel and Ethan Leech, Jonathan's friends. The lab made test standards of three different adult sized boots that had the best impressions. One print indicated that there was a hole in the shoe. Examiners collected and made test prints of the shoes from residents of Cog Lane and the surrounding homes leading to Hanging Lee. By overlaying the cast print against the test print of the resident's shoe, they found a match. It belonged to a man called Ron

Stevenson. Stevenson was sixty-six years old and lived with his wife in a row of terraced houses close to the Cook home. He was called in for questioning but later released without charge after he proved both he and wife were holidaying in southern Spain at the time of the disappearance. SOCO's assessment was clear; the clough had too many visitors to identify a suspect from the footprints alone. There were no recoverable fibres, traces of blood or hair.

"Shit!" Nolan said, throwing the sheet into the air.

He anticipated another night wrestling with theories into the early hours. Sleep compromised by exploring wild conjecture. A framed commendation from the Chief Constable for his diligence in all three cases leant against the wall near to where he was kneeling. He had contemplated hanging it but felt the act both hollow and insensitive in view of the fact his best efforts had failed to bring the children home. He leant over and picked up the frame. Light cast a ghostly reflection of himself in the glass. He was ashen and bloated, like a corpse of his younger self dredged from a riverbed. He wondered where the years had gone. He threw the picture frame against the wall and consoled himself in the sound of shattering glass landing on the floor. He then drained the tumbler beside him and walked to the living room window.

A single row of brick houses the color of a human tongue huddled together in the darkness beyond. Nolan knew the forename and surname of each of his neighbors. It was his job to know their movements, from the time they left for work, to the time they arrived home. Their car engines were to him as familiar as birdsong. A detective never turns off. They never rest. He spent about a minute gazing out of the window listlessly before a man entered his view, his pace set by an Alsatian that lurched into the coming winds with the grit of a husky. Nolan recognized the man as Brian Hughes. Hughes lived with his wife, Theresa, in a bungalow two streets away. He was in his late forties and had apparently atoned for the balding of his head by growing a beard and wearing a bandana, something Nolan thought both sad and pathetic.

"Out late tonight," Nolan said quietly. "You and Theresa had a falling out?"

Nolan was about to turn away when he noticed Wendy Hindle getting out of her car. Wendy usually attended an aerobic class between 6 PM and 8 PM. This was confirmed when he saw her pull a sports bag from the boot. Through the glass, he heard Hughes call out her name as he passed. Wendy waved back casually and then entered her home. Nolan studied the exchange and replayed it in his mind. Wendy Hindle hardly looked at Hughes when he called her name. She was neither threatened nor startled by him too, even though it was late and getting dark. Perhaps it was because, like him, she knew Hughes's voice and so didn't sense any danger. Perhaps, within a small community such as Stormer Hill, a place where everyone knew everyone's business, a person could move effortlessly and without consideration if they were known. Something struck Nolan. It felt like a cattle prod in his side. Nolan dashed to his armchair. He placed the tumbler down thoughtlessly on the floor causing bourbon to blot the paperwork belonging to George Levy. He wrote with pace and precision within his notepad. It was only a few lines, but right then, it felt like much more than all the paperwork surrounding him, much more than all the theories and conjectures on the wall. Nolan would later go to bed with all thoughts toward the case gagged and bound, and for the first time in weeks, he fell into a deep, peaceful sleep without concern. Beside his bed the pad remained opened at the page, and in small cursive writing it read: *Whoever took the children lives in Stormer Hill. They are known and liked.*

CHAPTER 13

THURSDAY

The library was a small compact building on one level. The petrichor smell of earth following rain, and the dust and leather scent from books that abut all four of its walls, gave Alex Palmer a warm feeling of nostalgia when he entered. He noticed a tall woman aligning chairs in rows of three, and assuming her to be the librarian, cleared his throat to catch her attention. She turned with a start, but upon seeing Palmer, the famous author, her face relaxed instantly. The hem of an accordion pleated skirt trailed along the floor as she approached nimbly and with haste to meet his hand.

"Mr. Palmer!" she exclaimed. "It's such an honour to have you here."

Palmer noted the librarian had wild hair with a sweep of gray at the temples, her lips overly rouged, as if the act of applying makeup was new to her.

"Don't mention it...." His voiced trailed in anticipation of a name.

"Angela Kowal," she replied, almost face-palming herself. "Your agent, Juliet, arranged to have your books sent up. I've stacked them on the table, as you can see."

She pointed to a small wooden trestle that looked to be struggling under the weight of the hardbacks. Angela turned back to Palmer, the glass in her spectacles magnifying the relief and veneration in her eyes. It was sickening to Palmer, but he smiled nonetheless.

"I can't thank you enough for doing this," she said. "It's such an honour to have you visit our ..." She paused for a moment, blushed and added sheepishly, "I've already said that, haven't I?

To make her feeling better, Palmer replied, "To be honest, you're helping me out. I've not done one of these things for a while and I need the practice."

"Is there anything I can get you? A coffee perhaps?"

The question was punctuated with a fleeting, but obvious, fluttering of eyelashes.

"Coffee would be good," he replied.

"There's a small kitchen in the back."

Angela guided Palmer to a small utility room with sink and a work surface large enough to hold a microwave and kettle and very little else.

"The coffee is instant, not ground."

"I'm just happy you have coffee. Since arriving here all I've been offered is tea."

"That's Yorkshire for you," Angela said, smirking.

The kettle rumbled beneath a wall-mounted clock that told Palmer it was 4 PM. The signing was in half an hour and the library was empty. He lent casually against the work surface and enquired about attendees.

With her back to him, Angela busied herself preparing the coffee.

"When your agent rang and said that you were coming, I requested that the signing take place at a time more convenient for residents, Mr. Palmer."

"It's okay to call me Alex," he said.

Angela turned and Palmer noticed her blushing. She continued stirring.

"People working full time jobs wouldn't be able to attend until after 6 PM, but cuts to the local authority budget meant that we had to fit in during core hours." Angela looked over her shoulder, "I'm sorry, Mr. Palmer. I did offer to work late without pay, but I couldn't persuade them to keep the library open."

She turned back to finish the coffee.

"So you're saying it's just you and me?"

"I'm not that lucky," Angela said, and then, as if abashed by the remark, handed Palmer the cup, adding quickly, "I'm expecting at least twenty, maybe even thirty people. It'll be the biggest gathering we've seen here."

Palmer usually drew in audiences nearing a hundred at signings. Thirty people seemed like an insult. But he reminded himself of what Juliet had said; this wasn't an exercise in promotion, but to appease suspicion and gain trust within the community. A cough from within the main library interrupted any further conversation. Angela took the opportunity to push past Palmer to exit the door. She smelt of fresh linen, something earthy too, like driftwood or lumber that had been left out in the rains. He assumed it was just the smell of the library, or her home, which he imagined to be small and chaotic, a home of a lonely person, with shelves filled with old paperbacks and knickknacks. That's what he could smell. It was loneliness.

Palmer entered the library and noted two women had arrived. Angela knew them all by their first name. She engaged in idle chitchat with one woman, presumably to obscure the passing of time while they waited for more people to turn up, but it was obvious to Palmer word had gotten out that he was there to gather material for a new book. The sum total of attendees eventually rose to three people. Angela gave an over ingratiating prelude to the question and answers section that made Palmer restive. He kept giving her glances in the hope it would rein her in, but it was obvious Angela had practiced the speech for some time. He waited it out. A forced applause followed, and Alex Palmer began by encouraging the attention of his audience by asking each one their name, something he felt wouldn't take too long considering the poor turnout. A mature woman with cropped hair the color of a knife blade spoke first. She had a saturnine expression, and when she introduced herself as Mrs. Thickett, her voice resonated with pomposity and sureness.

"You should know," she said, straightening her back, "I plan on asking you some very direct questions, Mr. Palmer. A person of your standing in the literary world may not be used to people being so blunt."

Palmer attempted a smile, "I'm sure it can't be worse than the time I attended a primary school during World Book Day. Those five year olds were ruthless."

Angela let out an audible chuckle, which was met with an icy glare from Mrs. Thickett.

"I'm no five-year-old child, Mr. Palmer," she said, addressing him again. "I'd like you to remember that should you attempt to speak to me like I'm one."

"I wasn't trying to imply ..."

Thickett cut him off, "I'm here not as a fan, Mr. Palmer, but in the capacity of reporter. I'll be transcribing the answers you provide today for the weekly Parish newsletter."

Palmer did his best to reassure Mrs. Thickett that he was pleased she was acting as a spokesperson for the community, and would welcome any questions she had, but by then she had reclined back in her chair, busying herself with a pen and pad. The second lady, who gave her name as Mary Albright, looked a similar age to Mrs. Thickett, but more genial.

"Have you read Ray Bradbury and Isaac Asimov?" she asked Palmer. He nodded his head. "My husband, Bernard, loved their novels. He was what you call a nerd." She added a little smile to assure the group it was meant in jest. "Angela will tell you. He was always asking for Science Fiction novels. Wasn't that right, Angela?"

Angela nodded reverentially, and Palmer inferred from Mary's use of past tense, and Angela's composed expression, that Mary Albright was a widow. The final attendee was sat on the back row nearest the Early Learning section. It was a man, probably in his mid-twenties. His hair had been shaved closed to the skull and he looked terribly thin. When Palmer asked his name, the man lowered his head and inspected the floor. Palmer waited for a few seconds, assuming he was shy and building the confident to speak, but the man remain mute. Angela gave Palmer a look that suggested it was best not to probe too much, so he didn't.

Palmer's inflection rarely lost its level of compassion during his introduction, and only wavered when Thickett began asking him questions.

"Do you think writing a novel on the subject of the missing children could be seen as insensitive to the community of Stormer Hill, Mr. Palmer?"

He paused for a second to gather his reply, and then responded warmly, "I can only offer reassurances that the misfortune of others is never something I feed from, Mrs. Thickett."

The woman wrote frantically in her notepad.

"Did you consider the impact your visit would have on the parents?" she asked.

"I'm not fortunate enough to be a parent," he said. "But that doesn't mean I don't know what it feels like to lose a child. Some of you may know that in my previous life I was a police officer in London. There was a girl down there called Amber Gouldner. She was six years old. Amber was pulled from the Thames two days after she went missing. I was one of the officers who attended the Gouldner home when they told the parents. It's a day that still haunts me. The job has a great way of darkening the heart, Mrs. Thickett. I can count on one hand the time I left the station feeling good about myself. Most things you get over, but knowing a parent will never wash their children's clothes anymore, or kiss them goodnight, that sticks with you. I'm fine with whatever people want to call me, but insensitive is something I can't accept."

Palmer missed a beat and used the time to survey the many spines of books uniformed like piano keys around the walls of the library. When he returned back to the three people he saw that each was staring at him, waiting. The pleats upon Thickett's brow had slackened a little, her lips unclasped.

"I know my writing can't bring the children back," he continued. "But knowing I can write a story where they do, well, that gives me hope. It'd please me to know it may do the same for the people of Stormer Hill."

Neither Mary nor the man tendered any questions, which brought the session to a premature end. Angela quickly corralled those to the table that wished to get a free copy of Palmer's novel. Palmer took a seat and sat with fingers laced. Thickett endured a few more moments in Palmer's company, stating his book could be used for the monthly Parish competition. Her matriarchal posturing never faltered, even when Palmer asked if she would like a personal inscription. Though she hesitated for the briefest of seconds, Thickett insisted the book was not for her but the community. She then left the library without another word. Mary Albright asked for an inscription and thanked Palmer for his time. She added that her husband would have liked him, but not his books, which Palmer accepted with the same level of humility an actor shows when receiving a bouquet. The person who interested Palmer the most was the last to approach the table. The man's bearing was clumsy, his manner awkward. Handing the book to Palmer, he exposed the skin on his hand, which had paled and assumed the profile of grilled cheese. He was quiet and appeared unconcerned to how he may be perceived, much like a child. Palmer was about to ask him if he wanted the book inscribing when he was taken by a sneeze, probably due to all the dust in the library.

"Bless you," said the man, quietly, and added, "My Momma says that if you don't bless a person quick enough, the Devil gets inside them. She's what they call an expert on these things."

Angela handed Palmer a small tissue, and used the moment to introduce the man.

"This is Gram Slade. Gram works in the local school and has a leaning toward sword and sorcery books, isn't that right Gram?"

Gram shifted his weight a little and looked at the ground.

"I'm not much of a reader. I like comics. They have pictures."

"I'm afraid there are no pictures in my book, Gram."

"It's okay," he said. "I'm getting a copy for my Momma. She reads all sorts."

"She sounds like an interesting woman."

"She'd tell you to wrap mint around your waist to remedy stomach pain, and that nettles from a churchyard boiled up will help with dropsy."

"And what does your mother suggest if there is no one around to bless you when you sneeze? Maybe Old Nick might use the opportunity to take advantage of loners."

Palmer was thinking the advice might be worthy of Angela Kowal's attention.

Gram retrieved a handkerchief from his pocket that had been tied into a knot.

"I carry this around. A knot keeps the Devil away."

Palmer gazed at it for a moment before saying, "But I don't own a handkerchief, Gram."

"Then sprinkle a little salt at the doorway. It'll stop evil entering."

Gram rubbed his hands together as a flush of blood warmed his cheeks. He seemed to console himself in movement, rolling his head from side to side slowly. He allowed the skin to rumple along the bridge of his nose, his eyelids to flicker. A finger traced the pen marks left by excited children on the trestle table, moving with the grace of a planchette across an Ouija board.

"Momma would like it if you wrote a few words," he finally said. "Something nice. She's a good woman."

"Sure. What's her name?"

"Zee."

Palmer retrieved one of the books and opened it at the title page. He established himself in the role of author, and with a few flourishes of the pen closed the book and handed it back to Gram. They were briefly connected, their hands a few inches from touching. In the exchange they looked at each other. It would be later, while in bed listening to the choir of angry winds outside his window, that Palmer found a suitable relationship between the shades of green found in Gram's eye to those within the common grape, and only after he turned off the lights, and retired for the evening, did he wonder what they had seen, and what Gram Slade knew about the children.

CHAPTER 14

THURSDAY

Nolan got the call from Coonan at 6.33 PM. He was sat at his desk updating the Operational Police Unit System when his mobile rang. The CID office was an open plan design the size of a tennis court. Florescent lighting made skin mortuary gray. Static charges built in the soles of shoes when officers walked the indigo nylon carpet, and were later discharged when they touched the metal frame of chairs or door handles. No workstation was personalized. Walls were painted in the same shades as those in psychiatric and hospital wards. It was a sterile and depressing place that seemed perfectly appropriate considering the jobs each detective had to deal with daily. When Coonan's name appeared on the mobile's screen, Nolan welcomed the break in monotony.

"I've just got off the phone with the BCU commander?"

Coonan's voice had a clinical edge, cold and direct. His words were never tendered for affect or exaggerated, and for that reason Nolan tuned his ear to the pattern and tempo so he didn't miss anything. His spare hand gripped a pen and hovered over a pad emblazoned with the Force's insignia.

"An hour ago, a ten year old girl called Amy Taylor was reported missing."

The pen slipped from Nolan's fingers. Air escaped from his mouth. He bent forward in his chair, adopting the posture of a shrimp as he lowered his head toward his knees. One hand screened his brow while the other pressed the mobile closer to his ear. He heard the roar of a car engine from the other end of the phone. Coonan was on route somewhere fast.

"Who made the call?" asked Nolan.

"The mother. Kristen Taylor. You know her?"

When Nolan was tasked with visiting the residents of Cog Lane, Kristen's home was the first he visited. The tragic events that led him there did not addle his brain from her beauty. She had met him at the door. The sun was bright and flooded her face, and even then, with her forehead in pleats and expression bent into a scowl, she was prettier than any woman Nolan had known. The only flaw she had, if it could be considered such, was that her right eye had a different pigment to the left. In sunlight, it shimmered in shades of amber, whereas her right eye remained the color of Moroccan dates. He later looked up the condition and found out it was a hereditary condition known as heterochromia. A small detail that lingered with him. Kristen had made coffee from a cafetiere and sung quietly to herself as the water percolated. Clothes seemed to look better on her, their colors brighter, or so Nolan thought. He assumed that any person meeting her for the first time would instantly warm to her nature, just as he had. He kept his questioning professional, but took the opportunity to ask about her partner, qualifying the enquiry as an act of procedure, as they may have seen something she didn't. Kristen spoke briefly of Paul, her husband, and that he had passed on. Nolan instantly apologized, and because she was used to this reaction, Kristen tendered a well-rehearsed smile.

"Paul gave me a wonderful daughter, Detective, many happy memories. I have no complaints. Better to live a moment in bliss than a lifetime in misery, right?"

Nolan nodded, but he sensed he had fallen into the latter of the two options. He asked a few more questions, finished his coffee and left. For a woman that had mourned the loss of her husband, sadness had yet to mark her skin. Grief had yet to darken her eyes. But now her daughter was missing, and Nolan wondered if that had changed.

"I've spoken with her in the past," Nolan said to Coonan, affirming his grip around the mobile. "How is she?"

"Wound tighter than a clock spring," Coonan replied. "Fortunately for us she's also paranoid."

"I'm not following, Boss."

"After Sarah Cook went missing she made Amy wear one of those GPS watches for kids. If the watch is removed, it activates an SOS call and sends a notification to the parent's mobile. It's been sending fifteen second audio recordings ever since."

"As it picked anything up?"

"Mostly ambient sound. I'm surprised we've got as much as we have. From what I'm told they're hardly the most reliable of things. We'll see if the Digital Investigation Unit can clean up the audio. If she was taken, we may be able to pick up a voice, which will at least give us a gender."

Coonan stopped talking. The engine noise amplified suggesting he was concentrating momentarily on a difficult manoeuvre. Nolan used the lull to establish a link between Amy Taylor and Sarah Cook. Kristen fell into the abductor's MO perfectly; single mother, child at the same school, home bordering Hanging Lee. Nolan felt a pinch in his stomach.

Coonan resumed the conversation, "I need you to get to the junction of Barrow Lane and Edgerton Road right away."

"You're not going to the Taylor home?"

"The GPS signal is our main priority. We think Amy may be close to Edgerton Road. Bob Wood and his team are on route, so are SOCO. I'll be there in two minutes."

"Didn't the Taylor home have CCTV?"

"Jesus, well remembered."

The way Coonan said this released a wave of pride through Nolan.

"It's a home kit that overlooks the garden," said Coonan. "Before Kristen rang the job in, she checked the footage. The first attending officer at the scene said that Kristen recognized someone walking close to her garden fence twenty minutes before Amy went missing."

"Did she give a name?" asked Nolan.

"Someone called Gram Slade. You heard of him?"

Nolan spun his mental Rolodex. He recalled the name, but couldn't remember from where.

"He sounds familiar. Do we need to bring him in?"

"Hanging Lee is common ground. People pass through there every day. It could have just been coincidence."

Nolan could sense Coonan going through the rationale behind the decision to arrest Slade. Coonan only needed grounds to suspect Slade was involved for an arrest to take place, but it brought with it various issues that needed considering, mostly relating to whether Slade posed a serious risk at the moment, or if he was likely to destroy, conceal or falsify evidence that would obstruct the investigation. Arresting him would also mean seizing his clothes, fast tracking them for forensic investigation, all of which costs money. There were custody arrangements to consider. If alibis needed corroborating then the custody sergeant may bail him, causing further distress if Slade had to return. But a man had been seen prior to Amy being taken. This was the most they've had to go on for four years. Coonan's reticence toward bringing Slade in for questioning posed a real threat to the investigation. The Force had come under scrutiny for not acting quickly enough. The media wanted answers, and following the other three missing children they had hanged Coonan like a human piñata until every journalist had taken a swing. The locals didn't trust him either, labelling him incompetent and cold. But Nolan knew that what Coonan lacked in bedside manner he made up for in experience. Before he joined West Yorkshire Police, Coonan had worked out of Greater Manchester taking down Organized Crime Groups. He was used to the hard edge of policing. Added to this, he'd also done several years in the MIT team, leading on three high profile murder investigations. There was a rumour going around, though no one was sure of its origin, that following the last investigation he had collapsed outside Force HQ of exhaustion. Soon after, he transferred to the Riding area. Whether his move was the result of fatigue, or a push, no one really knew, but it was clear Coonan took his role and the job seriously, even at the cost of his own health. Still, Nolan couldn't stand aside without trying to convince him to act, if only to protect Coonan's reputation.

"You still don't think there's enough to bring him in, Boss?"

"I've got the officer at the scene checking the footage," Coonan stated. "They'd be grounds to arrest if we have footage of him dragging Amy out of the garden and into Hanging Lee, but from the mother's first account, he wasn't seen with her."

Nolan cleared his throat and asked, "So you're treating this as a missing, not an abduction?"

The question sounded cynical, and he instantly regretted not framing it more cordially.

Coonan exhaled, "There a problem, Tom?"

"I just don't think the girl would walk."

"Look, I don't blame you for fearing the worst," Coonan said, refusing to soften his tone. "I'll give some thought to Slade. But right now I need you down at Edgerton Road, okay?"

Before Nolan had time to respond, the phone went dead. Nolan slipped into his jacket and logged off the computer. He was in his car less than a minute later.

***

A liveried van had been parked askew in the centre of the Edgerton road, blue lights flashing. The police officer tasked with redirecting traffic slowed Nolan's Mondeo to a crawl, but waved him in on seeing his warrant card. Two unmarked vehicles and a small white van with the words Crime Scene Investigator were parked up before the cordon tape, which had been stretched from one side of the road to the other. Nolan parked his car next to the CSI van and spent a minute watching a woman dressed in white coveralls kneeling on the road.

They must have found something, he thought.

Past the cordon, Nolan saw Coonan deep in conversation with a brawny looking man who he recognized as Bob Wood. Wood was one of the best PolSa officers Yorkshire Police Force had. He was genial and assiduous, and had the standing among his colleagues as a bloodhound when it came to tracking offenders. Wood's finger was tracing a route on a map he was holding, which Coonan followed with furrowed brow. He then looked up, scanning the flanking moorland as if translating its bleak terrain into viable routes and probable graves. When Nolan arrived, he did not interrupt the conversation, and redirected his attention to the SOCO officer as she rested on haunches. He watched as she placed a tape measure against two black marks scored into the road. Once fixed, she retrieved an expensive looking camera from an aluminium flight case and began taking photographs. The flash lit up the ground making the tracks look like an equal's sign in some bizarre mathematical sum drawn on the road.

"Tom, you know Bob?" said Coonan drawing Nolan's attention.

Nolan turned to the two men and canted his head.

"We worked on the Cook case," said Nolan.

"And Guffey, right?" confirmed Wood in a tone that could influence people to give up smoking or lose weight.

Nolan offered his hand before giving his attention back to Coonan.

"Did you find the watch?" he asked.

"We found it," replied Coonan, and produced a clear zip bag that contained a small watch with purple strap and yellow face. "It was discarded at the side of the road close to those tyre tracks." He nodded to the SOCO officer. "If Amy's a runner, could be she took it off."

Nolan waited for another theory.

"Or," Coonan continued. "Whoever took her didn't want us following them. Hopefully we can lift a few prints off it."

The tension eased in Nolan's stomach. Coonan was coming around to the idea of abduction, which would make his theory more palatable when the opportunity came to present it. Bob Wood folded the map and placed it in a Napoleon pocket on his waterproof jacket. He gestured to the end of the lane.

"Those car tracks suggest the vehicle came to a halt while heading out of the village. I was saying to the Boss that if it continued along this road it'll either go west, back toward the village, or east where it'll join the main arterial route out of Stormer Hill."

"You think the car was used to abduct Amy?"

Nolan was baiting his line. He knew tyre tracks were as unique as fingerprints. If SOCO could get a good cast they'll be able to determine the make and model, and based on wear, maybe even the age of the vehicle. The tread would have picked up traces of soil, sand, glass or other materials that could narrow down the search. It was a good lead.

"I've got officers deployed at the edge of Barkisland and Soyland to stop all vehicles leading out of both arterial routes," replied Coonan, ignoring the direct question. "We'll also check ANPR for any vehicle leaving Stormer shortly after Amy went off the radar."

"What's the timeline?" asked Nolan.

"At around 4.40 PM, Kristen Taylor was in the kitchen preparing dinner while Amy was in the garden playing. Ten minutes after that Kristen looked out of the kitchen window and saw Amy playing on the swing. She didn't look again until it was time to call her in. That was around 5.00 PM. The call came in at 5.43 PM."

Nolan verbalized his thoughts, "So we have a ten minute window when Amy left the garden and went into the Hanging Lee."

"The SOS call from Amy's watch was activated at 5.03 PM. Kristen then used the app on her phone to try and find Amy. The GPS signal showed her on Barrow Lane at 5.20 PM."

Nolan visualized the terrain and measured it accordingly.

"It'd take a competent runner to cross that distance in ten, maybe fifteen minutes."

Bob Wood chipped in, "We figured at least twenty minutes for an adult carrying a child. That gives us an approx time of around 4.55 PM when Amy was taken."

Nolan was struggling to give up with the maths, but remained deadpan so not to show his limitations.

Coonan continued, "The last GPS signal showed a stop in movement on Edgerton Road at 5.28 PM."

Happy he had a rough timeline in his head, Nolan asked, "Why so long?"

"What you thinking, Tom?" asked Coonan.

"If Amy was on Barrow Lane around 5.20 PM, why did it take eight minutes to get on Edgerton Road? That's a journey that would take no more than five minutes on foot."

"This is why we think a car was involved."

"There are fragments of a headlamp near to the tyre tracks," Wood said. "Judging by the marks on the road, it was involved in a RTA."

Coonan jostled for attention, "The most viable theory we have right now is that Amy was stuffed in a car on Barrow Lane at 5.20 PM. The car then turned on Edgerton Road before heading out of town. The driver got distracted, took their eyes off the road for minute and hit an oncoming vehicle."

Nolan chewed on this for a moment, "Which means someone will have seen them."

"That's what we're hoping," replied Coonan. "I'm going to get a holding statement together and send it to the media unit. Also, driving around with damage to a vehicle may raise suspicion."

"You think they may have dumped it before leaving the Hill?" asked Nolan.

"It's a possibility," Coonan replied. "A description has been passed to Comms for circulation on PNC. Amy has a distinctive birthmark on her neck so that should work in our favour. We're also making enquiries with the local hospitals and British Transport Police should she, or they, exit via train."

"What about air support?"

"They're caught up in a pursuit in Wakefield. Once they're done it'll be redirect over here."

A people carrier approached in the distance. Wood looked over and raised his hand to acknowledge the driver.

"The team's here, Boss. I figure we have less than four hours of good light so I'm going to start the ball rolling. As discussed, I'll put officers in Hanging Lee along the proposed route toward Barrow Lane. A second team will move along Edgerton Road. I'll keep you updated if we find anything."

Coonan turned to Bob Wood, "I'll be staying around if you need me."

Wood saluted the two men before walking toward the van. Turning back to Nolan, Coonan recovered his usual dour expression.

"I know you're not buying that Amy ran away."

"This follows the same MO as the previous missings," said Nolan, rubbing the back of his neck

"I know," replied Coonan. "Single mother and the kids are all under ten years of age."

"They're also from the same school."

"You think someone from the school is taking the kids?" asked Coonan.

"The abductor may be choosing them because they're easier to handle," he said. "I also think the children knew them."

Nolan's voice was twanging like a detuned guitar. When Coonan didn't disagree, he mustered up the strength to continue.

"I think it's trust, Boss. All those kids wouldn't have gone anywhere near a stranger, least not after Lucy Guffey went missing. Their parents would have drilled it into them. They trusted the person who took them, that's the only explanation to why there was no struggle, which means the person lives in the village. In the past, we've done house-to-house and an appealed for witnesses. No one has seen anything. But what if they did and discounted it because they were local?"

The corners of Coonan's eyes were red. Blood vessels branched toward his pupils. Nolan assumed it was inflammation, or the result of long work patterns, but it gave Coonan a menacing, demon-like look.

Nolan held his stare but it was uncomfortable. He felt coldness in his legs that made them twitch.

"You remember anything about Gram Slade?" Coonan asked.

Nolan had reason to hold on to Slade's name. It was different. Gram sounded like a surname. It was not common to Stormer Hill, and though Nolan used the journey from the office to Edgerton Road to try and recall why it resonated with him, he felt the answer was hidden behind a locked door in his mind.

"I'm still working on it," he replied.

"I need you to go to Kristen Taylor's house," Coonan said. "Speak with her. Find out if there is anything she's done tonight that was different. I want to know if her weekly routine had changed in anyway. The main priority is the CCTV. See if the officer attending has found anything else. I'd have good reason to bring Slade in if he's seen talking to the girl."

"What should I tell her about Amy? She'll want to know about the watch."

"She already knows the watch was dumped. Why do you think she rang us?"

Nolan began to feel all the credibility he had built up evaporate.

"Look, you're good with people, Tom. Tell her we're doing all we can. If you need an FLO, ring me. Dianne Crosby is on call. I need to go and speak with SOCO."

Coonan turned and approached the Crime Scene Investigator pouring gelatine onto the tyre mark. His stride was stalled by a hobble. Nolan had never noticed it before and couldn't remember if it had always been there or not. It was a detail he may have never acknowledged before or stored because it held no importance. Maybe this was why the children had slipped through his fingers in the past. Maybe he was missing the little details that hold the bigger clues. He glanced toward the moorland. His pupils dilated to take in the landscape, his eyelids blinking as they struggled to accept it scale. He observed the pylons tethered by electrical wire that sagged like hammocks. Cottongrass leaned away from winds. Sheets of gray cloud curtained the sky. Tom Nolan closed his eyes and endured the knowledge that once he opened them again another child would be gone from it, and there was nothing he had done to prevent it from happening.

CHAPTER 15

THURSDAY

The Police Constable at Kristen Taylor's house introduced herself to Nolan as Claire Mulvihill. She had blond hair and a face too young for the job. The second officer was in the spare bedroom reviewing the CCTV footage stored on a DVR. Nolan hovered in the hallway for a moment to ask Mulvihill if DNA had been seized, just in case. The young officer nodded and said she had bagged and tagged Amy's toothbrush. She then handed Nolan a photograph. It had been taken a few months ago at a tennis club. Amy was dressed in a blue polo shirt. Her skin was albumen white. Freckles decorated her nose. Her long neck displayed the birthmark Coonan had mentioned. It reminded Nolan of an autumn leaf. Nolan then tasked Mulvihill to help with house-to-house enquiries and to report directly back to him. He could see the disappointment in her eyes. Mulvihill must have wanted to hang around, be more directly linked to the case. She was probably fresh out of her probationary period, keen and equally green. Nolan tried to recall what that felt like. He gave back the photo and told to her to attach it to the Missing report.

"Claire, I need good officers to help find this girl," he said. "There may be someone out there who saw Amy talking with another person. That's all we need. Just one piece of the puzzle to get us started."

Mulvihill sighed and shouted up to her partner that she was helping with house-to-house, her tone flat and raw.

When Nolan entered the living room, Kristen Taylor was sat on the couch playing back the audio recordings sent from the GPS watch, the loud static hiss coming out of her mobile sounding like rain on corrugated steel. On seeing Nolan enter she pressed the stop button and looked at him with both fear and expectation. She was dressed in a long sleeve top the color of limestone. Tears flecked the cotton around her chest. A tissue was hidden under the cuff, furnishing her wrist with a tumor-like growth. Unlike the first time he met her, Nolan saw the widow in her, the way grief shrinks and reduces a person into a cadaver of their former self. Next to her was an older woman who he recognized as Linda Mossop. Linda owned a farmhouse and small rental cottage with her husband Bill. Nolan introduced himself and asked if he could sit down. Linda interceded.

"You can cut the pleasantries, Tom," she said. "We all know each other here. Have you found her?"

Nolan rolled his teeth along his bottom lip. He turned to Kristen and said, "No."

She inhaled deeply and let out a sound that persuaded Linda's arm to frame her back.

"Who's leading this," Linda asked.

"The SIO in charge is Detective Inspector Coonan," Nolan said. "He's a very competent detective."

"The same detective who brought back Sarah Cook and all those other children?" she asked.

"Oh, Jesus," Kristen said, and pulled the tissue from her sleeve.

Linda turned to Kristen and apologized. Nolan attempted to diffuse the tension with fact.

"Amy's watch helped us to gain a timeline of events, Mrs. Taylor. This means we have a viable parameter to work within. That was smart, getting her to wear it. I take it you've not been able to hear anything from the recordings?"

Kristen shook her head.

"We have people who may be able to clean up the audio," he replied. "Can you send the files via email?"

"I think so," she said, uncertain but appearing hopeful.

Nolan handed her a small card with his phone number and email.

"If you find a way, send them directly to me and I'll pass them on to the relevant department."

Nolan took a seat on an armchair opposite Kristen. He didn't recline but remained upright and engaged. Kristen placed the card on the arm of the chair, and with glazed eyes looked to the detective and asked, "Who would do this?"

Nolan wanted to offer some explanation that might temper her worry, some little bit of police knowledge or statistic that once tendered would ease the tension in her shoulders and reduce the lines in her forehead. But he knew there was nothing, not one thing he could say that would make her feel better.

"The truth is, I don't know. There are just some bad people in the world."

"What's happening to bring my baby home?"

"Things are moving faster than usual," Nolan said, his tone confident and more controlled. "DI Coonan is at the scene where the watch was abandoned. He's working with a Crime Scene Investigator and search party. The force helicopter will be doing an aerial search soon too. There will be a media statement released, which will include a description of Amy. We're hoping this will help bring forward witnesses. This same description has been circulated to all patrols just in case one of our officers sees her. PC Mulvihill is currently doing house-to-house enquiries to see if any of the neighbors saw anything. We're also looking into the ANPR cameras along both routes out of Stormer Hill."

"What's that?" asked Linda.

"Automatic Number Plate Recognition. The cameras are usually near traffic lights and they take photos of every car that passes them. Because we have a decent timeline, we'll be able to retrieve the registrations of every vehicle that left the village. I understand PC Mulvihill has gone through the other procedures with you, Mrs Taylor?"

There was a pause before Kristen spoke.

"You came to my house when Sarah Cook went missing."

Nolan nodded. He wondered if she recalled his awkwardness when they spoke, the shades of periwinkle under his eyes born of restless nights. He wondered if she thought about him in the same way he thought about her.

She asked, "Is it true that ninety nine percent of abducted children are killed in the first twenty four hours?"

Linda countered, "You shouldn't think like that, Kristen."

Kristen refused to avert her glare from Nolan. As a display of professionalism and empathy, he remained fixed on her. He sensed she was preparing herself for the news that her daughter was dead. He had seen it before. Like rooms in a mansion that cannot afford to be heated in the winter, Kristen was closing off parts of herself. She was now occupying the logical part of her brain in an attempt to ignore her heart.

"Linda is right," he replied. "Try to remain positive."

"PC Mulvihill took Amy's toothbrush. She reassured me it was policy. You need DNA in case a body is discovered."

"Did PC Mulvihill tell you that?" he asked.

"No."

Nolan looked to Linda and she shrugged. Kristen must have read it on the Internet, probably in the same article that gave her the morbid statistic. Nolan couldn't blame her, nor censure her thought process considering where she lived.

"We're throwing a lot of resources into finding Amy," he said calmly. "Right now we need to follow procedures to help us bring your daughter back home. PC Mulvihill was just following policy, Mrs. Taylor. That's all."

"We need to let the police do their job, Kristen," said Linda, her hand rubbing small circles between Kristen's shoulder blades.

Nolan ran his hand through his hair. It felt greasy against his palm. He couldn't remember the last time he washed it.

"PC Mulvihill has asked you a lot of questions already, but I need to know if you changed your routine tonight?"

"Routine?" she asked.

"What is it you do, Mrs Taylor?"

"For work?" she clarified. "I'm a personnel manager."

"Is it a full time position?"

"Yes, but I do compressed hours."

"You work longer some nights?"

"Every day but Thursday," she answered. There was a hint of suspicion in her voice. "Why?"

He didn't want to worry her so tried to keep it on track, "Do you work at all on Thursdays?"

Nolan was trying to establish if Kristen was home alone all day. If Slade was watching her, then he would know her schedule too.

"I use Thursdays to catch up on the chores and do the food shopping. My work is demanding, Detective. In the evenings I want to spend as much time with Amy before she goes to bed, not spend it cleaning the house."

"I understand," Nolan said. "On the nights you work late, who looks after Amy? A family member?

"My parents live in Buxton. My eldest brother, Michael, immigrated to Canada about eight years ago."

Linda jumped in quickly, "Bill and I have offered to pick Amy up after school, but Kristen didn't want to tie us down." She turned to Kristen. "We told you it would be no trouble, didn't we?"

The question was directed at Kristen, but it was pantomime for the benefit of Nolan. Linda didn't want to look like she wasn't supportive, considering all that Kristen had been through. Through the Stormer Hill grapevine Nolan knew Linda and Bill had revenue coming in from the cottage, as well as a private and work's pension. They lived a comfortable life with no commitments, and save for walking their dog twice daily, their days were quite mundane and uneventful. They could have done more to help Kristen, considering they had the time. It was clear this was now playing on Linda's conscience.

"I know," Kristen said to Linda. She returned back to Nolan. "The nights I work late, Amy goes to Bright Owls."

"Bright Owls?" he clarified.

"It's the before and after school club. They run it from the school for parents who can't make home time, or need time in the morning to drop their kids off so they can get to work."

"The school run it?" he asked.

"Actually, I think it's independent from the school."

"Like a private business?"

Nolan's mind was adding more numbers to the list of possible suspects.

Kristen nodded slowly, leaned forward and said, "You just assume your children will be safe on school grounds."

Nolan saw a worry rash hurrying up her neckline.

"What makes you think Amy wouldn't be safe?" he asked.

"Gram Slade," she replied, expressionless.

"Kristen's gone through this already with the female officer," said Linda, her tone suggesting she was close to losing her patience.

"Gram Slade was looking into my garden before Amy went out to play," said Kristen.

"DI Coonan is aware of this," he said. "And I'm sure we'll be talking to Mr. Slade in due course."

Kristen, her voice rising on the flow of emotion, said, "Did they not tell you that Gram works at Amy's school?"

Nolan felt the rise and fall of his Adam's apple. When he didn't speak, Kristen looked to Linda briefly and abdicated.

"Gram is a cleaner there," Linda said. "We were trying to figure out how long, but at a guess it must be a few years now. Amy knew him."

"How do you know?" asked Nolan.

"She used to speak with him at Bright Owls," replied Kristen, taking hold of her emotion. "He works before school begins and after home time. I've passed him in the corridor on the way to pick up Amy up several times."

"Did Amy ever tell you what they talked about?" asked Nolan.

Kristen considered the question for a moment before answering, "No. She just said that he was nice, and that some of the older kids call him names. Not to his face, but behind his back."

"What kind of names?"

Linda interjected, "I don't know the politically correct term, but in my day they'd call him retarded."

The noun caused Nolan to flinch. As a kid he suffered with allergies, still did during the summer season. This meant he had to breathe through his mouth most of the time. The children in his class would observe him sat alone, mouth breathing, and would call him retarded too. Even now, as an adult, the term was a cruel spear in his side.

"Did Amy ever say anything to make you think she'd go off with Gram?"

On hearing the question, Kristen straightened her back as if a cold finger had traced her spine.

"Do you have children, Detective?" she asked.

"No, ma'am."

There was regret in the reply, but not enough to stop Kristen from delivering her thoughts.

"Then don't assume I haven't done my fair share of counseling on the dangers of speaking with strangers."

Nolan wanted to qualify that his question wasn't aimed to disgrace or call in to question her parenting skills. He raised his palms toward her in protest, but she paid no heed and continued.

"I've raised Amy to be honest, to never hide secrets from me. If Amy was at risk, she'd tell me."

Linda tried to calm Kristen down by clasping her arm and whispering her name, but it made no difference. Kristen was a pressure cooker, and with every minute that lapsed without news of her daughter, composure grew more difficult to maintain.

"Every child in this village knows what happened in Hanging Lee," she added, spittle collecting at the corners of her mouth. "Do you honestly think Amy would go in there with someone she didn't know? I told her time and time again, don't leave the garden. Don't go anywhere on your own! We had passwords. I even acted out scenarios where I tried to abduct her. I made her scared of the world, Detective, but her safety was my only concern. After Lucy went missing the community put trust in the police to keep their children safe, and you failed them." Her body was shaking, the bottom lip trembling. "I've seen those mothers sob their hearts out in church and on the street. That wasn't going to happen to me. I wasn't going to be a victim, and neither was my daughter. I know people say things behind my back, call me paranoid for making her wear that watch. But it didn't help, did it? I failed her too, didn't I?"

Linda objected, "You mustn't blame yourself, Kristen. Tell her, Tom?"

Nolan was struck dumb. He's been to so many houses to deliver bad news, car accidents, fatal beatings, death, and each visit had scored his skin like the edge of a cold blade. He lived with those scars. But there was something about Kristen Taylor that cut him deeper than anyone else he had sat before. Maybe it was the accumulation of all the missing children finally taking their toll, or maybe it was the blame she had placed on the police that felt more personal now. Hearing Kristen reminded him of this hurt. Nolan didn't care what most people thought of him. He knew people in the office talked about him behind his back, just like the children did to Gram Slade. The hours put in weren't a commitment to the job but a reason not to return to an empty home. The smell of cigarette smoke on his clothes, the extra hole punched into his belt, they prompted nothing more than pity in the eyes of the other officers. But it was easier to ignore office tittle-tattle than it was to overlook what Kristen thought of him. As ludicrous as it was, Nolan cared for her, and even though he knew she was beyond his reach, he did not want Kristen to feel anything but admiration for him.

Her voice was a flame struggling in the wind, "Every time I think of her out there, scared and alone, I die a little. I've already lost one person I loved. I don't want to lose another, Detective."

Nolan was about to tender an apology when a male officer came into the room, cheeks flushed. He was tall, lank, a dense coating of hair along his jaw. On seeing Nolan he tried to rein in his enthusiasm. Nolan acknowledged him and ushered him out into the hall with just his eyes. Raising himself off the chair, the cracking sound from his knees causing Linda to blink, he made his excuses to the women and left the room.

CHAPTER 16

THURSDAY

Coonan sat in his car writing in his policy book. The radio had been tuned low to Radio 4. With each news broadcast that came and went, he was reminded another half hour had elapsed without any positive lines of enquiry. Then his mobile phone rang. Tom Nolan's name appeared on the screen.

There were no pleasantries or salutation when he spoke, "Tell me you've found something, Tom."

Nolan cleared his throat and said, "I've been racking my brains, Boss, trying to figure out how I knew the name Gram Slade. Then I saw him on the CCTV at the Taylor home and it came to me. It was during the Guffey case. A man had approached one of our officers asking if he could help with the search. When the officer said he couldn't because it might compromise the scene, the man started acting strange."

"Strange?" asked Coonan, picking at the word as if it was stuck between his teeth. "Shifty-strange?"

"No, not really. He was more, I don't know, friendly-strange."

"If you're remembering someone for being friendly, you've been a cop too long, Tom."

"No, it wasn't that he was being kind. He was over friendly. It wasn't normal, if that makes sense?"

"Not really," replied Coonan.

"I assumed he had mental health issues at first, autism or something like that. It was his manner, the way he avoided eye contact. The officer at the scene was struggling to explain the consequences of him helping with the search. I overheard the conversation and intervened. Slade got all upset. He kept saying he could help. I wouldn't have remembered any of this had it not been for what he said next."

"We're on the clock here. Cut to the chase, Tom."

"He said he wanted to help because he could see the dead."

Coonan paused as he processed what Nolan was saying. That Slade could see the dead meant the guy was a loon or a simpleton. Coonan had dealt with his fair share of each to know that either could be dangerous.

"And this man," Coonan said, "you think it's this Gram Slade?"

"His features are more recognizable than most."

Coonan asked, "He's disfigured?"

"No. He just looks different enough that you'd remember him."

"And what he said, about being able to see the dead, it didn't make you suspicious at the time?"

Coonan knew Nolan was experienced enough to realize the question was framed as an accusation of incompetence. When Nolan didn't reply, he let the silence run its course. Coonan admired, Nolan. He was a good detective, but sometimes he was too trusting of people. It was a weakness, and if Nolan ever wanted to rise through the rank, it was a trait he'd have to purge.

"It did," Nolan finally said. "I pressed him on what he meant, but he got all jittery and tongue-tied. I convinced him to take my contact details in case he heard or saw anything that might help with the enquiry. That allowed me to ask for his name. I remember doing a PNC check but he was clean, which is why I never raised it."

Coonan flipped open his Day Book and began writing. He underlined Gram Slade's name. Next to that, in parenthesis, he made a note to check the police system again.

Nolan added, "There's something else, Boss. The previous night, a few hours after the vigil in the Hanging Lee, a person was seen entering the Taylor garden. They sat on Amy Taylor's swing looking at the house for eight minutes before exiting through Hanging Lee. The PC found it while trawling the CCTV footage. It's too dark to get a positive ID, but based on what I could see, the person was of a similar height and build to Slade."

Coonan looked out of his windscreen at the road ahead. His car was still parked on the side of Edgerton Road. The sun was turning the bellies of clouds orange and red. Jackdaws stirred the air before settling on telephone wires like sots at a bar, and grazing sheep took the form of snowflakes on the hillsides. There was something perfect about Stormer Hill and that always left Coonan feeling unsettled. He estimated that the average person will pass at least one person who has killed another human being while walking on the street. That people tolerated this is down to simple ignorance. He wished for those moments of normalcy and routine, where strangers were not potential monsters, and their smiles were not veils hiding a horrible truth. But you can't forget what you know, and Stormer Hill may have looked perfect, but in Coonan's experience, evil is always attracted to paradise, because there it is free to exercise its fantasies.

"What else do you have?" Coonan asked.

"I spoke to Kristen Taylor about her routine," he continued. "It's fairly consistent. But I did find out that Amy Taylor goes to a breakfast and after school club called Bright Owls every day but Thursday. It's run from within Stormer Hill Primary. I plan on doing background checks on all the staff, but of all the people Kristen could have mentioned who worked at the club and the school, there was one name I didn't expect to hear."

Coonan finally broke from his trance to say, "Gram Slade."

"He is one of the cleaners in the school," replied Nolan. "Amy knew him, and from what Kristen told me, it wasn't uncommon for her to speak with him."

"I want to see the employment records for everyone at the school," said Coonan, his voice more alert and focused. "Get me a list of every member of staff that works at this Bright Owls too. The CCTV has given us a male with an approximate height, build, and age. We also have a time parameter to work with. Hanging Lee is common ground, which will broadened the search, but those living in or associated with the geographical area should be our main focus. It's not an exhaustive list, but helps construct a more accurate TIE strategy."

"You're not arresting Slade?" asked Nolan.

"He's of interest to this enquiry, but at the moment, no. Get a statement from him. I need to know where he was at the time Amy was taken. With his consent request DNA samples, fingerprints and footwear impression. Tom, I'm only looking to TIE Slade at this stage. Nevertheless, feed him some rope. If he says something you feel could implicate him, you ring me and I'll make the decision to arrest. Even if he howls at the moon, I want to know about it. You got that?"

Nolan agreed and added, "I take it Bob Wood hasn't found anything yet?"

"And you'd be right," replied Coonan. "I'll get SOCO to attend the Taylor home. They may be able to lift something from that swing. I'll also get someone at the station to run Slade's name through the Police National Database, see if we can pull up any Intel on him. To get a job at a school he will have gone through extensive vetting so he won't be a Registered Sex Offender or have any previous. But that doesn't mean we can't find out if he's been a victim of crime in the past." Coonan missed a beat before continuing, "If this guy is as vulnerable as you say, make sure there's an appropriate adult present before you start asking questions. I don't want it to look like we're taking advantage."

Coonan ended the call. He spent a moment gazing out of the window before saying, "Paradise sucks."

CHAPTER 17

THURSDAY

Palmer was packing his suitcase for the journey back to London when his mobile rang. He walked to a small wooden dresser and saw Juliet's name on the mobile's screen. He'd sent her a text about twenty minutes ago explaining that he was returning home the following day. He gave no reason to why his visit had ended so abruptly, but did add that the experience has given him greater compassion towards Dr. Frankenstein's Monster.

Juliet sounded punch-drunk when she greeted him, "What's going on, Alex?"

Palmer moved over to the bed and sat down beside the suitcase. He checked his watch. It was 8.56 PM.

"You fall asleep reading manuscripts again?" he asked.

"I had a meeting this afternoon in the city with a client. There were cocktails."

Palmer had only seen Juliet drunk once before. They were celebrating the release of his third novel and had gone for a drink in a sky bar that overlooked Canary Warf. Juliet had consumed two Mojitos when he realized she had thimble guts. Juliet had always remained professionally reserved whenever they spoke on the phone. If they met, she wore oversized black-rimmed glasses, low cut blouses and pencil skirts with block heel pumps. Her hair was always tied in a side braid that hung over her right shoulder like a black snake. If they small talked, she laughed. If they discussed work, she remained focused and stony. She never ventured too far into his personal life, and never her own. But that afternoon at the sky bar her eyes were a little wider. She had untied her braid allowing the hair to cascade over her shoulders. It was the first time Palmer had seen her professional mask slip. Palmer studied her face as she spoke spiritlessly of the burden leading bookstores placed on publishers, and how they were killing profits for most books published, and the more she spoke, the more she drank. Alcohol seasoned the dialogue and soon her voice sounded less snobbish. Palmer liked her when she wasn't so expeditious. That was also the day he heard Juliet swear for the first time. She ordered another Cosmo. Palmer progressed to an Old Fashioned. Then, unprompted, she revealed to him that she had a miscarriage the previous month. Palmer didn't know what to say, so that's the tact he took. He consoled her by placing his hand on hers. Juliet appeared embarrassed, as if coming to the realization she had crossed some ethical, or professional line. She backtracked for a moment, blaming the omission on alcohol and hormones. But something happened that day. Juliet became human in Palmer's eyes. Normally, if a woman showed some vulnerability, and was drunk, he would have taken advantage of the situation, but Juliet was his agent, and engaged to an architect called Corky. It would have done neither of them any good to sleep with each other, professionally, or personally. So Palmer did the one thing alien to him; he went against his natural instinct and encouraged talk of her wedding plans.

For nearly half an hour, Palmer endured talk of venues, cake and dresses. He found long-term commitment something of an anomaly in the genetic makeup of humans. There were advantages to it, the sharing of social norms, nesting and foraging. But neither proved to have enough pull for him to settle down. Each week he abdicated the chore of grocery shopping to some faceless person behind a computer screen. Interior design never piqued his interest either and had gone to the expense of hiring someone to decorate his apartment and furnish it accordingly when he moved in. Sure, Palmer could see the benefits of social monogamy, but failed to comprehend sexual monogamy, comparing it to a round peg in a square hole, a suitable analogy that, depending on his audience, would be altered slightly to include a triangular hole, not a square one. He had once read in a popular science periodical how DNA fingerprint technology had been used in animals to determine how promiscuous they were. It did not surprise him to understand that to guarantee their lineage the male species would spread their seed to multiple partners, meaning sexual monogamy was more an ideal than a practice in the animal kingdom. That polygamy was frowned upon, and in many cases, illegal, save for many Muslim countries, only bolstered Palmer's reasoning to never marry. He knew that if he did, it would only be a matter of time before he was caught in bed with someone else. In a weird sense of justification, he had avoided marriage to save any woman being hurt. To feed his sexual appetite, he paid for high-classed sex workers, the type that knew when, and how, to keep a secret. He never hired the same woman twice, and often engaged in threesomes where he spent most of the time watching the girl's limbs entwine on his bed. Sometimes he chose women because they looked like Juliet. He would get them to dress in office attire and wear their hair in a side braid. That he never took advantage of the moment in the sky bar, he believed, was a display of strength, because humans, regardless of their ethics and morals, were flawed. They all had weaknesses, and the greatest of them all was the need to be loved, something he did not need nor crave.

"Did something happen at the signing?" asked Juliet.

Palmer could almost smell the cocktail syrups on her breath coming through the phone.

"Three people turned up," he replied, the defeat in his voice evident. "Word had clearly gotten around the village why I was there."

"Three?" she asked. "The librarian assured me the place would be full!"

"It's not her fault," Palmer replied. "The community is still reeling from Sarah Cook. It was bad timing on my part. I've booked an early train to Euston tomorrow. I should be back in London for around 10 AM."

"So the trip proved fruitless?" she asked.

"Not entirely," Palmer replied. "The detective involved in all the cases took me to Hanging Lee."

"Hanging Lee?" Juliet repeated. "It sounds like a town straight out of a Spaghetti Western."

"It's where the children went missing. There was definitely something eerie about it," Palmer said. "You know that feeling when you walk into a dark room, and just before you turn on the light you sense someone there, waiting in the darkness?"

"No. But I will now," she said.

"It felt like we were being watched," Palmer continued. "There was a presence, something unworldly. I'm still trying to figure it out."

Palmer quickly recalled that first night in the cottage when he woke and saw someone in the garden.

"I did find out a little more about Sarah Cook's disappearance, which will help flesh out some of the story. The locals hold a vigil for all the missing children every three months. They light candles and say prayers. It's clear they're all still united by the tragedy. You forget how small some worlds are when you live in a city."

Juliet asked, "Do you think they'll ever find the children?"

Palmer didn't want to say aloud what everyone in the village was thinking. He knew, like them, it would be tempting fate to say that the probability of discovering either child alive now was unlikely. When he spoke to Nolan about this in The Old Swan, he had remained noncommittal, but deep down he was thinking the same thing as the detective; if the children weren't already victims of child sex exploitation or human trafficking, then there was a strong chance they were buried in the moorland.

"For all his faults," Palmer added, "the detective whose been showing me around has a grasp on things. Hopefully they'll find them soon."

"How long has it been since that Cook girl went missing?" asked Juliet.

"Going on six months," he replied, his tone smooth as glass.

"Jesus. I can't even imagine what the parents must be feeling."

"We can be thankful we're not in a position to know either," Palmer said, and realising how incentive that might sound after her miscarriage, changed the subject quickly. "So, have you missed me?"

"What?" she asked.

"I thought maybe when I get back, I'll pop over to the office. We can catch up."

"Erm, sure."

"You okay?"

"I'm fine. Just a little light headed. I tell you what; I'll take you out for lunch at that gaudy restaurant you like so much. You can tell me more about being driven out of the village by locals bearing pitchforks and torches."

Palmer smiled. "So you got the Frankenstein reference?"

"It was hardly subtle."

The conversation was drying up, and Palmer felt indebted to the yawn Juliet delivered.

"I'm such a light-weight when it comes to drinking," she said, and yawned a second time.

"You best get to bed, Aurora. We'll catch up soon. I'll text you when I land back in London."

Palmer ended the call. He placed the suitcase on the floor and looked out of the bedroom window. Wind turbines stood sentry across the hills in the distance. Silhouetted against the fading sun they looked more like colossal daisies that had most of their petals removed by the fingers of giants. If Palmer pressed his eye close enough to the pane, he could see the Mossop farmhouse to his left. A security light shone down over a gravelled area outside their door. Bill's moss-green Defender was parked outside; a faint glow of light came from the ground floor windows. There wouldn't be much time in the morning to explain why he was leaving, and he didn't really want to leave a note for Bill to find. He felt an obligation to speak to him in person.

"Best to be civil," he said to himself.

Palmer made his way downstairs, slipped into his jacket and took the short walk to the farmhouse.

***

Bill opened the door with a look that suggested Palmer had caught him some in lewd act. He was loose jawed, and his tongue could be seen flinching from within the darkness of his mouth.

"Have I come at a bad time?" asked Palmer.

Bill looked briefly over Palmer's shoulder, and then escorted him in as if he was bearing a secret only for Palmer's ears. The smell of burning wood and soup coming from the living area couldn't distract from the mustiness of Eli's pelt. The dog was found in its usual sanctuary under the large dining table, its legs twitching to a dream. Bill sat down at the table. He was dressed in an old red and blue plaid shirt buttoned to the neck. He had not shaved that day and the white buds of hair that sprouted from his skin gave him the appearance of an Arctic explorer. The table surface was cluttered with letters, the writing too small to read from where Palmer was stood. Bill gestured for him to sit, and as he pulled back the chair, the grating of wood on stone sounded like hunger pains.

"I wanted you to know that I'll be leaving early in the morning," Palmer said as he sat down.

Bill was busying himself arranging papers into neat little stacks. At the very least Palmer expected some investigation into the reason, but it was clear the man was consumed by something his brain was processing. Palmer looked around the room.

"Linda out?" he asked, hearing the cop in his voice surface again.

Bill placed the last sheet of paper on the pile and looked up. In contrast to his forehead, which was as rippled as tree bark, his skin was smooth around his face, almost transparent. A spiderweb of tiny red veins sat beneath each cheek, and pendulous skin hung under his eyes in shades of mulberry. Palmer couldn't tell if he was close to tears or that his eyes had, with age, developed a sheen that made them glisten.

"Better you hear it from me," Bill said, his voice raspy and seasoned with remorse. "Linda got a call from a friend of ours who lives in the village."

Bill rubbed his hands together as if trying to remove a stain that wasn't there. Palmer encouraged him to continue by saying, "I can fix you a drink if it'll help?"

Bill dismissed the offer by shaking his head. He labored his breath and said, "A few hours ago a little girl called Amy Taylor went missing."

Something lurched in Palmer's stomach, hitting its walls so hard he almost bent forward to reverse the feeling.

That makes four, he thought. *Four children in four years.*

His cold-gray eyes settled on Bill who was lost in the fine grain set within the table. Palmer looked around the room for a drink's cabinet.

"You keep any whiskey close by?" he asked.

Bill rubbed his hand over his balding pate, made a few noises that were too low and muddled to decipher, and then motioned over to a small cupboard on the wall. Palmer investigated and found a bottle of single malt. Taking two glasses from the cupboard, he returned with the bottle and poured them both a drink.

Bill spoke first, "Kristen, that's the mother of the girl, she's a widower. Her late husband was deployed to Afghanistan a few years back, but never returned home. Amy was their only child. She's around ten years old now. God only knows how Kristen raised that child after Paul died, but she's a tough one. Can't say how long a person can remain on their feet when life keeps trying to take their legs."

Bill brought the glass to his lips. Palmer saw his hand tremble, and for a while neither man said anything. No words of condolence. No admission of sadness. They each lifted their glass consecutively to allow the sting of alcohol to coat their lips and tongue. Palmer's chest warmed as the whiskey settled within him.

"I should be out there," Bill said, "helping to find her."

"You may end up hindering the search if you do," replied Palmer. "They'll have trained officers searching the area as we speak."

Something behind Bill's eyes lit up.

"You think they'll find her?" Bill asked, tendering a desperate gaze.

Palmer swirled the whiskey around the flanks of the glass, taking his time. He'd just gotten off the phone to Juliet who had already invited him to give his experience on these matters, and even with her he felt uncomfortable speaking aloud his own concerns. Bill was a local. He knew the mother. Whatever he said would probably be taken verbatim, and delivered to the locals accordingly. Palmer knocked back the whiskey and looked at Bill.

"She's got as good a chance as any right now," he conceded. "This may sound a little cold, but had those other children not gone missing, Amy might have been more at risk. I dare say there is a lot of officers out there right now closing the net, and with God on her side, she'll be reunited with her mother before nightfall."

Palmer hated bringing God into the conversation, but it was a comfort blanket for most people. When you don't have hard facts or evidence to justify your answers, then a little blind faith always smoothed the edges of hardship. The lines around Bill's eyes thinned out. His shoulders relaxed.

"I hope so," he said. "Poor kid."

A key entered the front door and awoke Eli from his slumber. The dog jumped up, knocking the table as it made a dash to the porch. Bill called its name and steadied his glass as he watched the door open and Linda walk in. Struggling to remove the key from the latch, Linda employed her leg to hold Eli back from jumping up at the woman waiting outside.

"Eli!" Linda shouted, pushing her shin into his neck. The dog turned its attention to the woman and began clawing at Linda's coat to get past. Bill moved his chair away and walked slowly toward Linda.

"Down, Eli!" Bill demanded.

On hearing his master's deep timbre, the dog turned and walked dejectedly back to the table where it circled for a moment before resting.

Bill had a good foot and a half over Linda. It was clear that all the years of adjusting his gaze downwards to meet her eyes had fashioned a slight stoop to his bearing. Linda exchanged a few hushed words that Palmer could not hear, but presumed it was why they had a visitor so late in the evening.

Bill returned back to the table, and said quietly, "The police have been to the house. Kristen doesn't want to stay there alone, so Linda has brought her back here."

"That's the mother?" asked, Palmer.

"She's shook up something bad, so tread lightly around her."

The noise of the front door slamming shut forced Palmer to look over. The soft light coming from a small lamp moved over Kristen Taylor as if trying to warm her. If she was wearing makeup, Palmer couldn't see any. He assumed most of it had been washed away by the tears, leaving her appearing natural and genuine. She was pretty, that much he was sure of. Linda removed her coat and gently guided Kristen to the room where both Palmer and Bill were waiting, their bodies awkwardly trying to adopt a casual position but instead made them look like scarecrows following a storm. Palmer stood to his feet when Kristen entered the room. She did not look at him at first, and trailed Linda blindly until she stopped before the table.

"Mr. Palmer," Linda said, her tone suggesting she was now in mother hen mode, "Bill tells me you know what's happened. I'm sure you'll appreciate this is a very stressful time for…"

Palmer cut her off, "You don't need me taking up anymore of your time, I'm quite sure of that."

He turned to Bill and said, "I'll post the keys through your letterbox before I leave tomorrow."

Bill nodded and offered his hand.

"Have a safe journey, Mr. Palmer," he said.

The two men shook hands before Palmer addressed the women. He wasn't really sure what to say. He knew he couldn't leave the room without offering some words of comfort, or acknowledgment to Kristen. He paused briefly to assemble the right amount of empathy, at which point she looked up at him. Her eyes were ink black, save for one that had tones of amber. The crescent of each eyebrow had long since yielded to the weight that had gathered around her forehead, and in that moment, caught between grief and fragility, she looked so sweet and innocent Palmer felt an overwhelming urge to gather her in his arms

"You're the writer," she said, voice honeyed and low.

Palmer considered the consequences of admitting that he was, that she might too follow the same cockeyed view of every townsfolk in Stormer Hill, but in the end he nodded. Kristen Taylor then smiled. It was not overstated, or offered carelessly, but subtle enough that Palmer felt wrong to accept it. He smiled back, then turned quickly to Linda and canted his head.

"You have a lovely cottage," he said.

She took this well and thanked him.

"You don't need to leave because of me," Kristen said stepping into his view.

Linda turned and said, "You should rest, Kristen. Conserve your energy."

Bill chimed in, "Linda's right. You need to relax."

Like most men when presented with a situation that demanded high levels of compassion, Bill decided to do the only thing that came natural to him.

"I'll go put the kettle on," he said, and vanished from sight.

In Bill's absence, Palmer could feel Linda's eyes burning through him like hot pokers. He was about to make his excuses when Kristen pulled up a chair at the table and sat down. She placed one of her hands over the other and looked up to Palmer.

"You going to write about the children?" she asked.

He responded cautiously. "I was considering it."

"What's changed?" she asked.

"Being here."

Kristen paused and added, "You're not wanted?"

He looked briefly to Linda before reclaiming his seat. He lent his body over the lip of the table and mimicked the same hand positioning as Kristen.

"I guess people have a way of letting you know when you're not wanted without actually saying it," he said. "You lived in the village long?"

"My husband thought it would be safer here than the city."

The irony wasn't wasted on Palmer.

"Bill told me about what happened to your husband. That must have been hard."

Linda took the chair where Bill had been sat earlier. Her movement quick and deliberate to draw attention away from Kristen. When she was settled, she shifted the conversation back to Palmer.

"So you've got things to take care of before you leave?" Linda asked.

"Not much," he said. "Suitcase is packed. I just need to book my train tickets."

Linda forced a smile.

"And where is it you live, Mr. Palmer?" Kristen asked.

"Call me Alex," he replied, amiably. "London."

"Must have been a culture shock coming to Stormer Hill?"

"The lack of McDonalds certainly threw me for a while," he said, smiling.

"I like the intimacy of a village," said Linda, using her words like a crowbar to get between them both. "People know you, and you know them. You don't get that in cities."

"Very true, Linda," replied Palmer. "But for me, that's a blessing."

There was a moment of silence before Kristen spoke again.

"Do you know my daughter has gone missing?" she asked.

Palmer nodded, and without prompt Linda's hand arranged itself on Kristen's.

"She'll be home soon, Kristen," Linda said, the words sounding rehearsed.

"Amy loved reading," Kristen said to Palmer. "She'd always have her head in a book. I'd catch her sometimes after she'd gone to bed, a flashlight under the covers. She told me she wanted to be a writer when she grows up." Kristen's voice wavered as the struggle to push out the words tore at her throat. "Maybe you could give her some advice. When she comes home?"

Palmer smiled.

"Do you have a pen, Linda?"

Linda retrieved a ballpoint from a small drawer and reluctantly handed Palmer. He scribbled down a phone number on a scrap piece of paper and passed it to Kristen.

"This is my personal mobile number," he said. "Tell Amy that whenever she wants to talk she can ring me. My agent represents a children's author too. I'll see if I can arrange to have some of their books sent over."

Kristen folded the paper and placed it before her. She didn't say thank you. It was evident from her expression the gesture was kindly received and valued. Palmer leaned back into his chair, physically uncoupling himself from Kristen's stare. He looked over to Linda and thanked her once again for her hospitality before regaining his height. There was a fleeting look exchanged between Kristen and Palmer, and though no words were spoken, he felt like a connection had been established. Since she entered the room he'd been drawn to her vulnerability. Behind all that grief he could see an attractive woman full of life, and he wondered in that moment if she felt anything for him. Did she find him attractive, mysterious, or exciting? He wondered if, like Juliet, she would share secrets with him too. Confide in him. Palmer said his farewells to the two women as Bill walked in carrying two cups of hot tea.

"Thought you'd already gone?" he asked.

Palmer nodded. "Just leaving, Bill. Got to book my train tickets," he said.

"Give my regards to the Big Smoke," Bill said placing the cups on the table.

Palmer nodded, and before leaving, turned one final time to look at Kristen. She was staring right at him.

CHAPTER 18

THURSDAY

The car journey from Kristen Taylor's place to the edge of Stormer Hill gave Nolan enough time to smoke two cigarettes, which he chained while waiting for Comms to conduct a voter's check to see where Gram Slade lived. The results came back as Nall Street, a small terrace the color of shale rock situated on the outskirts of the village and tucked away from the main road. Nolan got out of his car on the street and waited for a moment outside the property. It was one of seven on the row; red blistered and cracked window frames gave the house a look of abandonment; jaundice netting hid the rooms, the skirting of each dirtied by condensation.

Maybe they hide something else too, Nolan thought.

He knew this area. His old man used to drag him out here to ramble across the nearby fields when he was a teenager. Nolan hated the place back then, didn't care too much for now. The local water company owned some seventy thousand acres of the surrounding land, which was either used to collect the raw water that would be treated for drinking, or tenanted by farmers. Sheep grazed along the hills in the winter. Brown cows occupied it in the summer. Because it was classified as open access, ramblers, like his father, were free to roam the mix of rough acid and calcareous grassland without limitation. There were rudimentary roads etched through it like veins that led to small dams or pump houses. To the casual observer it was idyllic, picturesque, but to Nolan it was a place he once walked silently in the shadow of his father, breathless and bored. Now, it was the home to a monster.

The voter's check revealed a woman named Zerelda Anne Slade also lived at the address with Gram. Nolan assumed, due to her age, this was the mother. Coonan had given him the instruction to make sure an appropriate adult was present when he questioned Gram, then who better than the mother. While a blessing, he assumed

Zerelda would also be a real pain in his arse too. If she thought the visit was anything to do with the missing children, even if it was just a suspicion, she'd place a gag on her son as soon as he opened the door and turn on Nolan. If he left with just spit in his eye, Nolan would class the meeting as a success. He'd seen it before; mothers and fathers do all they can to protect their young, even if they know they've done wrong. But Gram was the first positive lead the police had in four years. Whatever Zerelda Slade was going to throw at him, it might be worth taking.

Nolan rapped the door with clenched fist. He waited and considered his words should Zerelda opened it. The light in the vestibule came on, bolts withdrew. The door opened and a man stood before him, shadows dripping off his forehead into inky and indistinct eyes.

"Gram Slade?" Nolan asked, seeming to struggle a little to get his words out.

"Yes, sir," replied Gram, politely.

Nolan didn't say anything for a moment. He just stared at him. The bones beneath Gram's clothes pointed out at angles giving him an ungainly posture that summoned up unease in him. It was fleeting but Nolan quickly checked Slade's hands to see if there were any traces of blood or fresh wounds that may denote a struggle had taken place, but the scar tissue that covered the backs of each was more disconcerting. He returned his gaze back to Slade's face.

"I was hoping to ask you a few questions, if that's not too much bother?" asked Nolan.

Gram nodded.

There seemed to be no fear in him, not even surprise. Nolan concluded that had the Devil or a hand cream salesman knocked on the door, Gram Slade would have greeted each in the same way. It didn't seem right, at least not to his detective instincts. A guilty person puts on a show for the police. They playact and offer up moments of feigned concern or compassion, mostly toward the victim they've murdered. They'll gasp, shield their mouth, pause dramatically and ask, *How* and *Why*. There is no malice or hatred in those waking moments. In truth, they show interest, maybe even offer to help the investigation. They do not reveal the evil within. But Nolan hadn't seen any of this on Gram Slade's face. He opened the door and was not struck dumb, nor did his eyes dilate to reveal shock. If anything, Slade appeared at ease, almost happy to see the detective. Nolan was about to ask if he could come into the house when a woman's voice rose up from behind Gram, shrill and narked.

"Who's calling so damn late?!" she yelled.

Gram turned and shouted, "It's the police, Momma."

Facing Nolan again, he offered his hand. The gesture took him by surprise. He shook it, feeling for the first time the strange landscape of Slade’s foreign skin. It was smooth, soft, and Nolan wondered for a brief moment if it had cradled Amy Taylor's face tenderly, or gripped tight her throat.

"How'd you know?" he asked Slade, extricating himself.

"What's that?" Slade asked.

"That I was a police officer," Nolan added, unsure if he had to spell everything out.

Gram ran his hand over the buzz-cut and replied, "Remembered you from..."

His voice trailed off. Nolan realized Slade was recalling the night Lucy Guffey went missing. He watched for a moment, looking for the signs on his face that would reveal he had played a part in her disappearance, a twitch of the eye, glance to the floor, the masking of his mouth with his hand. Nothing. The vestibule's door suddenly swung open. From behind Gram Slade came a wiry-looking woman with hair tied into a bun. Her body was arched over a walking stick, which she struggled to keep balanced. Gram turned and placed his arm around the woman's shoulder to support her frame.

"You shouldn't be walking too much, Momma," he said.

Zerelda Slade grunted and threw a stony glare toward Nolan.

"Who the fuck are you?" she asked.

"You can't cuss like that," Gram said.

"It's okay," said Nolan. "My name is Detective Tom Nolan."

"What business do you have coming here so late?" she asked. "Haven't got time for chewing the fat with some pig."

Gram now palmed his mouth.

"Police are good for nothing but catching geese," Zerelda said to Gram. "Bet my left eye on the geese winning out too."

"Sorry, sir," Gram said.

"Don't you be apologizing," she chided.

Gram shoe-gazed for a second, cheeks turning crimson, eyes blinking erratically.

Zerelda redirected her attention back to Nolan, "Now what is it you want, Mr. My tits are freezing off out here."

A light came on in the neighbor's bedroom. It was bright enough to catch Nolan's attention. He saw the twitching of curtains and the shadow of a man.

"Perhaps it would be best if we go inside," he said, his tone amiable but firm. "Wouldn't want to keep you on your feet too long, Mrs. Slade."

"You can say what you need to say out here," she replied sternly. "And it's Ms. Slade."

"If only to keep this matter private, I think it would be best to discuss things inside, nonetheless."

Nolan countered his head, gesturing toward the neighboring house. Zerelda Slade squinted at the wall beside her as if she could see through it to the occupants beyond. She conceded by curling her lip and turning back into the house. Gram stood for a moment watching her hobble inside before he gestured Nolan in with his hand.

"She's got the pain real bad today," Gram said quietly, closing the door as Nolan entered.

The detective nodded and asked, "What's wrong with her?"

Gram scratched his head as if he had been tasked with diagnosing an oil leak in a car.

"Momma calls it her bane. That's all I know it by. It makes her legs weak and she says it's like her spine is on fire. She's usually very nice," he added, almost as a reminder for him than an affidavit.

Gram closed the vestibule door and led Nolan to a small living area. Incense sticks charged the air with aromas of sandalwood, jasmine and lavender, their wisp of gray smoke curling like twine toward the ceiling. The decor had a South Asia and Morocco influence. A large Indian Mandala tapestry covered a blood red wall. Brass nails held aloft dream catchers and Rasai gold bells, and a macrame plant holder caged some kind of plant that had long since died from neglect. A porcelain reproduction of Ganesha sat on a shelf beside a wooden Kamadhenu with calf, and lining the windowsill was varying sized gourds and candles. As Nolan moved to the centre of the room, he saw fairy lights framing a large triptych painting fixed to the chimneybreast, all three panels rendering biblical scenes featuring Jesus, God and the Devil. The figures were all distorted, twisted, and Nolan couldn't help but stare at it with fascination.

"Bosch," replied Zerelda Slade.

She lowered itself to a leather couch festooned with sequined cushions. Gram helped lift her pale feet to a large tan leather pouffe, the scene well rehearsed and matter of practise.

"The Last Judgment," she continued, her breath labored. "I keep it there because it reminds me of my son."

Nolan gave Gram a quick look to see if he'd acknowledge Zerelda, but he was too busy positioning a throw over her legs. Nolan asked he could sit. Zerelda gestured to a small armchair the color of a rapeseed field. Springs pressed against his backside as he settled into the seat, and thought for a moment he felt one was trying to corkscrew up his arsehole. Gram sat down too, perching himself beside his mother. For a moment, Nolan couldn't think of anything but that old house at the back of the Bate's motel.

"I'm Detective Constable Tom Nolan," he began."It's not my intention to take up too much of your time, Ms. Slade, but I need to understand where Gram was today between the hours of 4 PM and 6 PM."

Gram looked to his mother, confused. Zerelda didn't turn or try and pacify him, but remained fixed on Nolan like a leopard stalking out its prey. Nolan allowed the silence to reach an uncomfortable stage. He was used to waiting and knew eventually someone would speak, and it sure wasn't going to be him.

"Cut the shit, Detective. What is it you think my son has done?" asked Zerelda.

"A person fitting Gram's description was seen close to a crime scene, Ms. Slade. We just want to eliminate Gram from our enquiries. That's all."

"What crime scene? You saying my boy did something bad? Look at him!" she said. Taking hold of Gram's hand, she added, "He ain't got one bad bone in his body!"

"As I said, we're just eliminating people from the enquiry. At this stage anyone fitting the description of the offender is being questioned." He turned his attention to Gram. "You don't need to worry, Gram. I just need to know where you were today between 4 and 6 PM. Can you remember?"

"You've not cautioned him," stated Zerelda. "Whatever he tells you is inadmissible, Gram. I know my shit, Detective."

"We're just trying to establish a few facts, Ms. Slade. That's all."

Zerelda turned to her son and rubbed his hand reassuringly, "Tell the detective where you were, Gram. It's okay."

Gram looked at his mother, and whatever muted conversation was had, it had given him the conviction to slowly turn his head and face Nolan.

"I was at the library, sir," he said.

"Did anyone see you there?" asked Nolan, trying his best not too sound too pissed off at the disclosure.

"Angela Kowal," he replied. "She's the librarian. Mrs. Albright was there too along with Mrs. Thickett."

"Claire Thickett?" asked Nolan, remembering her from parish meetings where her voice was felt like an earthquake.

Gram nodded and Nolan produced a small pocket notebook from his jacket and began writing.

"Do you know Mrs. Albright's first name?" Nolan asked, his hand busily guiding the pen.

"No, sir."

"You work at the local school, right?" He waited for Gram to nod his head before continuing to write. "And what are your normal working hours?"

"Work two times, sir; once in the morning before the children arrive, and then again after they leave."

"And what time do you normally leave, the second time?"

Nolan tried to adapt the same pattern of words as Gram to avoid confusion and potentially stalling the conversation.

"He leaves at 5 PM," interjected Zerelda, her tone suggesting she was growing impatient.

"But you were at the library at 4 PM? Is that right, Gram?"

"Yes, sir. I got to leave early, considering it was such a special event."

Nolan stopped writing and gave his full attention to Gram.

"What event?" he asked.

"Not every day we get someone famous in Stormer Hill," he replied.

Gram stood, walked to a small shelf in the corner of the room filled with two-tone earthenware bottles and a few books. He removed a hardback and handed it Nolan. The cover revealed a silhouetted man walking through woods. Snow bleached the ground and dusted the branches of trees. The typeface was bold and lilac revealing the name Alex Palmer. Nolan opened the book and saw the small inscription on the title page: *To Zee Slade. Should you ever forget to carry a knotted handkerchief.... Bless you. Alex Palmer.*

Gram sat back down with his mother and said, "I got it for my Momma."

"You went to see Alex Palmer, the author?" clarified Nolan, closing the book and putting it on the arm of the chair.

"He was very nice," replied Gram. "He wrote a message."

"I saw," said Nolan. "And this was at what time?"

Gram looked up trying to recall the exact time.

"4.30 PM, I think. I got there a little before though. Thought it might be busy, but I didn't need to worry. It was pretty empty. Then Mrs. Albright and Mrs. Thickett came, which was good thing because I would have felt bad for Mr. Palmer."

Nolan flipped closed his notepad and returned it to his jacket.

"Thank you, Gram," he said, reigning in his disappointment.

Gram looked at his mother and asked, "Did I do right, Momma?"

She nodded and stroked his face, "You did fine, son."

Nolan lifted himself from the chair. He considered extending his hand to Zerelda, but thought better of it. She'd probably bite him, and that'd mean an hour or two waiting in A&E for a tetanus shot. Instead, he asked her if it would be possible to obtain a sample of Gram's DNA.

"No you may not," she said, spitting out the words as if they were darts aimed at Nolan's head. "You want to frame my boy for something he didn't do!"

Nolan raised his hand, "Actually, the DNA would allow us to rule out Gram's connection."

"My boy has told you where he was!"

Zerelda's face was ruddy, hands trembling. Nolan half expected her to stand up like a congregation member of an evangelical church, miraculously cured of her aliments and all the power of Christ the Lord Saviour instilled within her arms to crack that walking stick over his head. Fortunately she remained seated. Instead, she pointed the stick in Nolan's direction like a bony finger.

"You calling my boy a liar?"

"The sample is voluntary, Ms. Slade. But should you refuse, I'll need to take a formal statement where I'll be asking for the reasons. And, should further evidence present itself that may link Gram to the scene, I'll be requesting that Gram comes down to the station for interviewing. I'll be able to obtain a sample then, which I'm sure will be more traumatic an experience for Gram and yourself to undergo. By getting a sample now, nothing gets written down, and it'll mean you'll probably never see me again."

Nolan could see the resignation settling into her eyes.

Gram finally spoke, his words soft and unhurried. "I don't mind. I done nothing wrong."

Zerelda glanced at her son. All the fire faded from her skin. She turned to Nolan and gave a nonverbal approval that allowed him to return back to his car and fetch the sample kit. He talked Gram through the procedure, swiped the inside of his mouth with a cotton bud, and placed it into a small plastic container, and put that in a zip bag.

"You did well," Nolan said.

Gram relaxed back into the chair and took his mother's hand again. Nolan was making his way to the door when Gram shuffled to the edge of the seat, as if about to escort him out.

"He knows the way," Zerelda said, and Gram froze still.

"You understand I'll have to check with those who attended the library to see if they corroborate Gram's account?" Nolan said to Zerelda.

Her eyes narrowed, forehead ruffled like an unmade bed.

"You waste as many hours as you like, Detective. Just don't be coming around here accusing my son of wrongdoing. He's a good boy, never been no harm to no one."

Nolan looked at the simple and guileless man.

Maybe she was right, he thought.

The evil he assumed was coursing through Gram's veins had been flushed out with displays of kindness toward his mother. There were still questions that needed answering concerning his whereabouts at the time of Amy's disappearance, something he wasn't going to dismiss solely based on Gram's performance today, but should Alex Palmer, or any of the other women corroborate

Gram's story, then it meant the abductor was still out there, and Nolan was no closer to finding them.

CHAPTER 19

THURSDAY

When Palmer returned to the cottage, the air in each room had cooled enough to tighten his skin. A large cast iron radiator stood against the wall in the living room, which he brushed his hand across; cold to the touch. He kicked the pipe that ran off from the supply valve as if testing the pressure of a car tyre.

"Piece of shit," he said to himself.

He thought about going over to see Bill again, but knew that with Kristen Taylor there he'd only raise more suspicion in Linda. He could tell from the way she acted as chaperon to the conversation she didn't trust him. Maybe Linda was right. Maybe if Palmer had been alone with Kristen, he would have taken advantage of her vulnerability, a sympathetic ear, a kind smile from time to time. If she broke down in tears, he'd offer a tissue. Maybe he'd even hold her hand, his thumb stroking her soft skin. He'd never break away from her eyes, soft words of understanding slipping from his lips, all measured and threaded together with one intention, which was to win her heart. Yes, maybe it wouldn't be the best thing returning to the farmhouse, for everyone's sake. This didn't help his current situation though. The cottage was cold, and the temperature would drop moving into the night. He recalled the moment Bill had refilled the heating system. The boiler was in the cellar, and from what he could remember it seemed like an easy process. All he would need to do is find the isolating valve and release fresh water into the system until it reached the desired pressure. Palmer still felt grounded in the real world to work this out.

The stairs leading to the cellar lay behind a narrow door in the living room. He released the latch that secured it and flicked the light switch. The bulb did not react. He tried it again, alternating rapidly between on and off. Blackness, rich and endless draped the stairs. He considered searching for a flashlight but instead produced his mobile and activated the torch. It produced enough constant light to illuminate five to six feet in front of him. Taking the steps cautiously, he arrived in the cellar unharmed and began to slowly navigate to where the boiler was situated.

The stucco walls were the color of roadside snow. Exposed pipes ran in and out of holes leading to different parts of the cottage, the copper lime green and resembling vines. Dusk breathed on the pane of a small window, its light diffused by a net of aged cobwebs. Palmer stumbled over a misplaced shovel as he inched toward the boiler and he blindly reached out to grab something with his spare hand, finding only the dank air to grapple with. Steadying himself against the nearest wall, he shone the light at the floor to make certain there were no more hazards. Rain, or possibly bilge water, had collected in pools on the gray slate. It was reasonable to assume that given the lack of light, and warmth, the cellar would always remain damp, but what caused him to stop and remain fixed on the ground was an impression of a boot left by the water. He assumed at first it was just a trick of the light, but as he knelt down and guided the mobile's light over the area, he saw the distinct print of its sole. He raised the mobile a few feet ahead and saw that the footprints were leading behind a small partition close to the boiler. He remembered the person in the garden that night, watching him.

Someone's broken in, he thought.

He carefully picked the shovel off the floor so not to produce a grating sound. Part of him wanted to announce his presence in the hope it would frighten the intruder and cause them to concede, but then the memory of Jason Legge came to him again like an ocean wave. *Live with it. Live with it.* Palmer felt himself tumbling under a riptide of panic. The mobile cast strange and monstrous shadows across the walls as his hands trembled with fear. In seconds, the shovel had gained weight and he began to struggle to keep hold of the handle. Palmer convinced himself he could hear someone's breathing, long and drawn out like a ghoul's song. He turned on his heels to face the stairs and lifted the light before him. He was right. There was someone down there with him. Sat on the bottom step, with head titled to one side, was the man he saw at the library.

"Gram?" he asked under his breath. "That you?"

The man's face looked like a Kabuki mask, body a skeleton draped in pale skin, hands gloved. His attire was so dark it almost seemed to be part of the gloom that surrounded him. Slade raised himself up from the step with the intent to rouse terror, which it did and forced Palmer to edge away.

"You're trespassing. I could call the police. But if you leave now, I won't tell anyone."

"Do I need to make this real for you?" Slade asked. "Do you need to feel scared?"

Palmer wanted to say he was scared, but volunteering his emotional state may put him at a disadvantage.

"Look, nothing has been stolen. I'll blame the broken window or lock on me. I'll tell Bill I got locked out and busted the door in, smashed the pane."

"You think I broke in?"

Palmer tried to remember if he'd locked all the doors before leaving for the farmhouse.

"You must have," he said.

"No," Slade said, smiling. "You let me in."

Palmer backed away. The light began to dim over Slade's face. As he came to a stop, Palmer felt another presence behind him. He didn't have time to turn before a sodden rag was pressed against his nose and mouth. Palmer struggled for a while against the intoxicating smell. He resisted for nearly a minute with eyes dilated and mouth bent by fear, kicking and throwing his arms erratically, the light from the mobile sending weird shadows across the room. He then fell on his back, the cold stone chilling his skin. Flashes of Slade's face loomed over him, smiling, divided equally in shade and light, then nothing. Palmer's grip on the phone loosened as his perception fogged. The room was plunged into darkness.

CHAPTER 20

THURSDAY

The woman's coat matched the color of her lips perfectly, a vibrant shade of Ferrari red. Coonan noticed her eyes weren't too far off the same shade, probably due to trawling the internet for a good story. This must have been how she found out about Amy Taylor's disappearance. The press statement hadn't been released, which meant one of the locals had leaked it on social media. Now this journalist, whatever her name was, had corralled a cameraman and hotfooted it over to Edgerton Road, waiting behind the police tape, back as stiff as the heels on her shoes, press card in hand as if redeeming loyalty points.

"Fucking parasites," Coonan said under his breath as he approached her with a confident stride, face stony and ashen.

The camera light was oppressive, equal to any of those found suspended above a dentist chair. He raised his hand as an official symbol of control, and adjusted his pattern of speech so it sounded officious and measured.

"This is how it's going work; I'll begin with the circumstances, and if there's any time after that, I'll answer any questions you may have. But you need to know that this investigation is time-sensitive. I may, and will terminate the interview at any given juncture to proceed with further lines of enquiry. These are my terms, which were non-negotiable."

The woman nodded. He felt there was no need to interrogate her on how she found out about Amy Taylor, as it would only mean more time in her company, and may infer he was rattled and unprepared.

"Detective, if I may..." she began, but stopped shortly after Coonan began shaking his head.

"No, you may not. I'd like to remind you that you're the first person I've spoken to from the press. Any deviation or cocksure attitude will result in you missing out on an exclusive. Now, are you going to keep butting in, or you going to let me speak?"

The tip of her tongue timidly ran along her bottom lip before withdrawing back into her mouth. Flirtation. It was deliberate and noted by Coonan with a wry smile. Her hand raised a microphone and Coonan began explaining the timeline of events, which began with the initial call from Kristen Taylor leading to the police arriving at Edgerton Road. He gave an accurate and detailed description of Amy Taylor but omitted any suggestion of Gram Slade being a prime suspect. Kristen was portrayed as a loving, and concerned mother, and Coonan encouraged anyone who may have been around, or near to Hanging Lee at the time of Amy's disappearance, to contact the police as soon as possible. Coonan had been talking, without interruption, for about five minutes when he felt his mobile vibrate against his left rib. Motioning with his hand, he put a halt to the recording.

"I need to get this," he said, reaching into his pocket.

The woman teeth-sucked and called out, "Detective, please, I have one question."

Coonan didn't take the bait and backed away with the phone held against his ear. She continued to call his name as he walked away.

"Who's that?" asked Nolan when Coonan accepted the call.

"Some local hack squeezing me for information. What did you find out?"

"I visited the Slade home," Nolan said. "Gram was there. He's says he was at the library when Amy was taken."

"Witnesses?" asked Coonan.

"A few," replied Nolan. "Turns out he was there to see Alex Palmer."

"That writer you've been babysitting?" he said, each word as taught as piano wire.

Coonan had made it known in the office that he thought it would be in the taxpayer's interest to have the police out on the streets solving and preventing crime, not hand holding some inquisitive author from London.

Nolan mumbled a few vowels before continuing, "I'm pulling in to the Mossop place where he's staying. I'll check out if the story stands up with Palmer."

"Who else was at the library?" asked Coonan. .

"A librarian called, Angela Kowal," he replied. "And you may know Claire Thickett. She's been involved in a few community meetings. There was another lady there too called Albright, but Gram didn't know her first name."

"I'll get a couple of officers to go and speak with Kowal and Thickett. Anything else?" he asked.

"If I'm being honest, Boss," Nolan said. "Gram didn't strike me as the type to hurt a fly. Maybe it was act, but he wasn't fazed when I turned up at his door. And throughout the interview, he seemed more interested in the wellbeing of his mother."

"I'm sure that's what they thought about Norman Bates," retorted Coonan. "Once you speak with Palmer, let me know." And with that he hung up.

CHAPTER 21

THURSDAY

Nolan slowly pulled into the Mossop driveway. The rental cottage was immediately on the left. All curtains were drawn. He looked over to the farmhouse and noticed Bill's Defender parked out front. A little further up the driveway was Linda's Saab. When he attended Kristen's house earlier, Linda had told him she would be returning back to the farmhouse with Kristen. She wasn't asking for permission. To try and rein her in, and keep some control, Nolan had agreed under the proviso Kristen keep her mobile close by should he need to contact her urgently. The truth was Nolan was thankful Kristen would be with someone he knew. Bill and Linda were good people. They would look after her, keep her fed, and more importantly, stop her from doing anything silly like visit Gram or try to find Amy. Nolan considered dropping into the farmhouse after speaking with Palmer, but felt it would be too contrived and may escalate her emotions on seeing him.

Later, he thought. *When I've got something positive to offer*. Nolan corrected himself. *If I get something positive.*

The door leading into the small porch had been left open. The front door to the cottage was ajar. Nolan pushed it open and called out for Palmer. When he didn't get a reply he entered. There was a chill in the air, which he assumed was due to the door being open. He walked into the living room and smoothed his hand over the radiator. It was cold. He shouted again for Palmer as he navigated the rooms. No reply came back. He reached the bottom of the stairs and shouted up before ascending, slowly. Something wasn't right. He could feel it. With each step his brain manufactured different explanations or possible outcomes to why the cottage was left open. At best, Palmer was at the Mossop's place, maybe complaining about the lack of heating. Worst case, Palmer was lay unconscious on the bedroom carpet. He was partly relieved to find no body in the main bedroom, but equally perturbed by the packed suitcase resting on the bed.

He must have gone over to see Bill and Linda to pay the rental charges, Nolan thought. If nothing else, it gave him a legitimate reason to visit.

Linda opened the door and seemed surprised to see the detective.

"You got news, Tom?" she asked.

"Sorry," he replied, pausing briefly to warm his hands with his breath. "I'm here to speak with Alex Palmer."

Linda looked over her shoulder to make sure Kristen hadn't heard. Nolan glanced over too and saw Kristen scratching Eli's belly. Linda turned back to Nolan and pushed him onto the driveway. Closing the door behind her she grabbed him by his arm and walked him toward the rental cottage.

"It's important we don't upset Kristen unnecessarily, Tom," she said. "Her nerves are at breaking point. If she sees you she'll assume you've found Amy or...." She trailed off briefly. "I'm sure you'll agree it'll be best all around if you visit with news relating to the investigation, not to catch up with Mr. Palmer."

Nolan waited before speaking. "I am here on police business, Linda."

Linda stopped and turned to face Nolan, "Alex Palmer is involved in Amy's disappearance?" She chewed on this revelation for a moment before straightening her back and raising her finger in front of Nolan's nose. "I knew there was something about that man I didn't trust. Just moments ago he was sat at our table all fulsome and reeking of shameful intentions."

Nolan asked, "He was at the farmhouse?"

"Yes," she replied. "I'd brought Kristen back with me. When we arrived he was sat at the table drinking whiskey with William. As soon as he saw poor Kristen he was like a moth to a flame. Oh, I could see right through him the moment they began speaking."

Nolan felt a pang of jealously in the pit of his stomach.

"And he's not there now?"

"God no. He had the good grace to leave. He said he was returning back to London in the morning. Good riddance, if you want my honest opinion. I'm sorry, Tom, but that man was a leech."

"Mr. Palmer isn't involved in the investigation directly," he confessed, his ability to suppress his emotions becoming easier in public. "I just need to speak with him to confirm some information we've received. Now, you said he was with you earlier. How long ago was that?"

"I don't know, maybe twenty, thirty minutes ago. He was heading back to the cottage. Your car is out front so I'm assuming you've already checked?"

Nolan nodded, "The door was open."

"Huh. Maybe he called a taxi and left already."

"His suitcase is still there," replied Nolan. "Did Mr. Palmer say anything else to you? Did he mention visiting anyone else before he left?"

"No," she replied. "He came over to thank us and that he was cutting short his stay. That's all he said. You don't think?"

Nolan didn't offer any reply. He exhaled a cloud of breath into the night, one that held the knowledge he now had another missing person to search for.

CHAPTER 22

THURSDAY

Drops of water fell on Palmer's dry, cracked lips. He opened his eyes. A small wall mounted lamp revealed various industrial pipes, some the width of his thigh, some narrower, like those that carry water. Rust had settled over valves and release levers attached to some of the thicker pipes. Cylindrical bodies belonging to engineering machinery sprung up from the ground, their paintwork chipped and flaking. Wherever he was it had long been abandoned. Palmer felt the strain of a rope cut into its wrists. He pushed his body forward and realized he was tied to another large pipe that ran from the floor to the ceiling. The water that had awaked him came from an overhead duct. It now tapped the top of his head like a finger.

"Where the fuck is this?" he said to himself.

A dull throb like a heartbeat radiated from his jaw when he spoke. Dredging his memory, he remembered the face of Gram Slade. The man had presented himself as gentle, vulnerable, with a simple mind that welcomed the attention of anyone willing to listen at the library. But the man he saw in the cellar was nothing like this. That man was possessed, but controlled, menacing but understated. If it was Gram Slade, he had let his mask slip, and the face that lay behind had chilled Palmer to the bone. It was possible. Though he never voiced it aloud, Palmer had always considered the majority of his fans unhinged. When he gave reading, he would look up at the crowds and see in their faces a rich satisfaction for the blood he issued upon each page. The merest whiff of destruction or death excited them. The more pain, heartache, misery and violence he tendered, the more they came back wanting more. His success had taught him that people endure life so they can, for a few hours a day, be immersed in books that offer something else. It was a release, a break from normality, and what Palmer offered was the darker side of life. He gave good people the opportunity to understand the minds of the sick and depraved, to walk with serial killers, to be in the room when they exercised their will. But the one thing that allowed him to sleep better at night was the knowledge that most of his readership would never braid fiction with reality. They knew the difference between the two. But there were exceptions. Gram Slade was one of those exceptions.

The clang of a heavy lock followed the sliding of metal. The room temperature dropped as a door opened in the distance. Palmer's body stiffened as footsteps approached from a place he couldn't see.

"Who's there?" he asked, nervously.

Slade came into view, his attire befitting that of a cat burglar; black sweater, dark cargo trousers, tight-fitting donkey jacket. His skin had all the color of moonlight punched through a stormy night. He stopped a few feet in front of Palmer, pointing a gun at his head. Before he squeezed his eyes tightly closed, waiting for the snap of its hammer, the gunpowder thunderclap that pre-empts an eternity of blackness, Palmer noted it was an automatic, 9mm. But there came no noise. No end. Palmer opened his eyes again.

"I didn't want to tie you up," Slade said, tilting the handgun sideways, the nozzle of the gun partly obscuring his mouth. "But you were struggling too much."

"They'll come looking for me," Palmer said. "If I don't make it back to London by tomorrow, they'll call the police."

Slade cocked his head to the side as if recalling something. Perching himself beside Palmer like a gargoyle, he asked, "Who?"

"My agent," replied Palmer. "She's expecting me back at 10 AM. And if—"

Slade cut him off.

"Enough!"

Palmer anticipated the edge of the gun's grip across his nose, or side of the head, a quick, hard strike that would render him unconscious. But Slade placed the gun on the floor, and began instead to untie the rope. Palmer eyed the abandoned gun. If his hands were free, he figured it would take less a two seconds to reach.

"It's not worth it," anticipated Slade, as if reading Palmer's thoughts.

Slade stopped fumbling with the rope to look directly at Palmer. Long lashes canopied eyes the color of charcoal. Looking into them was like staring down a deep, dark well, one where light cannot reach its end, and what lies beyond the murk is unknown but worrisome. Slade returned to the rope, his work hindered by the gloves. Once the rope was removed, Palmer massaged the skin that banded his wrist. Slade returned to his feet with gun in hand.

"Stand up," he instructed, the muzzle aimed directly at Palmer's head.

"Where are we going?" asked Palmer, stalling to assess the probability of rushing Slade and taking him down before he could release a shot.

He was about three feet away. A lunge would do it. But Palmer's legs were fatigued from being sat for so long. If he tried anything too impulsive he'd no doubt keel. Slade pointed the gun toward a door on the other side of the room.

"I want you to see something," he said.

"What?" asked Palmer.

"The reason why you're here," he replied.

Small lanterns, similar to those that lined Hanging Lee, lit up the corridor leading out of the holding cell. Slade remained behind Palmer with the gun held in front.

"When you get to the end, turn left," he said.

Palmer shuffled his body forward slowly so not to trip on debris of broken plaster, rotten door sections, splintered pieces of aged window frames. A few of the candles in the lamps had burnt out creating pockets of darkness. One darkened area caused Palmer to bark his shin on an upturned filing cabinet. He cursed and limped a few steps as the pain took over him. That Slade hadn't changed his pace in the darkness assured Palmer that the man could easily find his way out of this place blindfolded. The corridor finally reached an impasse where only a right or left turn could be made.

"Left," instructed Slade.

Palmer followed reaching a corridor punctuated by three doors.

"Take the second," directed Slade. "It's open."

Palmer asked, "This thing you me to see, does it have anything to do with the missing children?"

"The second door," he repeated.

Palmer slowed purposely to avoid entering the room. He looked up. Pipes lagged in silver foil hung over his head. Wind could be heard wandering the corridors like ghosts. Things creaked and moaned giving the whole building a sense that it was alive.

"You're slowing," said Slade.

"What's in the room?"

"The beginning."

The door was made of reinforced steel painted military gray. The keyhole had at some time been forced to gain entry and was now secured by a large padlock and hasp, which had been left open. Slade pressed the muzzle of the gun into Palmer's back, pushing him forward. Palmer clasped the handle, the cold metal doing nothing to moderate the sweat on his palm. The lock's mechanism sobbed. The room exhaled. The door swung back, and there, lingering beyond the threshold was nothing. Slade entered first. If there was a moment to run, it was now. Palmer stood beyond the door's divide on the corridor, heart-gathering pace. He looked right and saw a dead end marked with a brick wall. He looked left and saw the route he had already taken. It felt like he was in an elaborate maze or something like the Minotaur's labyrinth. His heart quickened. Adrenalin pulled tight the muscles in his legs. A noise, similar to a lawnmower being started, froze Palmer to the spot. The room instantly grew bright. Slade arrived at the door and stood to one side, adopting the stance of a concierge welcoming in a guest to a hotel room. Palmer entered cautiously, his mind conditioning itself for the image of Sarah Cook's corpse, or the remains of Lucy Guffey and George Levy.

The room beyond the door was sparse, but cleaner than the one he had awaked in. The engine noise came from a diesel generator that powered a light stand and industrial size dehumidifier. The walls were covered in plastic sheets, the floor a mosaic of terracotta tiles, many of which were cracked. Centre stage was a large metal table over which a large white sheet had been draped, hiding something, or someone beneath. A blue plastic chair was placed before the table. Palmer was instructed to sit. His body felt like it had gained several pounds as he lowered himself to the seat. Slade walked to the opposite side of the table and belted the gun.

"Who's that?" asked Palmer, looking at the table.

Slade tendered a slow, overstated intake of breath before withdrawing the sheet with a grand gesture. Lay decumbent, as if sleeping, was the naked cadaver of a heavyset woman in her mid-50s. A sheet of parchment sat beneath her body like the kind used in baking. Her skin was the color of goose fat, eyes and mouth closed; lips purple and dry. Blue veins traversed her thighs and arms, converging within blue-violet bruises, some as small as a thumb, some as big as a fist. Two sagging breasts parted for an incision that ran from the groin to the neck, and Palmer could see that her insides had been removed. A fetid scent charged the air, reminding him of the times when, as a police officer, a decomposing body was found, usually that of an old person in their bed. But this smell was more diluted than that, probably because the organs that would have been affected by bacteria and gasses had been removed. The possibility that they were removed while she was still alive turned Palmer's stomach. He dropped his head to the side, throat undulating as he drank down the bile rising in his gut. The change in him seemed to satisfy Slade.

"They'll find you?" Palmer said, gaining enough self-control to look back toward Slade. "The police are looking for Amy Taylor."

Slade retrieved a large kitchen knife from under the table. He displayed it like a magician would a long sword before thrusting it into the box containing his glamorous assistant. Holding it over the woman's leg, he drove it down with force, the movement fast and without warning. The knife entering the skin in short stabbing actions sounded like a sheet of paper being torn into strips. Slade's breathing became more noticeable too the faster his arm worked the skin.

"To improve the cure, the salt needs to penetrate the flesh," Slade remarked casually.

The knife charted the woman's body, the whisper of flesh being cut changing to a harsh snapping noise similar to ice cubes cracking in a glass of water. Slade was striking bone. Palmer winced and felt his own bones ache. Slade stopped for a moment, wiped the sweat from his brow and fetched a hessian bag filled with salt from under the table. He cut a hole in the fabric and poured the salt over the body, scattering it evenly over every inch of the woman's skin. When all the contents had been used, he retrieved another and followed the same procedure.

Working the salt into the skin, Slade turned to Palmer and said, "The body will rest for seven days. That'll be long enough for all the moisture to be drawn away from the flesh. I will wash and dry the body before wrapping it in cheesecloth to wick out any moisture forming around the skin. It will then hang for an additional two months before being cut free."

Palmer couldn't help notice how Slade referred to the woman as the "body". He was detaching himself from the person lay before him.

"You listening to me?" Slade asked, wiping his hands.

He walked to Palmer, squatted down, and taking the tip of his gloved finger, rolled it along Palmer's lips. Traces of salt leached into his mouth causing Palmer to heave.

"They all begged," he said. "They all cried and pleaded for me to let them go." His breath was a mix of late nights and hunger. "Do you hear their voices too?"

Palmer curled in on himself, still, impassive. Slade stroked his hand against Palmer's cheek.

"What we're doing here is important, you know that."

"Important?" Palmer repeated.

"People won't understand it, not right away. But in time, they'll understand."

Palmer kept his head bowed. He tasted copper, and realized that for the past few minutes he'd been biting his bottom lip. He swallowed the blood and said, "No, they won't."

"Why? Why won't they understand?" asked Slade.

"Because you're crazy."

Slade smiled, and said, "Galileo was convicted of heresy because he didn't believe the earth was the immovable centre of the universe. He too refused to accept the order of things, and they called him crazy too."

It was getting hard to accept this man was the same person he saw in the library. He had the same face, but none of the kindness he had seen in Gram. He was educated too, more self-assured. It was if a fiendish spirit had possessed the sweet, gentle Gram Slade introduced to him by Angela Kowal.

Palmer looked over at the fat woman hollowed out like a Halloween pumpkin.

"You're inhuman," he said quietly.

"Now you're beginning to remember."

Palmer turned to Slade.

"Remember?" Palmer repeated, wearily.

"Damnation awaits man, not us. Do you remember?"

"Damnation? I don't anything about that. All I know is killing is wrong."

"It's not!" Slade interjected. His hand viced Palmer's face. "Know that you are the temple of God, and that the spirit of God dwelleth within. Do you remember?"

Slade stood, releasing Palmer from his grip.

"And if any man defile the temple of God, him shall God destroy; for the temple of God is holy. Do you remember?"

Palmer searched every sentence he had shaped over the years, every damn word he had chosen and committed to page, but there was nothing he could recall that mirrored Slade's words. Nothing he had created or fashioned from his experiences as a cop resembled Slade's thinking, which was that this man before him saw himself as something more than human; but what? A higher force. A deity? God?

Slade asked, "Now do you remember?"

"What? What the fuck am I supposed to remember?"

Slade's gun struck Palmer across his head. The force was so great it knocked him clean off the chair. His face was the first thing to hit the tiled floor. Blood poured into his left eye, and in that bleak landscape where nightmares await, Palmer heard Slade's voice call out to him.

"All of this," he said. "You need to remember all of this."

CHAPTER 23

THURSDAY

After realising Palmer was missing, Nolan had called his sergeant, Paul Cornwell. Cornwell was as near to retirement as he was type II diabetes. His desk, which faced Nolan's, had an ongoing joke that its drawers contained more biscuits than solved cases. There was some truth to this, mainly because Cornwell had begun coasting toward retirement five years leading up to it. Sure, he was happy to control the ship, if the ship only needed a slight push to keep it on course. He didn't want headaches, so allowed his staff to take more control of the cases they were working on. This was why Nolan had been given latitude to pursue his hypothesis on the missing children between other less demanding jobs. It was also why there was little resistance from Cornwell when Nolan informed him that he would be traveling to Manchester. The news of Palmer going missing hit Cornwell like a ball of shit. Nolan knew senior command would need informing of this at the next PACE setter, and because Palmer was such a high profile person, Cornwell would be the one tasked with informing the Superintendent, which would mean more work, more questions, all of which Cornwell didn't need right now.

"If it's any consolation," Nolan said, stood before Cornwell's desk. "I'm fairly confident DI Coonan will take the Palmer case on as part of his ongoing enquiries in Stormer Hill."

Cornwell wiped the sweat off his brow with a handkerchief. Like Nolan, he was carrying more weight than he should. His neck was aligned perfectly with his jaw giving his face the appearance of a thumb poked through the neck of a shirt. Even if it was a few degrees above freezing, the man could be found sweating worse than two rats fucking in a wool sock.

"What makes you think Coonan wants the hassle?" asked Cornwell.

"I think it might be linked with the missing girl," Nolan replied.

"Sarah Cook?"

"No, Amy Taylor. But yeah, Sarah Cook too. Too many missings in one place for it to be coincidence."

"That right?"

Nolan could almost hear the relief in Cornwell's voice.

"So, everything okay with me crossing over to Manchester?"

Cornwell wasn't even looking at him now. His eyes were fixed on the desk's third drawer.

"Manchester? Yeah, sure."

"Do you want to contact Coonan about Palmer going missing, or should I?"

Cornwell looked up, his eyes widening at the thought.

"You're working with him on this case. No point in me muddying the water. Keep me updated though. I'll need to keep SLT abreast of the situation. Hopefully he's on a long walk or fucking some book-geek." He paused for a moment in reflection before adding, "Jesus, if anything has happened to him, we'll be in for a shit-storm."

"I can't see it," replied, Nolan. "The abductor just takes children. Adults are not part of their MO."

Nolan was about to walk away when Cornwell threw out a perfunctory remark about time management and traveling expenses, which Nolan acknowledged dutifully. As he left the office, he heard the drawer open on Cornwell's desk, and the familiar sound of biscuit packaging being opened.

***

Coonan didn't take the news of Palmer's disappearance as well. Nolan had called him on his mobile and had to wait over a minute listening to him kick the shit out of waste paper basket before he returned to the phone.

"If the media gets on this we're fucked!" he said, his breathing overstated. "What is it with that village? It's like the Bermuda-fucking-Triangle!"

Nolan knew when to stay quiet.

"I also got word Kowal and Thickett," Coonan continued. "They corroborated Slade's whereabouts at the time Amy went missing, leaving him in the clear. This fucking village!"

A lull came as Coonan calmed himself. Nolan used the time to fill him in on the details he had found since leaving the Slade home.

"Boss, I checked to see if there was any Intel on either Zerelda or Gram Slade. PND brought up several reports of antisocial behaviour toward the family from local youths in their hometown of Manchester dating back over seven years ago. The last was seven months prior to them moving to Stormer Hill."

"And?"

"The details were sparse, but it showed that Gram had been subjected to false imprisonment after he was locked for several hours in their garden shed. No arrests were made because Gram couldn't identify any of the offenders. Zerelda reported it. The records show she also reported four other incidents of harassment, all accumulating in an arson attempt on their home in 2006. No arrests were made due to lack of evidence and no witnesses."

"Arson?" asked Coonan, his voice calmer now.

"A petrol bomb. It was thrown through the window while Zerelda and Gram were inside. Gram was rushed to hospital with severe burns to his hands and arms"

Nolan recalled the moment he looked down at Slade's hands. It wasn't uncommon for families to be victims of ASB, especially in poorer areas, but it probably didn't help that Gram had learning difficulties. The kids would have seen him as an easy target. The more Nolan thought about Slade, the more he felt sorry for him.

Coonan broke his concentration, "This theory of yours, about the children knowing the person who took them, maybe you're onto something, Tom."

He wasn't used to praise from Coonan, so struggled to respond appropriately. In the end he decided to remain quiet.

"I've got officers checking all the other staff at the school as we speak. But if you're right, we could be looking at anyone from the village."

"I know, we're casting a huge net. That's why I want to do a little more research on Gram. He didn't seem the type to do this to the children, and now he's got witnesses who saw him at the library at the time of Amy's disappearance. But he still remains a stone in my shoe."

"What are you thinking, Tom?"

"I was hoping to go to Manchester, see what I can dredge up there," said Nolan. "I'm going to start with Ravenswood Academy. Gram attended there between 92 to 97. I'm hoping they'll still have records on him. Can't see it hurting to understand what he was like as a kid. I also get that kids can be cruel, and the whole locking him in the shed thing was bad, but the arson attack was brutal. That could of cost lives. Bullies don't tend to go to such extremes. Maybe someone down there can tell me why someone would risk going to prison for some kid who to me looks like they wouldn't hurt a fly."

Coonan paused for second before replying, "Okay. See what you can find. I'll get in touch with the MET and get a couple of their officers to attend Palmer's place in London. I'm going to text you over a number for Palmer's agent. Her name is Juliet Klein. Tomorrow morning, ring her to see if she's heard anything. Don't panic her. Best case scenario for me right now is that she's spoken to him. If she knows anything, let me know. Get some rest, Tom. You'll need it for tomorrow.

CHAPTER 24

THURSDAY

Palmer emerged from the blackout with blood staining his eye, arms bound to that same pipe, and the early stages of anxiety creeping up on him. A sharp pain ran through his head as if a white-hot needle had been plunged into his skull. He shuffled his whole body ninety degrees and found himself facing a wall. He remembered visiting the CIRQUE *du Soleil* in Germany during one of his book tours. Lithe figures in Lycra jumped from poles fifty feet high and landed like cats without a scratch. Ta-Da! He also saw a man shimmy his whole body between two fake stone pillars using his feet and back only.

*How hard could it b*e? Palmer thought.

He outstretched his legs and laid the soles of his feet against the brickwork. Pressing his back into the pipe, he began walking slowly up the wall, each step short and quick. He gained about eight inches before he lost his footing and collapsed, smacking the bone of his arse against the floor.

"Fuck!"

Pain ran through him like iced water, starting at his buttocks and running all the way to his head. He leaned to one side to ease the pressure, sucked in the stale air threw gritted teeth. When his breathing settled, he heard something. Concentrating on the noise, he realized it was coming from a small airbrick in the wall.

"Hello? Is anyone there?"

It was the faint sound of a child crying. Palmer held his breath for a few seconds and listened again. He remembered the girl in Hanging Lee and outside The Old Swan pub. Sarah Cook. But it wasn't Sarah Cook. It was just his mind playing a trick on him, the sum of too much time searching archived material about Stormer Hill. Sarah's face had imprinted itself into his conscious mind, like the flash from a camera that lingers in the eye, distorting the vision and resonating in every blink. She was not real. She was just an echo of something that once existed, and was now gone. It was probably the same now with the noise; the echo of a child's cry. But he heard it again, clearer this time, a faint and undeniable sound of sniffling.

"Hello? Is someone there? Can you hear me?"

The crying poured through the small airbrick, amplifying the noise so Palmer could hear soft mumble words too.

"Yes."

The voice belonged to a girl.

"Amy? Amy Taylor? Is that you?"

He could hear Amy's labored breath like an ocean ebbing and flowing along a shoreline.

"Don't worry, Amy. I know your mother, Kristen. We spoke today at Bill and Linda's. She told me you want to be a writer. Is that true?"

He waited .When she didn't respond, he continued, "I'm a writer, Amy. My name is Alex Palmer."

"I'm scared," she said.

"Me too," Palmer replied, relieved. "Me too. Are you hurt?"

"No."

"Good. The police are aware you're missing," he said. "They'll be coming for you soon."

"I don't like it here," she said.

"Me neither. Could you do me a favour; can you describe your room to me?"

Amy didn't answer straight away.

"A good writer needs to describe what they see and hear to help their readers see it to. I can be your reader, Amy. Tell me what you see and I'll see if I can imagine it."

Amy stalled for a moment and then replied, "It a big room. There are plastic containers and brown glass bottles on the floor."

"Can you read any of the labels?" Palmer asked.

He heard her strain and then her reply, "Thymol Blue Solution."

Palmer thought for a moment but couldn't draw any comparison.

"Okay. I'm still here, Amy. Are there any windows?"

"No," she replied. "But there are candles."

"Is there a door?"

"Yes, but it's locked."

"How do you know?" asked Palmer.

"I've tried to open it."

It occurred to him that Amy wasn't tied up.

Amy added, "And there's a big round thing in the middle of the room. I don't know what it is, but it looks like what you see on the back of lorries."

"A tanker?" Palmer asked.

"Maybe."

"You're doing great, Amy. Is there anything there you might be able to use for a weapon? Like a piece of pipe or wood?"

"I don't want to play this game anymore."

Palmer could hear nerves creeping into Amy's voice.

"I'm sorry. Let's try something else. Is there anything like an access panel in the ceiling?"

"What's that?" she asked.

"It may look like a little square door cut into the ceiling. It won't be big. Maybe wide enough for a person to squeeze through."

There was a long pause before she returned to the airbrick.

"I think I've found one."

"Do you think you could climb up to it?"

"I could try and climb the metal thing in the middle of the room. But I'm scared."

"Don't be. The large thing in the middle of the room, is it directly below the panel in the ceiling?"

"To the side of it."

"Do you think you'll be able to reach it without falling?"

"Maybe," she replied.

Palmer spent the following minutes persuading Amy to climb the tanker to see if she could reach the hatch. Wheedling what courage lay within her, he instructed her to use as many pipes as possible along the wall to secure her footing. Palmer could hear her movements from the airbrick. He pictured her hoisting herself up using inlet pipes and opening the hatch.

"How's it going?" he asked.

Her voice was more distance, "It's too smooth. Can't get a good grip."

He heard her land on the ground with a thump.

"I can't do it," she said, nearing the airbrick.

He tried not to reveal his disappointment, "It's okay. You tried. Is there any other way you could reach the access panel?"

"No, I've looked. There is no way out!"

Amy was getting more upset. The clock was ticking. Palmer didn't know how long they had before Slade would return. Images of that woman lay splayed on the metal gurney eroded commonsense and raised his anxiety.

"You need to try, Amy! You need to get out while there's time!"

Palmer could hear every hurried breath and sniffle. He tried freeing himself from the rope binding his wrist. He pulled and yanked his limbs and felt skin tear. He screamed out, kicking his feet and craning his head toward the ceiling in a performance befitting the metamorphosis from human to werewolf. Then, when his energy abated, his head fell forward, chin resting on his chest. He was exhausted and wanted to close his eyes again. He wanted to sleep and wake up in his apartment in London, around familiar furniture, familiar smells. His eyes felt heavy. His limbs too.

"Mr. Palmer?" Amy called out. "Are you there?"

Palmer had already closed his eyes. He was now awaiting the Sandman to take him to a better place, but he knew deep down what awaited him was only nightmare, one occupied by the long, gaunt figure of Gram Slade.

CHAPTER 25

FRIDAY

A skin of gray cloud hung over Death Valley. Nolan pulled up on the hard shoulder of the M60 motorway and pressed the redial button again on his mobile. He had been trying to make contact with Palmer's agent all morning, but no one in the office was answering. He hung up and tried it again. On the third attempt a woman with a soft voice and good diction answered.

"Korpon and Gowin Agency."

"This is Detective Constable Tom Nolan of West Yorkshire Police. I need to speak with a Juliet Klein. Is she available?"

The woman paused. There was a strong chance she had never spoken to a police officer before and it must have taken her by surprise. Nolan allowed her time to adjust and filled the moment by looking out of the window. It was a thirty-minute drive along the M62 from Stormer Hill to Death Valley. When he left his home earlier that morning there were no clouds above him, but less than twenty-five miles down the motorway the sun appeared silver in the sky, almost identical to the moon. Bad weather was following him.

The receptionist spoke. "I'll transfer you now, Detective."

A truck drove past sending the Mondeo rocking to one side. Nolan watched the road ahead and saw a car pull out late in the middle lane. A white BMW discharged its horn in protest. This stretch of motorway ran along the periphery of Manchester and had gained its title due to the frequency of accidents. Nolan could see why.

"Juliet Klein," said a voice from within his mobile. To Nolan's ear she sounded educated, good diction like the receptionist.

"Ms. Klein, my name is Tom Nolan. I'm a detective working out of West Yorkshire Police Force. I need to ask you some questions concerning a client of yours. Alex Palmer."

"Is everything okay?" she asked.

"I was wondering if you've spoken with Mr. Palmer recently?" he asked.

Juliet missed a beat and replied, "We spoke yesterday over the phone. He called to tell me he was returning back to London, today."

"When exactly was this?"

"Around 8 PM last night, maybe later. Why? Has something happened to him?"

"I attended the cottage he's been renting last night, and again this morning. It appears Mr. Palmer hasn't been seen there since last night."

"Have you tried his mobile?" she asked, her voice rising.

"His mobile and his suitcase are still at the cottage," Nolan replied calmly. "We also found his wallet and house keys in his coat pocket."

"My God. Should I be worried?"

"I'm sure he's fine, Ms. Klein. You said he was returning to London, today; did he mention what time? The station perhaps?"

"Euston, about ten. We were supposed to be meeting for lunch. Is there something I should do?"

Nolan felt his car rock again as another lorry past him doing over 50mph. He raised his voice over the traffic noise so there was no misinterpretation.

"We believe he's in no immediate danger and may have just wandered off and will return in due course. Does he have any family you're aware of that he might go and visit in Yorkshire?"

"His parents died a few years back. He was an only child. Not many extended family members that I'm aware of. Alex keeps a very low profile, Detective, and rarely leaves his apartment. He doesn't even have a partner, or many friends."

That didn't surprise Nolan, but he refrained from voicing it.

"I'm following up on another investigation, but I want you to take my number. If you hear from Mr. Palmer, you let me know, okay?"

"I will," she replied. "Should I go to his apartment?"

"That won't be necessary. We have police officers in London who will be attending shortly. I know you're concerned, but I'm sure nothing has happened. If you do hear anything from him though, you must let us know immediately."

Juliet agreed. Nolan provided her with his mobile number.

She then asked, "Are you the detective that's been helping him in Stormer Hill?"

"That's correct, Ms. Klein."

"Alex spoke about you," she said.

"Let me assure you I'm not as grumpy as Mr. Palmer may have made me out to be."

The humor he hoped would help break some of the tension and worry.

"You don't think Alex's disappearance has anything to do with the children?"

"In what respect?"

"The person who took the children, could they be responsible for Alex going missing?"

Nolan held his tongue. It was a possibility, but he didn't want to worry her anymore.

"If Mr. Palmer turns up, I'll let you know."

Juliet thanked him for calling her. Though she sounded composed, Nolan believed there would be a moment following the end of the conversation where she would be contemplating the worst. For the rest of the day her mind would be occupied with memories of Alex Palmer, and until he was found, she would not embrace her life so willingly, because it was clear, at least to Nolan, she cared for him.

***

The small car park overlooked an oppressive building fenced by iron railings. It had the appearance of an asylum, or some gateway to a prison. Above the door, chiselled out of limestone, was a date: 1897. The windows were original wood, separated into four panes. Most were unadorned save for a few which had crude paintings of paper flowers and malformed birds pinned to them. Nolan removed his mobile from the cradle and locked his car. A sign directed him to the reception, above which was the name of the school, Ravenswood.

Children's voices grew from the distance. A xylophone, or possibly a glockenspiel, struck clumsily from a nearby room and launched other instruments into action; a trumpet, piano, a chorus of falsetto voices. All Things Bright and Beautiful. Nolan pressed a small intercom fixed to the main entrance doorframe. The woman on the other end sounded robotic.

"Hello?"

"My name is Tom Nolan. I'm a Detective working out of West Yorkshire Police. Would it be possible to speak with the Head of school?"

A short, harsh buzz released the lock and Nolan entered. The smell from the grand hallway reminded him of old linen. Parquet flooring stretched out to a wooden staircase that coiled upwards like a watchful cobra. The furnishings were dreary, Dickensian, and the only color came from crepe-paper collages festooning all its walls. A woman in her early thirties arrived from a doorway.

"I'm sorry Detective," she said, hooking her hair behind her ear. "Has something happened?"

Her face was pretty, mouse-like.

"I need to speak with the Head Teacher," Nolan said, adding, "If that's not too much of an inconvenience?"

"I've contacted Mrs. Sheldon and she's on her way down," she said, warmly. "Would you care to sit? There are chairs in the office."

She pointed briefly to the room she had exited.

"I'm fine," he replied.

"Here she is now," said the woman, pointing to the staircase.

Patricia Sheldon was in her late fifties, well dressed with good posture. She descended the staircase with all the grace of Ginger Rogers.

"Detective Nolan?" she asked, extending her hand as she approached.

On closer inspection Nolan noted her skin was pebble-smooth, well cared for, but her eyes were polished with distrust, a small detail that complimented a matriarchal tone resonating in her voice.

"Is there someplace we can speak, Mrs. Sheldon?" he asked, letting go off her hand.

"We can use my office."

Patricia guided him down a long corridor lined with glass cabinets holding trophies, bygone uniforms, and clay structures fashioned by young hands. A tiled floor exaggerated her step, the heel of her shoe as loud as the blacksmith's hammer on an anvil. She paused before a large door bearing a gold plaque with her title etched into it. She directed him to a comfortable chair inside and offered him a cup of tea. Nolan refused, not wishing to spend too much time should his questions lead to dead ends. Patricia levelled out her skirt and lowered herself to a tanned leather chair behind the desk. Her hands neatly laced together, her expression, impassive.

"How can I help?" she said.

"I'm currently involved in an investigation that may involve a previous pupil of Ravenswood."

Nolan reached into his pocket and pulled out his notebook. He opened it up at a random page, looked at it briefly and then addressed the Headmistress again.

"Do you recall a pupil by the name of Gram Slade, Mrs. Sheldon?"

"Gram? Yes. It's not a name you forget, really." Patricia looked up momentarily as if drawing from memory. "He had learning difficulties. William's Syndrome, if I'm not mistaken. Ravenswood is the only school in the area that receives special education and related services, so we were able to made reasonable adjustments to accommodate him. He was a good pupil, from what I recall."

"Do you have any old school records that I might be able to take back to the station?"

"I'd have to check. That is to say, I don't have them to hand, Detective. Depending on how it's been since the pupil left, records can be archived here, off site, or transferred to the county record office."

"I understand," replied Nolan. "If it helps, Gram attended between 1992 and 97."

"97? Well, we won't have the admissions register; they generally get destroyed after about three years. But we should have things like his graded tests, report cards and IEP."

"Forgive me, Mrs. Sheldon... IEP?"

"Sorry." Her apology seemed insincere. "An Individual Education Program. It's an official document bespoke to the child's needs. In Gram Slade's case it would have provided the school, parents and related service personnel to work together in improving his education each term."

"Would it have revealed any signs of violence or if he had been referred to social care?"

"I'm sorry, Detective. Has something happened to him?"

Nolan shifted his weight in the chair.

"We have suspicion to believe that he may be involved with an ongoing investigation in the village of Stormer Hill," he replied.

"You specifically mentioned violence," she said. "From what I recall, Gram was a gentle boy. If anything, his condition made him very sociable and friendly towards the other children. The only issues we experienced concerned things like spatial relations, numbers, and abstract reasoning. Violent? No, Detective. Gram was never violent."

"Would it be possible to get a copy of his IEP?"

"I'll have to contact the administration. I wouldn't hold your breath though. From experience, these things take a little time."

There was a pause as Nolan recalibrated.

"Is there anything else I help you with, perhaps?" asked Patricia.

Nolan glanced at his notebook then back to her.

"You mentioned Gram wasn't violent. How can you be sure?"

Patricia's brow pinched and her eyes narrowed.

"I don't understand?" she said.

"It's been nearly fifteen years since Gram attended," Nolan added. "That's a long time and a lot of pupils have been and gone between. How can you recall one pupil so very long ago being non-violent?"

Patricia Sheldon raised herself up from the chair and walked slowly to the front of the desk. Leaning against it, she extended her hand toward him to examine. Nolan noted two rings on her middle finger. One was an old antique moonstone, probably given to mark her engagement. The other was an Art Deco solitaire wedding ring. The bands were gold, the skin beneath swollen. Nolan assumed he was supposed to see something in the rings, and when he couldn't he looked to her briefly for an explanation.

"It's faded over time," she replied, "but if you look, you'll see the impression of teeth."

She angled her hand toward him, as though waiting for it to be kissed. Nolan leaned in and there it was; four small dimples in the skin.

"Gram Slade's teeth were widely spaced," she went on to say. "This impression came from a normal set of teeth. You asked me how I could remember why Gram was non-violent. It was because I was able to measure him against his brother."

Nolan leaned back into the chair.

"Gram has a brother?" he asked.

"Had," she replied, returning to her chair. "Layton Slade died, Detective. It must be going on five years now."

"What do you remember about Layton?"

"He and Gram enrolled at the same time. From what I recall things were okay at the start. But shortly into the second term I started getting a lot of complaints from the teachers. Layton showed little to no respect toward them and was being disruptive in class. The mother was a single parent, I believe. She had health issues. I spoke with her several times concerning Layton's behaviour. She was apologetic, as most parents are, and assured me she would address his conduct appropriately. She had a strange name too." Patricia adjusted her wording so not to sound disparaging or discriminatory. "Not strange, different."

"Zerelda," Nolan interjected.

Patricia nodded, as if remembering and then resumed her account.

"She was nice. I felt for her. It's not easy being a single mother. Maybe that's why we made so many allowances."

"Allowances?" asked Nolan, pen poised over his notepad.

"We attempt to manage disruption in class at all times, Detective. Bad behaviour, in any form, won't be tolerated at Ravenswood, and the standard punishment for not following the ground rules needs consistency and a united front. Layton was taken out of class whenever he played up. I had also arranged he meet with the school pastor three times per week as an intervention tactic. We persevered, and for a while it looked like we were making progress. But then things took a turn for the worse." She missed a beat to rub the teeth marks on her hand, as if releasing the pain that still resonated there. "I was called to the playground by one of the teachers. Something had happened to Layton. When I arrived I found his hands were covered in blood. His shirt too. I assumed he'd cut himself. I panicked, as you can imagine. But the blood was not his."

"Another child's?"

"No. When I approached, I saw he was holding a dead pigeon. It came apparent Layton had used a penknife to cut it open in front of the children. He then chased them around the playground, waving the bloody mess in front of their faces. A male teacher had to restrain him, but on seeing me he began to scream and kick, saying the most awful things."

"What kind of things, Mrs. Sheldon, if you can remember?"

"I can't recall the exact words, Detective. Mostly expletives. Colorful language. The kind not befitting the reputation of our school."

Nolan waved his hand dismissively.

"I wasn't trying to lure you into repeating the terms exactly. I'm more interested if Layton said anything racial perhaps, slang, or derogatory."

"Like silly old bitch; is that the kind of thing you mean?"

There was a cutting tone to the way Patricia delivered her remark, leaving Nolan feeling scolded and abashed. She had clearly perfected it over the years for the children and parents and could exercise it without consideration or effort.

"Was any of this reported?" he asked, wondering why it hasn't shown up on any police system.

Patricia looked up from her hand and said, "Zerelda was struggling enough at home raising one child with learning difficulties, and another that was feral. It was agreed the incident be dealt with by the school. It was recorded, as were the sessions with the pastor."

"And the bite mark?" asked Nolan.

"My own fault. I tried to lead Layton back into the school following the incident by the hand. He was agitated, most probably scared of the repercussions."

"And the pastor, where are they now?"

"I believe he retired and moved over to Ireland."

"You remember his name?"

"John McCormick," she said. "I'm sorry that I can't offer you anything other than my word, Detective."

"That's okay, Mrs. Sheldon. You've been a great help. May I ask one more thing?"

Patricia feigned a smile and nodded.

"Do you recall how Layton Slade died?"

She lowered her head for a moment, found solace in the moonstone ring, and then returned her gaze before answering.

"He threw himself off a bridge onto Death Valley," she said. "Though he made our lives hell, it was still a shock when we read about it."

"It was reported by the local newspapers?"

"Yes," she said.

"Was there mention of a suicide note?"

"Perhaps. I think so. I'm sure the police here in Manchester would have a copy."

"I'm sure they will. I'm sorry to keep pressing you on this, Mrs. Sheldon, but can you remember anything else? Other incidents that happened?"

"I can't say that there was any one incident more visceral than cutting open a pigeon. If you're asking me to recall the smaller incidents in class, I'd be struggling to say anything more than disruption and misbehaviour. And for those, intervention and measures were put in place."

Nolan stopped writing and clicked his pen closed, giving Patricia a moment to reflect.

"We were all deeply saddened by Layton's passing," she said. "I've been at this school for over twenty-six years. In my time I've grown close to many of the children, some more than others. Layton Slade was someone I believed I could help."

"Speaking from the perspective of a long in the tooth cop, regardless of what action we take, if a person doesn't want to be saved, sometimes there isn't much we can do."

"I can't accept that, even if it is true, Detective" she said.

Nolan spent a brief moment listening to the children singing somewhere in the building. They sounded so innocent. So pure. He wondered if Layton had once sung too.

"Of all my responsibilities as Head Teacher here at Ravenswood," Patricia Sheldon said, bringing him back to the room, "the one I draw the greatest pleasure from is shoelaces."

"Shoelaces?" Nolan confirmed.

"Yes. I've taught hundreds of children to tie their shoelaces. It is the most menial and ignored of all the things I do, but to me, it is the most rewarding. Knowing that a child won't trip and hurt themselves brings me happiness, Detective. I know it sounds silly, but it's the truth. The day I saw Layton Slade in that playground, I wasn't shocked at what he did. I was shocked that his shoes were untied. I knew then, no matter what I did, that boy would never change his ways."

A smile hesitatingly pulled at the corners of her lips. A faint slackening of the jaw. Window dressing, Nolan considered. Of all the learning she had given to these children, she had failed to study the art of the lie. Layton Slade was still haunting her. Nolan could see it.

"Is there anything else I can help you with, Detective?" she asked, as if marking the conversation with a period.

Nolan lifted himself from the seat and placed his notepad in his inside pocket. He thanked her for her time and was about to leave the room when he paused. There was still something he felt had not been addressed; he ran through the case notes quickly in his head and all the information he had gleaned up to that point.

Turning, he said, "I'm sorry. I do have one more thing you may be able to help me with. Do you know why Zerelda Slade moved out of Manchester?"

"If I kept abreast of every child that left Ravenswood, I'd have no time to do my job, Detective."

"I appreciate that, Mrs. Sheldon," he said. "But prior to Layton's death, and Zerelda and Gram leaving, was there anything you heard or remember?"

Like that feigned smile she presented so readily, Patricia Sheldon didn't have the competence to disguise her thoughts. It was evident she knew something. Her breathing had changed. Her voice was shallower, a direct result of her heart rate and blood pressure variation. Her hand had also trailed the length of her neck, stopping to rub the skin around her throat before finally moving over to her lips. The neck was a vulnerable spot and she was subconsciously hiding it. There was something she wanted to say but was afraid to, which is why she hid her lips. Nolan tried to reassure her.

"Mrs. Sheldon, you're not under investigation here. I'm only trying to establish facts that may help us understand more about the Slade family. If you feel uncomfortable, we can end the conversation now and I'll be on my way. But if there is anything you can tell me, it would be greatly appreciated."

She removed her hand from her mouth and said, "They were being harassed."

The fishing line was twitching.

"By who?"

She exhaled, "I'm sure you could retrieve that information on your police systems."

"I intend to, Mrs. Sheldon, but sometimes the intelligence we hold leads to more questions, and finding the answers takes time."

She pondered before replying, "There was a boy who attended here. His name was, let me think ... Myers. Peter. One of the teachers overheard him bragging in class about his brother's gang. Apparently, they were well known in the local area and had a reputation. I'm not saying I saw any of this myself. This is all third hand."

"That's okay, Mrs. Sheldon. Please, carry on."

"It must have been eight, maybe nine years since Gram had left Ravenswood. Then, out of the blue, I hear his name again."

"From this Peter Myers?"

"No, I heard it from Mrs. Connelly. She used to teach music here. Due to Gram's condition, it was the only subject he fully engaged with. Naturally the school encourage him to participate as much as possible in the subject. We also arranged one to one tuition with Mrs. Connelly. When Peter said Gram's name, Mrs. Connelly tuned in to the conversation, remembering Gram fondly. That was when she overheard the episode involving the shed."

Playing dumb Nolan asked, "The shed?"

"Gram had been subjected to an unspeakable ordeal."

She paused in reflection, or perhaps regret. Nolan found it hard to read in her expression.

"Some of the members of the gang, they locked him away in the family shed. Now, before you ask, Detective, we did pursue this information with Peter. That it wasn't reported to the police wasn't negligence on my part. It's just that after we spoke with Peter we realized the incident was historic."

Nolan slowly walked back toward her desk. He didn't sit, but instead hovered over her like a buzzard.

"When did the incident happen?"

"I would say, conservatively speaking, twelve months before Gram and his mother moved out of Manchester."

"And Peter, you think his brother was involved in locking Gram in the shed?"

"The way he was bragging it, I would say so."

"Can I speak with Mrs. Connelly, to see if she remembers anything else Peter said?"

"I'm afraid she's left the school now. She took a job in Macclesfield. That said I might have the details for where she is currently working."

"That would be useful, Mrs. Sheldon."

"Maybe I could email them over to you?"

Nolan handed her one of his business cards. His name was written in a font that gave it a clinical impression. Estrangelo Edessa. Gautami. He could never remember.

"Should I struggle to speak with Mrs. Connelly; can you recall the name of Peter Myer's brother?"

"James, or Jimmy. I can't quite recall."

"There's something about the shed incident that doesn't quite fit," he asked. "It doesn't seem enough of a reason for Zerelda to move her and Gram away? I'm sure it was harrowing for Gram, but why go to all that trouble to move them both out?"

"It was the fire at their home that forced her to leave. Someone threw a petrol bomb through the downstairs window. Gram and Zerelda were upstairs asleep. I don't believe Layton was home at the time. They lost everything, Detective. Had it not been for Gram pulling his mother out of that house, it could have been a lot worse. Gram wasn't a violent person because he knew how it felt to be hurt. Boys a lot stronger and bigger than him locked him in a shed until he begged for his life; all because he was different. All because he wasn't like them. I don't blame her for leaving. If it meant they could live in peace, then so be it."

"And how soon after the house fire did they move out of Manchester?"

She thought for a moment before replying.

"Gram was in hospital for a while recovering from burns. Zee moved in with a neighbor. From what I heard Layton took the law into his own hands. He had a temper, the likes of which leaves scars, as you've seen."

"Layton knew who set fire to the house?"

"People said he ran around in those circles. I guess we'll never know."

"Can you remember the name of the neighbor, the one Zerelda stayed with?" asked Nolan.

"Sally, I believe. Her kids are pupils here."

"Surname?"

"Anderson."

Patricia glanced at a gold-framed photograph on her desk. Nolan followed her gaze and saw a girl about sixteen years old wearing a summer hat. Her jeans were rolled up to the shin, pale feet submersed in the clear waters belonging to some faraway ocean. She was pretty and tall and Nolan considered her build and hair similar to the younger Lucy Guffey, had she lived beyond the ungenerous seven years of her life. There was another photograph next to it showing the same girl against a white background. A professional photo shoot families indulge in from time to time. Her skin was blanched. Perfect makeup.

"Your daughter?" he asked.

"Daughters," she corrected him. "Grace and Holly."

"Twins?" he asked, scrutinizing the photographs in attempt to see any differences. Save for one of them having a slight indent at the bridge of her nose, the girls were near identical.

"That was another reason I warmed to the Slade boys. I can't imagine how devastating that was for Gram. Twins have that special connection, don't they? Losing a sibling is hard enough, but losing your twin."

Nolan's eyes shut down. He was looking at Patricia Sheldon but he was blind. Conjectures and theories overruled every sense he had. He placed himself back at Zerelda Slade's house in Stormer Hill; the Moroccan influences, the triptych hung on the wall, the candles and the cheap ornaments, all slowly faded away in his mind. There was something missing that he hadn't realized when he first attended. It was the one thing that every home has - photographs. There were no photographs of Gram or Layton.

They lost everything, Patricia had said.

The ticking of a clock fell around Nolan like raindrops, incessant and with rhythm.

"If you can remember anything else, you have my contact details," Nolan said.

Patricia held up the card and tapped it gently on the side of her hip.

"I will," she replied.

She walked him down the corridor. There was small talk, history of the school, questions that were born of civility, and though her replies were articulated with a deep sense of pride, Nolan could not recall any of the detail. His only lasting impression of Patricia Sheldon came from when they were out of the building, children milling around her feet. He saw her kneel down before a young boy, her hands carefully, and with great attention, tying his shoelaces.

CHAPTER 26

FRIDAY

Palmer awoke with a start. He looked around the plant room half expecting Slade to be stood over him, waiting. But he was alone. The water dripped persistently beside him, reminding him he needed to piss. His hands were tied, the industrial looking pipe bolted to the floor too stubborn to budge an inch. He called out Slade's name. This time there was no sliding of a bolt. No footsteps. Just a gentle humming of machinery from another room. Palmer relieved himself where he sat. The piss warmed his crotch, and within a minute or two turned cold. It was a sensation he was all too familiar with.

Following the death of Christie Purlow, Palmer had fallen into a depressive state. To shorten the days, he employed the services of Jack Daniels and the good old company of Coca-Cola to numb him to the world. He'd frequent pubs, some of which he knew, others he didn't, installing himself in threadbare chairs and drinking until blind. Back then he wasn't famous. He could stumble into people without fear of being recognized. There were no column inches dedicated to him in highbrow tabloids, no interviews on TV, or critiques on culture shows. No, back then he was invisible, and of no interest to anyone but bartenders. It was a dark and strange time. He'd often awake in strange rooms, clothes abandoned on the floor, mouth arid and brain beating like a second heart. Whatever bed he found himself in smelt of cheap sex and even cheaper perfume, sheets stained from fake tan, the naked body of some faceless woman he had persuaded, though God knows how, to take him back to her place for a good fucking. He'd call them Honey, Princess, Angel; terms of endearment reserved for lovers, but in Palmer's case he used them to detach from the real person. He never knew their real names. He didn't want to. Sometimes he called them Juliet.

From time to time, he would wake and find the bed stained with blood, mostly his, but sometimes it belonged to other people. He didn't mind that. Palmer figured whoever had gotten in his face the previous night deserved to bleed. They were probably arseholes, opportunists or other drunks. He'd awake with raw and bloody knuckles, a busted lip and donut eye. He could cope with these things. But a broken tooth, a scar perhaps that ran from his eye to his mouth? That always worried him. He still liked that women found him attractive. His good looks were his one gift, the one thing that put him higher up in the male food chain. But scars aren't something you can wash away under the tap, or temper with ice packs. He began to choose his fights more carefully after he noticed a cut just a few millimetres below his right eye. If a drunk with a few inches on him started to push or call him a cocksucker, he'd back off. If there were more than one person, he'd apologize for whatever indiscretion had riled them up. It got to be that after a while he heard the term pussy thrown at him so many times he began to think he owned one. To make up for this, and install some confidence again, he began fights with vagrants, smaller people, weaker people, those he knew he could handle quickly and mercilessly. He was no pussy, he kept telling himself, and with every fist he threw that dislocated a jaw or broke a nose, he imagined he was strong, big, and dangerous. He imagined he was someone else. He imagined he was Jason Legge.

Back in the plant room, Palmer could now feel the first prickle of anxiety. He needed his meds. His fingers, the palms of his hands, the skin along his arm, they were all sensitive. Sweat made his forehead and armpits itch. Knees began to tremble. He was drawn to the changes, but equally perturbed and appalled by them, and likened the sensation of his skin similar to fingers that had been immersed in water and then rubbed together. Palmer wondered how long he could last without the Paxil. A year ago he had stayed over at a hotel in Italy for a book signing and left his medication there. He landed in Calgary the following day edgy and uptight and had to arrange with the local hospital to forward his prescription from the U.K. He'd gone a little over twenty-four hours without Paxil and felt like shit. He was now beyond that. His visions of Jason Legge were stronger. The feeling of him stood beside him almost too real. Palmer called out Amy's name to the small airbrick, and when she didn't respond he began to worry.

Had Slade taken her already? Was she now under a sheet too, her body waiting to be cured like some pig?

A swell of nausea rose up from his gut. Palmer unleashed Slade's name into the room once again, his throat tearing like paper. The noise leaked out under the door, along the narrow corridor where it lost momentum in a room much larger than the one he was in, a room where the faces of thirty-three preserved bodies lay bent in death.

CHAPTER 27

FRIDAY

Coonan was talking to Bob Wood at the police station when he got a call a young man was at the front desk wanting to speak with someone connected to the Amy Taylor case. He went down straight away. The Enquiry Counter officer pointed to a kid in his early twenties and looked like he was about to shit a brick. A small silver ring hung from his nose, pimples speckled his chin. Coonan approached with a lumbered stride. If figured him for a junkie bearing false claims so he could get a pardon for some misdemeanour.

"My name is Mark Coonan," he said towering above the kid. "I was told you had some information regarding Amy Taylor."

"Can we speak someplace a little more private," he asked, eyes shifting around the room to the scattering of people sat in the waiting area.

Coonan tilted his head to one side, and the kid stood, following him into one of the interview suites like a lap dog. The room was sparse; a small table with recording equipment, two chairs. Coonan pointed to one and the kid sat down. Coonan sat opposite and arranged his tie.

"Let's start with your name, shall we?" said Coonan, his tone suggesting he wasn't in the mood for any shenanigans.

"Stephen Tremblay, sir."

"Call me Mark."

Tremblay tried to smile, but it gave his face a peculiar look, a kind of mix between fear and constipation.

"I was a little reluctant to come forward earlier," he said. "The thing is ..." Tremblay paused and looked at the recording machine on the table. "Is this being recorded?"

Coonan had a holding statement to prepare, strategies and hypothesis to document in his policy book, not to mention parameter searches to discuss with Bob Wood. He didn't need some paranoid junkie taking up his time. He stared the kid right in the eye and sighed heavily. It was enough to wipe the feigned grin off Tremblay's face.

"The thing is," continued Tremblay. "I heard about that girl going missing on the radio."

"Amy Taylor," Coonan confirmed.

"Yeah, that's her. I heard the news say she'd gone missing near Hanging Lee. That's when I thought I better come in."

What was this? Coonan thought. *A confession?*

Tremblay supplicated, "The thing is... Oh, man. Okay, I'm sorry, it's just I've never spoken to a police officer before."

"We're not getting any younger here, Stephen. You want to tell me what happened."

Tremblay lowered his gaze to the table.

"I just didn't want to get in trouble, that's all."

Coonan grabbed an MG11 form and began writing. Tremblay continued his account, jumping from moment to moment like they were hot rocks in his hands.

"I've only had the car for a few weeks. It's my first one. Cost my parents a small fortune. They said they'd buy it as long as I paid for the insurance. That was the deal. Only, after I got a quote, I couldn't afford it. It was well over two grand. Subway pay me peanuts. You know, right?"

"You're telling me you've been driving around with no insurance?"

"My parents will kill me if they find out."

"What's this got to do with Amy Taylor?"

Tremblay looked up, big pitiful eyes glazing over.

"I took my eyes off the road for a second. A second."

Coonan began to wonder if this kid had hit Amy in his car, panicked and drove off. He certainly had all the jitters of someone who might be involved in a hit and run. Then it suddenly dawned on Coonan that his hypothesis had never considered Amy getting struck by a car. The damage he had seen on Edgerton Road had led him to think it was an accident involving two cars. But what if Tremblay had looked up too late? If Amy was running across the road and he couldn't stop in time? It was possible. Bob Wood had searched the area and found no body. There weren't even any traces of blood. Could Tremblay have hit her and dragged her into his car without leaving any trace of DNA? Could the abductor have waited until Tremblay drove off and then picked up the pieces of Amy Taylor? That didn't explain the lack of blood.

"Stephen, are you telling me you saw Amy Taylor the evening she went missing?"

"Amy? No. No, sir. Sorry, Mark. I didn't see her."

"Then maybe you can tell me why you're here."

"I hit another car. It came out of nowhere. I didn't stand a chance. I looked up and there it was. I've never been in an accident before. I wasn't going fast, honestly. But I couldn't stop and I went into the back of it. The sound. My God, it was so loud. When I realized what had happened, I began to worry."

"No insurance, right?"

Tremblay nodded.

"I knew we'd have to exchange insurance details. My old man had drilled it into me. He said if I ever get into an accident, first I should take photographs of the damage on my mobile phone and the reg plate, just in case they try and drive off. Then exchange insurance details. But I was the one thinking of driving off. All I kept thinking was my parents were going to kill me."

"Then what happened?"

"So this guy gets out and goes straight to the back of the car. I'm thinking he's checking the damage, right? Probably wants to see how bad it is. But no, the dude didn't even look at the damage. He pops the boot open, takes a look inside, and then closes it again. I thought for sure he had a baseball bat in there, you know, and he was going to crack my head open. But that was it. He looked inside, shut the boot and drove off. I gotta say I was relieved."

"You get a good look at this guy?"

"Sort of. He was thin with a shaved head."

"White?"

"Yes, sir. I mean, yes, Mark."

"Remember what he was wearing? Age?"

"He was dressed all in black. Had a black coat too. Looked more like a shadow than a person. I guess he was about mid-twenties, maybe earlier thirties. I don't really know. I wasn't thinking too straight."

"Was there anyone else in the car?" Coonan asked.

Tremblay began chewing his fingernail again.

"Possibly, it was hard to see through the back windscreen. There could have been someone else."

"And the vehicle you hit, you take your father's advice and take photos?"

Tremblay shook his head.

"Can you remember anything about it? The color, make?"

Tremblay spat out a tiny fragment of fingernail and said, "It was an old one. A silver Volvo Wentworth estate. I know because my dad had one a few years back."

"You remember any of the number plate?"

"Not really." Tremblay started gnawing frantically at the skin around the nail. Coonan looked on in disgust.

"You won't have enough room for dinner if you carry on eating your hand like that," he said.

Tremblay apologized, swallowed and added, "The last three letters of the reg. I remember them if it helps. EBB. You know, like the tide."

Coonan got Tremblay to sign the bottom of the MG11 and thanked him for his time.

"You think any of that will help you find the girl?" Tremblay asked. There was a pathctic look in his eyes that reeked of inexperience.

"You should have come forward sooner, but yeah, I think it'll help with the investigation."

"I was worried I'd lose my license." Tremblay waited for Coonan to add his opinion, and when he didn't he asked, "So, is that it? I'm okay to leave?"

"You're not under arrest, if that's what you're worried about. But you will need to hang on a little longer. Another officer will be with you shortly."

"But, I told you everything I know."

"We still need to issue a fixed penalty for driving with no insurance. You're looking at a fair few points on your license and a hefty fine. Maybe next time you'll reconsider taking your eyes off the road. Thanks again for all your help, Stephen."

And with that, Coonan left to the sound of Tremblay chewing on his fingers.

***

A VODS check on the partial registration number brought up two possibilities in the local area. Neither vehicle had been reported stolen. The nearest to the scene where Amy was taken was an address in Soyland. The registered keeper was a Peter Thompson. Coonan did a PNC check on him but he came up clean. No priors or warning markers on the address. He checked the other name, Colin Wilton. Save for a few domestic incidents, Wilton didn't seem a likely candidate to abduct a child. But that didn't mean either Thompson or Wilton couldn't. He tasked the Wilton job to a DC who was doing some of the legwork now Nolan was in Manchester. Coonan let his team know he would go and check Thompson out.

***

The small key ring contained a photo of Mark Coonan's two children, Freddy and Erin. It had been a present from his ex wife, Nicola, back when buying presents was thought out and planned. The photograph was sandwiched inside a small acrylic case and was taken when Freddy and Erin were still in nursery; their infant faces rounder, skin unblemished. Freddy was now fifteen. Erin, two years behind him. Neither had much to say whenever their father visited them. They would sit on the sofa lost in the television, or often staring blankly into a handheld device. Sometimes Erin would be mimicking the dancers she saw in pop videos, her moves crude and awkward. The only time they feigned interest was when he brought gifts. It wasn't an easy task buying for teenagers. Coonan often deferred to Nicola for any advice or guidance, but it was clear whatever she suggested was going to cost him. Under the supervision of Nicola, Coonan would hand out the presents, see a momentarily glimpse of excitement light up his children's faces, then spend the rest of the visit asking them about school, or what they'd been up to. Later, back at his small apartment, he would stitch together their monosyllabic replies with the diligence of a code breaker. Because he did not influence or control their daily lives, Freddy and Erin never measured their father with the same level of respect and tolerance they showed Nicola, and to some degree, her new husband, Edward. Mark Coonan was considered the same way as an uncle might be, a fleeting visitor baring gifts sand smiles, but with no true understanding or insight into who they were or what they truly liked. Coonan had resigned himself long ago to the simple fact his kids were drifting further away from him with every passing day, and the only way he could get close to them now was staring at photographs, or consoling himself in the act of holding the key ring.

He had the key ring in his hand while sat in his car outside a small bungalow on an estate at the edge of Soyland. Sycamore Drive had a wholesome feel to it. The road was clean, lawns neatly trimmed. Vehicles were purchased for their dependability, not their speed or design. When Coonan pulled his BMW to the kerb he noticed several curtains twitch. It was obvious the residents knew each other well. Strangers were like dark clouds preceding a thunderstorm. The car he was searching for was sat on the drive belonging to Peter and Fiona Thompson. He could see that the rear bumper had been cracked; the right taillight had been damaged appropriate to the fragments found on Edgerton Road. Coonan placed the key ring back in his pocket and locked his vehicle. A cursory glance at the vehicle on the driveway revealed damage to the door lock too. It was an older model, like Tremblay had described, dating back to the early 1990s. It had a keyhole under the driver's side door that had been punched out. Looking through the windscreen he saw it had been hot-wired. If the vehicle had been stolen, why return to the Thompson residence?

Coonan knocked on the porch door. No reply. He tried the doorbell, its faint warble resonating through the house. He tried the porch door but it was locked. Correspondence was building on the mat. Either the Thompson's were very popular, or they'd gone away and had yet to return. Coonan went around the side of the house to check. A low, waney lap fence ran from the garage to a wooden gate. He slid back a bolt and entered the back. The garden, like many others on the road, was well kept, its boarders filled with pretty flowers. A large tree bearing fruit grew from the centre of a verdant lawn, the length of grass suggesting it hadn't been cut for a week or so, which considering the effort taken to maintain the garden, seemed odd to Coonan. A conservatory had been built on the back of the property. Coonan delicately pulled at the handle, trying best not to smudge any latent prints. It gave to his pressure and opened. The patio led directly into the living room where the smell of expired meat was great. The television, which looked expensive, was still there. No ornaments had been smashed. Paintings were aligned and fixed to the wall. Everything seemed in its rightful place and untouched, or at least looked that way. Coonan went from room to room, checking to see if there was any damage elsewhere, but found no signs to suggest a robbery had taken place. The only room that did show any signs of disorder was the kitchen. Breadcrumbs covered the work surface. A butter knife and coffee cup sulked in the sink, a fine crack running the flank of the cup. The smell of rancid meat was also stronger in the kitchen. Coonan checked inside the bin to find out if something was in there that had gone off, but found only an empty pizza box and soda cans. A tall, integrated refrigerator gurgled in the corner of the room. Coonan pulled his shirtsleeve down over his hand and yanked back the door. The smell of decay hit him like a fist. He reared back on his heels. By the time his eyes adjusted to the interior light, he had his sleeve against his mouth. Eleven clear plastic Tupperware boxes of various sizes were laid out on the shelves. Coonan could see they contained meat of some kind, some a purple black color, others paler and redder. The largest of the boxes took up the whole bottom shelf and had something written on it with black marker. Coonan leaned in and read it aloud, "Peter."

He found a pair of Marigolds under the sink and slipped them on. A domestic peg was employed to block the stench from entering his nose. The first Tupperware box contained something more like a large disused ball of chewing gum. It was only when he took a closer look he realize it was a human brain. The other boxes contained various organs, from the heart to the kidneys. The stench from the small intestine had been so pungent it had pushed its way past the peg on his nose making him heave violently. Peter Thompson's lungs were found in the largest of the container on the bottom of the shelf, but the inventory of every major organ did not prepare him for the horror of seeing Peter's Thompson's face in a container within the crisping drawer. It had been carefully removed and flattened out giving the expression a weird and abstract appearance. Without cartilage to give it shape, the nose remained flat and pugilistic, lips lilac and cheeks waxy. It was the face of a burn's victim, or something found in a traveling freak show. Coonan made it to the garden before purging his guts over the flower's pretty little heads. He would never recall how long he actual spent in the garden following the discovery of Peter Thompson. He only remembered reaching into his pocket for the key ring, and how the act of believing he was back with his children steadied his hand from shaking.

CHAPTER 28

FRIDAY

After leaving the school, Nolan had tasked the HUB to run a check on anyone living in the Manchester area called Myers, narrowing it down to either James or Jimmy. The results came back with three potential matches. PNC records for two showed up nothing, but the third revealed a man in his early thirties with prior convictions for GBH, domestic violence, and theft of a motor vehicle. He had also done time for aggravated robbery five years back. It sounded like the type of person who wouldn't think twice about locking up a weaker kid in a shed. He also asked for a check on a Sally Anderson living on the street where the arson attack had gutted Zerelda Slade's house. It came back with a positive hit for Anderson, and showed she still lived there. Nolan made that his first call.

Sally Anderson was in her late forties, buxom. She reminded Nolan of the cartoon housewives depicted in saucy seaside postcards who are about to get more than just a pint of milk from the local milkman. Her husband was a long distance lorry driver working for a respectable haulage company based out of Oldham. He was away for days at a time, which further bolstered Nolan's theory Sally spent most of her time alone and was probably happy for the distraction of speaking with someone, even if it was a police officer. She offered tea, and they sat for a while at a small table in the kitchen. After

Nolan explained his reasons for being there, Sally relaxed and went into offering her opinion of Zerelda Slade.

"She's a good woman. Thinks the world of Gram. You met her?"

Nolan nodded, refusing to add that he thought she was a belligerent old hag.

"We've not spoken much since she and Gram moved out of Manchester. We used to write every now and then, exchange Christmas cards. That's stopped now. Figure life's got in the way for her. It happens to us all. But for a while, we were pretty close. You know, the first time I met her I thought she was mad."

"Why's that?" Nolan asked.

"She dressed like a gypsy woman, said she was into the occult. Things like that. She didn't have a job and when people asked what she did, she'd described herself as a chirologist, cartomancer, you know, someone who does palmistry and Tarot. She did a reading for me back in the day. Said I was due a change in my luck. That was about ten years ago and I'm still waiting."

Sally smiled and sipped at her tea.

"How's she doing now?" she asked placing the cup on the table.

Nolan cleared his throat.

"She didn't look too well, if I'm being honest."

Sally reflected on this for a moment and thinned her lips.

"Yeah, Zee used to get this chronic burning pain in her lower back and legs. Some days it was so bad she couldn't walk without a stick. It'd make her as mad as a hornet."

Nolan agreed, realising he may have been too hasty in his assessment of Zerelda.

"I told her time and time again that she'd be able to manage it better with pain killers, but Zee wasn't one for Western medicine."

"Why's that?" asked Nolan.

"She used to tell me that the pharmaceutical companies were slowly poisoning the world, tablet by tablet. That's how they control the numbers, or so she claimed."

"She wasn't taking medicine for the pain?"

"No. She'd get Gram to rub an embrocation into her back instead. She made it herself out of lavender, clary sage and ginger oil. She used to make me up batches, but it stunk something horrid. You know she never went to a doctor her whole life. Well, maybe as a baby, but not as an adult. At first I thought she was joking. But it's true. Can you believe that? No prescriptions? Not even a visit to the dentist."

"Zee was against dentists too?"

"I think that was more a fear than any conspiracy theory she had."

"Zee had two boys, twins, Gram and Layton, right?"

"That's right."

"She never let them go to the doctors or dentist either?"

Sally shook her head, and if realising this could be misconstrued as child abuse, quickly came to Zerelda's defence.

"Zee's a little quirky, but there's no way she'd put her kids in danger, or see them go through pain. I think it was mostly her. She once told me she suffered with urinary infections, and instead of going to the docs she'd drink a quart of baking soda with eight ounces of water once a day until it cleared up. It worked too. I learnt quite a lot about home remedies from Zee. Did you know if you sprinkle cloves on open cuts, they'll stop infection, and you can cover warts with Duct tape?"

"Is that so?"

"Yes, Zee was resourceful. When Gram developed his nose thing in his early twenties, Zee made him inhale vinegar twice a day and chew regularly on horseradish. If he awoke with headaches she would sit him down and put a pencil between his teeth and tell him not to bite down, just to keep the pencil in his mouth and things would get better."

"You sure Zee wasn't allowing them kids to suffer?" asked Nolan.

Sally's neck reddened.

"I swear to God, those boys never had a cold. Not even the runs."

Sally moved away a little from the table as if distancing herself from the conversation. Nolan didn't want to lose her, not now she was being so open about Zerelda's past. He let the matter drop about possible child neglect and moved onto biology.

"What happened to Gram's father?"

"Last I heard he lives on a narrow boat on the Calder and Hebble canal. He was a carpenter. Had a flair for Marquetry, or so Zee told me. They met at a small craft festival in Hebden Bridge where Zee was offering readings. He chose the Hangman card. It's supposed to mean a person has arrived at a fork in the road of life and now was a time to act. He did just that. She later told me the card meant sacrifice, selfishness and hidden motives, presumably reasons she used to explain why he disappeared soon after she revealed she was pregnant with twins."

"What can you tell me about the boys?"

"Gram grew up different than most. His teeth were smaller, widely spaced. No matter how much sleep he had his eyes always looked puffy. He had this weird white pattern too surrounding the iris that Zee called, angel's halo. I don't think he said his first words until he was three years old. Maybe I'm remembering that wrong. But I do remember that boy was a pleasure to be around. He would give out hugs if he knew you from old or had just met you. But he was dumb, you know, simple?"

Sally suddenly became animated.

"I remember now," she said snapping her fingers. "Gram was referred for assessments at the Royal Infirmary. That's where he was diagnosed with Williams Syndrome. See, those boys did go to the hospital, if it was essential."

"So they'll be hospital records, appointments, blood tests, things like that?"

"Maybe. Zee took it upon herself to never let the condition control Gram's life, or rule it. To her, Gram didn't need men pocking and prodding him. He didn't need to be told by strangers that he wouldn't be able to do things other children could. If she saw him looking at other children who were more able than him, you know what'd she say? Gram, pay no mind to those other children. They'll never have the eyes of angels. As I said, Detective, she was a good mother."

"And Layton?" asked Nolan.

Sally turned away to the window for a second. When she returned, her skin had taken on the pallor similar in color to slate.

"He was different."

"You mean, he didn't have William's Syndrome?"

"No, he had the fire of Hell in him. From an early age that boy got into all kinds of trouble. Turned Zee's hair white as hospital sheets. If he was my boy, I would have tanned his arse, I don't mind admitting. But Zee, she always made excuses for Layton. Once the pain took hold of her, Layton had to take care of Gram more and more. I guess him rebelling the way he did was excusable in Zee's eyes because he had to grow up quicker than most kids."

"I spoke with the school earlier. The Head Teacher said that Zee stayed with you after the arson attack on their home."

"That's right. The damage to the house was valued lower than Zee expected. She hired an independent loss assessor to negotiate with the insurer on her behalf, and while that was underway, she stayed with me. The fire service report confirmed a vessel had initiated the blaze that ripped through the house. The crime report was submitted to the insurance company, and the independent loss assessor got Zee the full market value for the house. Zee told Gram they now had the money to rebuild their home, but she felt the house was now cursed so they would never live it in again. Zee was going to move them to rented accommodation out of the area, and once the house had been refurbished, she would sell it and use the money to pay the rent and live a modest life somewhere new. She told Gram they were going to move to Stormer Hill. Gram asked how far it was from Manchester, and Zee shown him on a map, estimating it a good twenty, maybe thirty miles away. I was there that day. Gram looked happy as Larry when she told him."

"The fire, did Zee ever say who she thought had done it?"

"Mrs. Sheldon tell you that some youths locked Gram in a shed?"

Nolan nodded.

"Then you'll know it was a reprisal attack. Layton went off to find those that had hurt his brother. It was probably the kindest thing he ever did for Gram. I guess those involved didn't take kindly to this. That petrol bomb wasn't meant for Zee or Gram. It was meant for Layton. You heard he killed himself?"

Nolan nodded. Sally Anderson paused, took a sip from her cup and smiled.

"Layton committed suicide to save Zee and Gram."

"From what I've been told, self-sacrifice doesn't seem the thing Layton would do."

"I saw what Layton put his mother and brother through, the tantrums, the fighting, the getting in trouble, and I hated him for it. But in the end, when it really mattered, he did the right thing by his family. Once he was out of the picture, things stopped. There were no more attacks, no more bullying. Zee and Gram stayed with me for a while Gram got better. The old house got rebuilt. Zee sold it and moved on. The last I heard, she was happy in Stormer Hill. Gram had even landed a job. Even if she wanted to come back and try and resurrect her life here, there was no way that was going to happen now. I was happy for her, and Gram. They'd been through a lot and they deserve their happiness too."

Nolan thanked her for her time, finished his tea quickly and offered his card. On the back, he scribbled down the Nall Street address.

"I'm sure she'd welcome another letter," he said

Sally took the card and for a moment Nolan assumed she might place it in her bra, or follow with a smutty reply, but instead she just held it before her, staring wistfully at the address.

***

James Myers lived twenty minutes away on a housing estate where locking your vehicle didn't really make much difference. The address had warning markers for violence, but none for weapons. Nolan considered calling up for local assistance in case Myers got a little rough, but whether it came down to time, or that he felt he was nearing an answer to a puzzle that had thwarted him for years, he disregarded his own safety and knocked on Myer's front door. It turned out he wasn't home. The neighbors must have developed a nose for smelling out a cop as neither answered when he knocked on their door. He was about to get back into his car when old man approached.

"If you're looking for that low life piece of shit, he isn't home."

Nolan didn't even attempt a smile.

"You know James Myers?"

"Know of him. Sick to the back teeth of his antics, especially the music he plays late into the night. You a cop?"

"Why do you ask?"

"Only two types knock on for Myers; druggies and cops. You don't strike me as the type looking to score."

"I'm trying to locate James regarding an investigation in Yorkshire. Would you know where I might be able to find him?"

"More than likely he'll be at Edgehill Industrial Estate. Works out of a place called J.M. Motors."

Nolan considered asking the old man more, but thought better of it. If any of the neighbors were watching him, the old man might get into bother if word got back to Myers. He thanked him for the information and got back into his car. The old man approached, tapped on the window. Nolan rolled it down and the man leaned in.

"I wouldn't piss on that boy if he was on fire."

Nolan nodded, rolled up the window and backed the Mondeo out of the estate.

***

J.M. Motors ran out of a small unit on the Edgehill Industrial Estate close to the area of Pendleton. It was hard to see off the main drag. Nolan had to pass its main access road twice before he realized any units were there. Most were unoccupied. Doors had been secured with padlocks the size of fists and chains that could support a ship's anchor. The J.M. Motors sign hung over a large access door, the letters crude and uniformed. Elevated on a ramp inside was a small transit van. Beneath it stood a thickset man examining the exhaust with a cone shaped lamp. Nolan got out of the car and approached cautiously. The radio playing in the garage was loud, the sparse walls and concrete floor helping to amplify the sound. To get Myers attention, Nolan shouted. Myers lowered his lamp and placed it on a hook at the side of the ramp. Wiping his hands on a rag, he stepped over the threshold of the garage door into the sunlight. He was a little over six feet tall, tapered with short brown hair that had been gelled back.

"Need help?" Myers yelled, placing the rag in his pocket, voice deep and thunderous.

Nolan pointed at the Mondeo and said, "Car seems to have developed a ticking."

Myers held up his hand. Nolan watched him return to the garage and enter a small office at the back. A few seconds later the music lowered. Birdsong surfaced from the hush. Myers walked back out into the sunlight and Nolan continued, "She's developed a ticking sound this past week. I was wondering if you'd take a look."

"Checked the oil recently?" Myers asked, adding more sarcasm than needed.

"It was serviced about a month ago. Figure I didn't need to."

"Pop the bonnet."

Nolan opened the driver's side door, bent down and flipped the release lever. He looked briefly around the foot well for anything he could use should things get out of hand, but all he found were disused tissues and an old air fresher.

"Turn the engine over!" Myers shouted from the front of the car.

Nolan turned the key and walked to the front of the car where he found Myers looking at the engine.

"Can't hear anything," he said, his hands poking and pushing various pipes and wires. "How long has it been happening?"

"A week," repeated Nolan.

Even to his untrained ear he could tell there was no noise like the one he described. He leant over the engine, mimicking the same quizzical expression on Myer's face.

"Strangest thing," Nolan said. "I've been traveling to work every day this week and it's sounded like a fucking woodpecker was nesting in there."

"Looks like it's flown away," Myers said, lowering the hood strut and shutting the bonnet. "Keep an eye on it. Not much else I can do until it starts up again."

Nolan nodded appreciatively. The two men engaged in a silent assessment of each other. Myers broke the silence, presenting an open question that would work in Nolan's favour.

"How did you find out about me?" he asked.

"Someone I knew recommended you," replied Nolan. "A guy called Gram Slade."

Myers repeated thc name aloud, shifted his eyes skyward briefly and stroked his chin.

"Can't say I recall knowing anyone by that name. But hey, if he recommended me then I must have left a good impression, right?"

Nolan smirked, "You certainly did that."

The tone in Nolan's reply revealed more derision than he intended. It goaded Myers into biting.

"Meaning?" he asked, eyes tightening.

Nolan displayed his palms, "Didn't mean anything by it, James. Is it James, right?"

Myers reluctance to respond pushed Nolan to continue.

"The car was an excuse. The truth is I'm trying to find someone. There's this woman. She hired me to track down her ex. This guy screwed her out of some money and it's my job to find people. I got a lead and chased it here. Someone said you might know him. His name is Layton Slade."

"You expect me to buy that?" said Myers, wiping his mouth. He leaned forward and sniffed the air around Nolan. "You got a funny smell, mister. It reminds me of something." He breathed up through his nose a little harder."A horse, maybe? No. Bull? Yeah, I certainly smell bull. No, wait ... I got it." Myers leaned back, his eyelids low and menacing. "I smell pig. I fucking hate the smell of pig."

Myers walked back to the garage. Nolan watched him continue to inspect the underbelly of the transit like he didn't have a care in the world. It was clear Myers was too smart to talk to a cop and Nolan felt too vulnerable to try and press him for a confession. He needed leverage. The van on the ramp looked too old to be a ringer. Couldn't use that. The garage could be a front to launder money, but without access to the account books it would be an empty threat Myers would bat off easily. Nolan walked to the side of the premises, past oil drums and worn tires stacked on top of each other. Nestling under the shade of an awning at the back of the garage was a charcoal gray Range Rover Evoque. Nolan checked the door. Locked. Peering through the window, he saw no signs of damage to the steering column or ignition, but that didn't mean it wasn't stolen. Thieves had been taking advantage of a weakness in the Crypto system used on most high-end vehicles for years. There was a strong chance the key had been cloned at some point, or had been stolen from the house of the registered keeper, but running the VRN through the system would prove time consuming and ineffective. The vehicle with the same number plate would show up having an owner; albeit they would have no idea their registration had been copied. The only way to substantiate his theory that the car was a ringer would be to check the small plate riveted to the chassis to see if it had been tampered with, but without the keys Nolan was going on blind faith. He returned to the garage. Myers was no longer under the van. Nolan looked around and saw he was sat in the small office at the back, studying some paperwork. He tapped on the office door and Myers looked up. Seeing Nolan, he rolled his eyes and motioned him in.

"Thought you'd gone," he muttered.

Nolan hovered for a while at the door, inspecting the dingy, poorly lit room. There was a smell of grease and cooked noodles in the air. The painted breezeblock walls were a gallery of bawdy posters featuring women dressed in underwear straddled over tyre tubes and car bonnets. This room wasn't for the eyes of the paying customer.

"There is no woman," Nolan said shutting the door behind him. "No money either. There isn't really a Layton Slade, because as you already know, Layton died a few years back. Do you mind if I sit?"

Myers shrugged and Nolan positioned a small office chair so it was facing him.

"So you the ghost of Christmas past?" asked Myers with a smile.

"Actually, I'm more the ghost of Christmas future. I'm here to show you what things could be like if you don't play the game."

"And what game is that, officer?"

Nolan looked around the room, and then back to Myers. He allowed his eyes to linger on his dirty overalls before readdressing his eyes.

"This really ain't your place, is it?" asked Nolan.

"What makes you think that?"

"Hands are too rough to be a boss. I figure you're a middleman, a name above the door. I'm guessing the people who really run this place only pop in from time to time to pick up vehicles, like that Range Rover out there."

Myers stood up, towering over the desk like some giant plucked from an old fable.

"Sit down, James," said Nolan. "I'm not here to bust you."

Myers paused for a moment and lowered himself back to his chair.

"I'm interested in what you know about Layton Slade."

Myers frowned.

"Like you say, he's dead."

"Maybe so, but back in the day I heard you and a few other kids liked harassing the Slade family. You locked Layton's brother in a shed until he begged for his life. I hear that right?"

The laugh that squeezed out of Myer's mouth sounded forced.

"You've been misinformed."

"If not you, then who did?"

"It's not safe for customers to be back here. All kinds of sharp objects about. I wouldn't want you getting cut."

A threat. Nolan decided to play his card.

"You think you're the only person able to break into cars?"

"I'm not following, officer. I don't steal cars. I'm just a working man who gets fucked in the arse every month by the taxman."

"I hear that," Nolan said with a smirk. "But the thing is, I checked the chassis plate of that Evoque out back and it's been tampered with. The rivets are new. It's a ringer, probably stolen to order. I'm guessing your boss is going to send over one of his goons to pick it up soon. I'm also guessing he wouldn't take kindly to finding half a dozen police officers rifling through his finances when they arrive."

Myers jaws clenched.

"Bullshit."

"Don't worry, James. We'll make sure you were given a pardon for assisting us. It's the least we could do."

Myers fixed his gaze on him and said, "That car outside is mine. Business has been doing well."

Nolan looked around the room again, assessing it with the curiosity of a homemaker.

"Business isn't doing *that* well."

"You ain't ever broken into a car. Shit, man, I'm surprised you can even fit into one."

"I'm no psychic, but I'm pretty sure if I run that plate it's going to show up the address of the real owner. All I'm asking for is a little information, James. Then I'll leave you alone."

Myers exhaled as if blowing smoke from a cigarette to the ceiling.

"It was a fuckin' lifetime ago. Why you dragging this shit up now?"

"Because I don't think Layton Slade's dead."

A smile crept over Myer's face, menacing and full of intent.

"Oh he's dead, alright."

"What makes you so sure?"

"Because killing himself was better than the alternative."

"Meaning?"

Myers leaned back, feet outstretched and crossed. Linking his hands behind his head, he said, "There's a guy called Paul Keenan. He ran things. Paul and me grew up on the same street together. He was the one that locked Layton's brother in the shed, not me."

"What did Keenan have against Gram?"

"Easy prey," Myers qualified. "Look, I don't know what went on in Keenan's head. All I knew was not to fuck with him. Shame Layton didn't realize this too. He was pretty tough though, Layton. He knew how to handle a knife. Guess it was cutting up all those pigs."

"What's that?" asked Nolan.

"He used to work at the butcher's over on Kent Road. My old man would send me over there to pick up tripe every Saturday morning. I saw him a few times, apron all bloody with a fucking cleaver in his hand. The way that thing came down whenever he saw me, it was like he was imaging me on that chopping board."

"So Layton went after Keenan with a knife?"

"Uh-huh."

"You see this happen?"

"Nope."

"So how can you be sure?"

"We used to run with a guy called Jockey. Him and Keenan were leaving The Duke of Wellington pub one night when Layton came up to them. He started talking about how he'd cut Keenan up if he ever laid a finger on his brother again. Pulled a knife to prove it. Jockey said he was bold as brass, started poking his finger in Keenan's chest."

Myers mimicked the action, jabbing his finger at the empty space before him.

"If you touch my fucking brother again, I'll cut your heart out. That's what he said, or words to that effect. Jockey said he didn't even see Keenan move, but the next he knew Layton was on the deck holding his jaw. Keenan grabbed Layton's knife and started talking like a fucking madman. Jockey thought he was going to stab Layton, but instead he took his finger, the same one he used to poke his chest."

"Took his finger?"

"Yeah, cut it off."

Nolan winced as his body registered the image. Phantom pains radiated along his own finger as he imagined that blade pushing down, firstly through the flesh, then the bone.

"Did Layton do anything after that?"

Myers missed a beat, "A month went by, maybe longer, can't remember; Keenan was leaving his girlfriend's house when Layton jumped him. Caught Keenan off-guard. Layton pulled a knife and this time cut Keenan. Probably would have seen him off too had it not been for Keenan's bird. She ran out, started hitting Layton on the head with the heel of her shoe. Crazy bitch did a good job too. Layton ran off while Keenan was on the deck, holding his side. That was when Keenan decided to torch the Slade house."

Myers reached over to a grimy looking cup and took a long swig. Placing it back on the desk he addressed Nolan earnestly.

"You want to know what I think?"

Nolan gestured with his hand.

"Keenan was scared of Layton. The way Jockey spoke about him, I'd be scared of him too."

"How do you mean?"

"Some people in the world go running with the tail between their legs if you fuck with them. Some are willing to give it back. Then there are those like Layton; you fuck with people like that and you know it's not going to end well. You end up the one running."

"So where's Keenan now?" asked Nolan, trying to establish if he had been involved directly in Slade's suicide.

"He was charged with possession and distribution a few weeks after the Slade place was burnt down. Did some time in Strangeways."

"He wasn't around at the time of Layton Slade's death?"

"He wasn't even alive when Slade committed suicide. You think I'd be telling you any of this if he was? Keenan would slice my throat if he knew I'd been jabbering to the cops. No, the idiot pushed his luck in prison and was found dead in his cell one morning by the screws. Some sick bastard in there had cut out his heart and wrapped it in paper."

Nolan knew from his years as a cop that the leading killer in prison was cancer, followed by heart disease, and then liver disease. Homicide was way down the list and was trumped easily by suicide. Whoever took the time to cut out a man's heart had both time and reason. But what troubled him more was why they wrapped the heart in paper. That was more than being expedient. They were sending a message. He explored this with Myers.

"The paper they used, was it a note?"

"Jesus. I don't remember," Myers exclaimed. "It could have been fucking toilet paper for all I know." Myers paused for a moment as if recalling something. "There was something now I come to think of it ... A painting, I think."

"Art? Like a print?"

"Yeah," Myers began to scratch the back of his neck. "There was this girl who used to drink in a pub I'd go in. Jesus, what was her name? Her boyfriend was inside at the time Keenan was killed. She mentioned the painting. Fuck, what was her name?"

"Can you remember the name of the painting?" asked Nolan, pushing Myer's thoughts back on track.

"Something biblical, I think."

Nolan mentally constructed Zee Slade's living room in his mind. His subconscious constructed walls, positioned furniture appropriately, arranged ornaments and drove in nails. He could smell the sweet incense filtering the air and the malleability of the carpet under his shoes. The faint roar of cars passing beyond the window fought against the sound of Gram's breathing. Nolan found himself stood before the chimneybreast where a web of fairly lights framed a painting depicting God and demons. He heard Zerelda's dissonant voice crawl up his spine and enter his ear like a spider, its legs beating out three words over and over.

"The Last Judgment," Nolan said aloud, speaking as though he just awoke from a long and deep sleep.

Myers didn't offer a reply immediately. He sat and let the words settle before he spoke.

"That's it. The Last Judgment."

CHAPTER 29

FRIDAY

Layton Slade shared the same face and build as his brother, but that's where all comparisons ended. He saw his brother as dim-witted, guileless and naïve, with the capacity to show compassion toward people he hardly knew. If he did something wrong, Gram cried and carried the weight of his actions like a ten ton chain around his neck. Layton's conscience was mute. He refused to reflect on any act he undertook with regret or remorse. He was stronger than his brother in every way, except for one.

At the age of thirteen, a young girl called Jackie Quigley once revealed her vagina to Layton behind the science rooms of Ravenswood Academy. Jackie was plump, round-faced with full breasts. She worked hard at being friendly with boys, and they would often take advantage of this. Layton had overheard the stories of curious fingers exploring the mysteries that lay beneath her shirt, and the topography of warm flesh resting there. Her kisses left lips sodden and smelling of Parma Violets. Eczema on her hands left her touch comparable to sandpaper. She was spoiled, used, and for that reason Layton did not entertain her command to touch it. The rebuke needled Jackie. The next day, word had gotten around school that Layton Slade was a weirdo and pervert and had tried to show her his penis, which by then had gained the dishonour as being compared to the size of a light switch. The days following, girls sniggered whenever Layton passed them on the school corridors. He would hear their derision over the sound of his feet gathering pace. But the image of Jackie Quigley with her skirt held aloft remained with him. He found comfort in rendering this image on blank sheets of white paper, which he kept hidden in a small tin box under his bed. The sketches were crude, and would often be accompanied with monsters that spilled from between her legs; their hands prying open the vertical cleft like it was a grand curtain on a stage. Eight years later, Layton saw Jackie in a rock bar in Manchester. He was there alone. She was with a friend who had taken a liking to lank haired guy with pot-marked skin and a black Metallica t-shirt five sizes too big for his frame. Jackie was drunk, and whatever memory she had of Layton seemed hazy when they began to talk. Layton remained affable, attentive. Slowly she began to remember him, or at least pretended to. They left the club together and returned to a small flat Layton was renting close to his mother's place. Jackie's intemperance with alcohol allowed him the freedom to strip away her clothes for the purpose of photographing her body in poses designed by his curiosity. She had agreed to this at the club, but presumably didn't believe he would go through with it. Too drunk to object, Jackie lay on his bed in just her underwear. He removed her knickers gently, and remembering that time behind the science rooms, stared at her vagina once again. The hair had been groomed, reduced to a line no thicker than a toothpick. He smelt her breath and it came back sour, not sweet, as he had once been told. Her lips were dry when he pressed his mouth against them, the skin on her hands, smooth and soft. Layton lay with her on his bed until she passed out an hour later. By dawn's light, he had cut her open from the groin to the breastbone, removing the offal and transferring it into bin liners. Even when he took the butcher's knife stolen from his workplace and severed each limb, pooling into buckets what blood leached from the wounds, he remained calm, serene. It was his first kill and he enjoyed it.

In the following months, sex workers of either gender were paid to accompany Layton to the same flat. There he would drug them, or feign perversions that allowed for belts or scarves to be attached around their necks, making it easier to later constrict their breathing and cause blackouts. Leaning on his butchering tutorage, bodies were cut up evenly to disguise their human form, and then transported in industrial bags to the Gremstall Abattoir along with spoiled stock from the butcher's shop. Outside the abattoir, enormous containers held animal leftovers that would be heat-treated and sanitized before being disposed of in municipal sewers, or incineration. No one ever found the bodies of his victims. Save for Jackie, all his victims were sex workers. He never frequented the same red-light areas twice, nor did he engage in the act of sex with any of them. That was too physical, too personal. Any sexual gratification came from documenting their genitals. Spurred by the memory of Jackie Quigley raising her skirt to him as a young boy, once the victim had passed out, Layton produced a small digital camera and took various photos from varying angles, and then subsequently masturbated to each. He then stored these images on a memory stick, which he kept hidden behind a loose section of skirting in his bedroom, inside the same tin box that housed his adolescent sketches. To him he felt no different than the philatelist and numismatists of the world, gathering a collection of work that reflected an activity he pursued with great curiosity and enjoyment, a collection that Layton believed should be shared. It took many years before he realized there was a place that would allow him to do this. That place was called the Dark Web.

Layton's journey began with the more common encryption tool, Tor, which served to spoof his IP Address so he appeared in a different country to the one he was in. It was secure, so be believed. Even the NSA couldn't hack it. But Layton soon found it a playground for charlatans and opportunists selling low-grade drugs with the same patter as a fishmonger. Sex, in its many varying forms, was on hand too, with doors left ajar to wicked and perverse rooms, all of which were too pedestrian for Layton. When he moved to Garlic Routing, things changed. Aware that his work may be too extreme for many, for a long time Layton remained guarded around the many faceless concurring souls that festered behind weird avatars and aliases along the Silk Road. Then, one day, he met someone who went by the name of Ragman.

Layton and the Ragman spoke covertly on secure servers for nearly two months. It was the Ragman who first allowed Slade access to his own FTTP where he kept various images from his own works. His victims were always women, pretty and well kept, many of whom he had met in bars, seduced and then choked to death. After that, Slade began to exchange images of the sex workers. It was this parallel, of bringing people back to their homes under some sexual pretense, that united Layton and the Ragman. They began to write letters to each other using methods such as Steganography, or the

Cesar Shift Cipher, should a clumsy postal worker rip the edge of the envelope and decide to read one. In a heavily encrypted message, Layton discovered the Ragman chose his name after his use of a rag soaked in chloroform to help induce sleep in his victims before photographing them. He was also an amateur tattooist with a keen interest in body modification, and had gone so far as to allow Layton into a secured area of his site where various images were stored, which revealed his body, but never his face. Layton saw that the Ragman was physically strong, muscular, tapering to thin, boyish legs. A mélange of biblical images based on the works of Hieronymus Bosch inked his skin from below the neckline. A God rendered in a mandorla sat atop his right deltoid while hundreds of tiny winged angels led by Lucifer battled each other down thick forearms. In the crease of his elbow, a tree baring fruit of temptation scored the skin. A robed Jesus extracting Eve from Adam's side was positioned along his wrist in whispers of gray and black. Christ clung to his sternum while angels with golden trumpets announced the end of time either side of his chest. His torso revealed the edges of Hell, a limbo filled with scenes of torture inflicted by fantastical insects, demonic frogs and imps. The sins of man were the scaffold to the Ragman's ribs and stomach in startling and horrific detail; a fat man being fed the excrement of a demon, a naked woman being led to her fate by a dragon. The left arm was reserved for Hell. The forearm revealed a clergy-like Satan with black face meting judgment, and above him, along the curvature of the bicep, a band of wailing, lamenting dammed huddled in their misery as brimstone and fire rained down from his deltoid. There was no skin visible. No section of his torso virgin to the needle. The frenulum running on the underside of his penis had been pierced, along with both nipples. It was a lesson in patience and commitment, and Layton was in awe. Like Bosch, the Ragman prescribed to the unorthodox Pantheon ideology of freethinking and considered himself a practising member of an ancient cult he referred to as, The Brethren.

"God is good," the Ragman would write. "God is love. He is incarnate in everything, meaning everything is God, and so everything is good. This is why there can be no such thing as sin, and why what we do is God's work."

And so it began that the Ragman and Layton would share their labors proudly and without judgment, because, as the Ragman would often say, "No one can judge God."

Alex Palmer now heard those same words leave Layton's mouth as he threaded rope through the frame of a wooden chair in was sat on, then around his wrists. A small cone lamp lay beside the chair. Palmer tried to estimate the size of the room. Darkness screened all four horizons. Though he would not appreciate it right then, the lack of light had saved him from understanding what existed beyond his narrowed vision.

"I swore I would never lie to you," Layton Slade said, and then leaning toward Palmer, added, "All the work that's been done. All the sacrifices made, I thought you of all people would appreciate the effort it has taken to get here, to this exact moment in time."

Palmer struggled, testing to see if there was any weakness in the knot that now secured his hands. It didn't budge. Slade stood up and tied a strip of linen over his mouth, tight so he could hardly breathe through it. Sweat marched across Palmer's brow like ants. He drew in the scent of the room through his nose and was reminded of a glasshouse, that mix of mildew and condensation. And something else too. Palmer had once visited a slaughterhouse a few years back while researching a novel. The owner had guided him to the back of the gassing machines where people in white boiler suits and hairnets guided pigs from a lairage into a bloodletting area. Here they gas-stunned the pigs using a high concentration of CO2, instantly killing them. Palmer watched their bodies hanged by trotters over large grates. He saw the knife, the cutting of its pale flesh, and the issue of blood. This was what he smelt now, the act of bloodletting.

Slade stood and moved to a different part of the room, taking with him the lamp. The light revealed large pupa-like objects lay on the dusty floor. Slade produced a knife from his belt and, kneeling before one of white shapes, ran the blade from pole to pole. When he pulled away the sheath, Palmer finally saw what lay beneath. It was no beetle or butterfly, but a human cadaver. Palmer writhed in the chair and moaned through the gag. Slade looked up and smiled.

"She's pretty," he said, and returned to tearing away the muslin.

Framed in an ethereal light, pale as stone, was a young woman, skinny and barely out of her teens. Slade scored the knife through the material of another human cocoon next to her, this one exposing a man's arm held aloft as if haling a cab.

"It might be difficult to see the cut," Slade said, tracing his finger from the man's groin to his neck. "But inside, I've packed the body with salt to help preserve it."

Palmer made a noise through the gag, a primal scream.

"We're not hurting these people," Slade said with a smile. "We're *curing* them."

Slade laughed, the baleful sound stirring sleeping pigeons roosting in the cavities of the walls high above them. He then walked around the room, slowly unsheathing more of the dead. Palmer wanted to look away, but he was drawn to the gruesome scene the same way motorists are drawn to a fatal crash as they pass it. Some of the bodies were set in position; hands screening eyes as if blinded by the sun, others listened to their palms as if impersonating the agonizing expression found in Edvard Munich's, The Scream. When Slade returned to Palmer, his breathing was overstated, as if the act of revealing the dead had truly excited him. As light from the lamp shifted across his face, hollowing out his cheeks and eyes, Palmer noted a change in Layton's expression. He was giddy. Happy. This adjustment was more unsettling to Palmer than the evil countenance he saw in the cellar back at the Moffet cottage. Slade reached out and pulled down the gag. The relief of being able to breathe again through his mouth caused Palmer to respire hungrily on the dank air.

"Where's... Amy Taylor?" he asked.

Slade combed the knife's edge over his eyebrow and replied gravely, "Waiting."

"You don't need her. You have me now."

"But I don't have you, not yet."

"I can't go anywhere," he replied, adding a short-lived struggle with the ropes binding his hands to emphasize the point.

"Where are you, Alex Palmer?"

Palmer looked around the dark room. It reminded him of photographs he had seen of old, derelict asylums long since abandoned but still retaining the spirits of its patients.

"I don't know."

"Yes you do. Where are you?"

"An old hospital, maybe a warehouse?" Palmer submitted.

Slade struck Palmer across the face with his hand.

"Where are you?" he repeated.

Palmer shook the sting off and replied, "I don't know!"

Slade struck him again.

"Fuck," Palmer said behind gritted teeth. "What do you want me to say?!"

"The truth," replied Slade. "Where are you?"

Palmer slowed his breathing.

"Perdition," he said.

Slade smiled and stood

"What's my name?" he asked.

Palmer lowered his head.

"Gram. You work at the primary school and have a mother called Zee who is superstitious. You carry a handkerchief in your pocket tied into a knot to stop the Devil entering you if you sneeze."

Slade pulled out the lining of his trouser pockets for Palmer to see.

"No hanky," he said.

To underline Palmer's confusion, Slade removed the glove on his right hand and held it in front of Palmer's face. The index finger had been cut down to the knuckle, the nub healed and stout against its slender cousins. Unlike Gram's, the skin covering Layton's hands was smooth and unblemished. He slipped the glove back on and squatted down again.

"You know I'm not Gram. You've known since the time you saw me in Bill and Linda's basement. Now, who am I?"

Palmer shook his head, "I don't fucking know."

"Okay, let's try something else. Who are you?"

Palmer complied, "My name is Alex Palmer. I live in London and–"

"No! Who are you *now*?!"

As a cop, Palmer had done is fair share of talking with the crazies in the world to find common ground in an attempt to control an escalating situation, but there was something in Slade's eyes that worried him. He tried anyway.

"I'm the reason."

"Good," replied Slade.

"I'm the reason all this exists."

"Yes."

"You created it for me. You made it real."

"Yes."

"You made this from the stories I write. But my books don't mean anything," Palmer said. "They're fantasy. No one gets hurt. No one dies."

Slade stood up slowly, eyebrows bucking.

"You're still not getting it," Slade said. "This isn't fiction."

He began pacing in small circles, head bowed, internally conversing, rationalizing, muttering stunted little questions that caused head-shaking and grand sweeping motions with his hands.

Palmer figured the police would be looking for him now. Bill or Linda would have called it in. With searches for Amy ongoing, they'd request more resources, more officers. It was only a matter of time before they found this place, wherever it was, and all of this would be over. He just needed a little more time. He knew it would be easier to prevail upon Slade's own delusions and pander to his stronger self, because Palmer had done the same when he kowtowed to that evil and stronger person within him, Jason Legge. The stronger character within was always the one listening more closely.

"I just want to understand," said Palmer. "Help me understand?"

Slade turned back to him, "But you know. You've always known."

Looking into the darkness, Palmer said, "That's right. I have always known. You punish them because they're weak, right? They're weaker than you, and you don't like weakness."

Slade continued to stare at Palmer and said, "I can be judged for what I do no more than a cat for killing a mouse. It is what comes natural to me."

"That's right. You can't be judged for something you have no control over."

Slade rushed toward Palmer and pressed the knife against his throat. Its blade broke the skin. Slade then placed his spare hand on the side of Palmer's face, supporting the jaw in his palm.

"No one can judge God," Slade said. "You'll see."

He reached his full height again and walked away to a darkened area of the room. The noise of a diesel engine suddenly bounced off all four walls. A line of upright lights came to life. The smell of bloodletting magnified as light crept over unsheathed bodies left naked atop of tin foil sheets, their skin sallow and lustreless. Many of the dead were bound and cloaked in white cheesecloth, their faces indistinct and mysterious. Palmer moved his gaze to Slade, who was now stood before a large sheet of tarpaulin covering the far wall, gripping a length of rope attached to the tarp. Palmer was sure he was about to make an announcement, something profound like when a person reveals a plaque set into a wall to commemorate the memory of those who had lost their life in war, or sacrificed it to stop one. But Slade didn't. He just stopped and looked out toward Palmer with a blank expression. It was then Palmer instantly felt a presence close to him, one that seemed to have rule over everything in the room, from extracting the wind out of Palmer's lungs, to wrenching the shadows off walls. Ambient sounds turned muted as they waited for this other person to speak. Slade's expression then changed to wonderment. Palmer tried to see who Slade was looking at, but couldn't turn his head. But he could feel them, behind him. Slade abandoned the rope and walked past Palmer. Then, in a low, almost sexual whisper, Slade whispered close to Palmer's ear. "You finally made it."

CHAPTER 30

FRIDAY

Nolan had telephoned Coonan while heading towards Kent Road. After his chat with James Myers he wanted to speak with the butcher who hired Layton Slade, but on hearing Coonan articulate that moment he found Peter Thompson, had stopped the car and pulled over to the lay-by. A rush of saliva in his mouth made it near impossible to speak, allowing time for Coonan to decanter the news and his own frustrations in equal measure.

"I'm still at the scene," Coonan said, dismally. "SOCO are trying to lift prints from the car and the house. Save for some white dust in the car's foot well, everywhere is clean. We're assuming for now the Perp wore gloves. We found a couple of soda cans in the bin, and a cup in the sink. With any luck they'll get DNA from those. There's no sign of any struggle, no blood or secretions on the preliminary search. Whoever murdered Mr. Thompson was careful and clearly knew what they were doing. The victim had a wife too, Fiona, but we've been unable to locate her. I'm about to prepare a handover for the SIO and then I'm going back to the station to follow up on any leads concerning Amy Taylor. You should know I got a call from Superintendent Roberts. He got wind that Palmer was on the system. Apparently they go way back and now he's chewing my arse to find him."

Nolan heard Coonan move his mouth away from the phone to speak with someone. The faint sound of an officer was informing

Coonan the DCI was ten minutes away. When Coonan returned to the call he sounded agitated.

"They've allocated Darren Healey from MIT to the Thompson case. He'll be here in about ten minutes so I haven't got long to speak. What have you found out?"

Nolan wiped his mouth and off loaded, concisely, what he had gleaned from his visit to Manchester, including accounts from Slade's old head teacher, Sally Anderson and James Myers. He let the information settle before adding, "What's your thoughts on exhuming the remains of Layton Slade?"

The proposal stunned Coonan into silence.

Nolan jumped in, "If we can gain a warrant from the coroner to exhume his body, it'll prove whether Layton Slade is dead. Kristen Taylor identified Gram Slade from the CCTV footage at her home. Or at least someone who looked a lot like Gram Slade. But as we know Gram couldn't have been in Hanging Lee at the time Amy was abducted because he was at the library." Nolan waited a beat to see if any of this was sticking. Coonan remained silent. "What I'm struggling with is why Layton killed himself? There was no threat because Keenan was dead way before he committed suicide. Something else Myers mentioned; while in prison, Keenan's heart had been cut out and wrapped in the print of a painting called, The Last Judgment. The same painting was hung on the wall at the Slade's place. The mother said it was her son's favourite, but at the time I assumed she meant Gram. I looked up the painter it was done by some guy called Hieronymus Bosch."

Coonan jumped back into the conversation.

"That's fucking twice I've heard that name today."

"Bosch?" asked Nolan, clarifying.

"One my DCs at the school were interviewing staff to see if anyone suspicious was hanging around prior to Amy's disappearance. Though none of them one saw anyone, the caretaker, Len Critchley, discovered something unusual a couple of days before she went missing. It was a baby pig. It had been left to rot in one of the industrial bins. Critchley assumed it was kids screwing around at first, which is why he never reported it to the police. Critchley said the pig had been splayed. Its insides removed."

"He thought that wasn't worth mentioning?"

"Apparently not. He also said its eyes were inked-black and it had the words, The Devil's Ass is Hell's Gateway, tattooed on its hide. The DC did a search on the phrase. Turns out it was a Dutch proverb dating back to the late Middle Ages. It inspired a section of, The Temptation of Saint Anthony. A painting by—"

"Don't tell me," Nolan interjected. "Hieronymus Bosch."

"Pigs are used by tattooists to practise on." said Coonan.

"You think our guy is a tattooist?"

"I'm not ruling it out."

"So where is it now, the pig?"

"Critchley thought it best no one see it. The next day refuge collectors emptied the bins. Any evidence we may have had was lost." Coonan sighed, "It's easy to make connections, Tom. What I need now are facts. So why exhume the grave?"

"I know it's rare these days, but what about presumptive identification? Slade's body was dragged along the M60. Chances are a full ID would have been difficult. If all the details suggest probable identification, but without complete certainty due to a lack of DNA or dental, wouldn't this lead to the coroner allowing the body to be released for burial?"

"The body would have to be the same height and build for one. Plus, they'd have to be so disfigured it would be near impossible to distinguish from recent photographs and dental. But even then, they'd bring in qualified specialists in comparative osteology and craniometry. The coroner wouldn't accept the body because they had the person's ID and suicide note in their pocket." Coonan added, "I guess DNA would be the only key to match the body to the person, but considering the Slade brothers never showed up on any of our records, it's safe to assume we hold none for either of them. That's the only explanation to maybe why the coroner allowed the body to be released."

"I have Gram Slade's DNA," Nolan said. "He volunteered it when I was over at his place. If we can extract DNA from the bones of the body and match it again the DNA I took from Gram Slade, we'll be able to determine if that really is Layton buried in Agecroft Cemetery."

"It doesn't change anything, Tom. All it gives us is a name and description, one of which we already have. Then there's the emotional strain on the family when we tell them we're digging up the remains because we believe their son is still alive and is going around abducting little children. What if we're wrong?"

Nolan could feel Coonan drifting so attempted to reel him back in.

"You said that the remains of Peter Thompson were removed proficiently. Myers said that Layton was skilled with a knife due his job as a butcher. I think these two cases are linked, Boss. The car seen on Edgerton Road prior to Amy Taylor's abduction suddenly turns up at a house where a body has been butchered like ..."

Nolan paused as all the pieces came together in his head

"A pig," Coonan said.

"Layton Slade is using his likeness to Gram to get close to the children. He's abducting them and my worry is we're going to find more containers, only this time with tiny pieces of children inside."

It was a shocking image, but Nolan felt he needed a sledgehammer to hit home his hypothesis and bring Coonan back to the moment.

"Kristen Taylor said Amy would have never gone off with a stranger. Layton Slade was able to take these children because they knew him, or at least they thought they could trust him because they believed he was Gram."

In the silence that followed, Nolan heard from the other end of the phone the hubbub of police officers and support staff against the faint rumble of helicopter blades churning the air. He leaned over and switched his car radio on and tuned it to a news channel. He kept the volume low as he waited for Coonan to speak again.

"We're on the clock," Coonan finally said. "Exhuming the body and getting a match will take time, time we don't have. Go and see the coroner's officer. Speak with them and find out as much as you can about Slade's body. I know him from my time at GMP. His name is Ken Teller. I'll ring ahead and tell him you're on your way. They'll be records. If you feel there may have been probable misidentification based on the evidence in the report, let me know and I'll apply for the warrant. In the meantime, I'll wait around here in the hope forensics can lift something from the scene. If you're right, about Layton Slade, I don't think he's doing this alone."

It had never occurred to Nolan that two people might be involved. He had been so preoccupied getting the evidence to suggest Layton Slade was the abductor there had been no room to consider an accomplice. But it made sense. Slade would need a second person to help him move the bodies, or take the children by surprise.

"I'm going to get one of the team to speak with the prison warden at the time Keenan was serving," said Coonan. "See if we can pull the release records of all inmates within a year of Keenan's death. Anyone skilled with a knife or experience in tattooing will be coming in for questioning."

Before ending the call, Coonan's tone dropped and lost its formality, "Tom ..."

Nolan waited, but he sensed the detective would never finish the sentence. This wasn't the time for sentimentality or praise. Seconds were dropping like rain around them and with each one that fell, Layton Slade was becoming stronger and more dangerous. He had chosen his victims based on their vulnerability, and wouldn't stop taking lives until the police found him. Nolan didn't wait any longer. He started the car's engine and pulled out onto the road. The phone's screen finally dimmed as news broke on the radio the body of Peter Thompson had been found.

CHAPTER 31

FRIDAY

Ken Teller had the appearance of a fished pulled from the water. His eyes were round and dead, skin pale. The collar of his white cotton shirt hung from his neck like quoits over a wooden peg. When he shook Nolan's hand, it came back clammy and cold. Dead man's hands.

"You one of Coonan's boys?" Teller asked, settling into his chair.

The way he said "boys" made it sound like Nolan was one of Coonan's sons working in the pasture, tilling soil for a good harvest.

"I'm just helping out on a case."

"How is he?"

Teller's tone suggested this was more than just a regular enquiry. His job was to unearth social and medical history of any deceased brought to the coroner's attention, and gather the evidence to assist the coroner in establishing the identity of the deceased. In short, Teller was paid to discover more about a person than they probably knew about themselves. Asking about Coonan's wellbeing wasn't convivial chitchat. He was being loyal to his natural instincts and wanted the satisfaction of knowing more than anyone else about Coonan's current mental state.

"He's doing fine," replied Nolan, tactfully.

Teller looked down his nose and said, "Job treating him well?"

Nolan didn't bite.

"We're all overworked and underpaid. But there's only three years until he retires so there's light at the end of his tunnel."

Teller's face creased into an uncomfortable smile.

"Let's not waste anymore time, Detective. I dug out the records for Layton Slade as requested." Teller pushed a manila folder across his desk. "Mark said you were investigating Slade's twin brother for a crime in the West Riding area. Gram. But he's gone missing, or something. He wanted to know if we extracted tissue sample or bloods from Layton Slade's body so you could match DNA found at the scene."

"That's right," Nolan said.

He was thankful Coonan had done most of the back story. Too many questions concerning the autopsy would infer something was missed, which would eventually lead toward misidentification. Teller might not like that. It would infer he was incompetent. To make matters worse, the person they assumed was dead was now abducting children and performing human evisceration based on the oversight. The press feed on that kind of story for years. No, the missing story was good, suitably vague.

Teller cleared his throat, "The conditions surrounding the death of Layton Slade resulted in the decision to release the body for burial shortly after post mortem. You'll read from my report that tissue blocks and slides normally stored in the medical pathology records were disposed of by incineration following no match on any police records, and that the cause of death seemed apparent enough."

"Suicide," Nolan confirmed.

"Not for the faint of heart," Teller said with a smile that sent a chill running through Nolan's bones. "Did a dive off the bridge at junction 16 of the M60."

"Can a fall like really do so much damage?"

"It wasn't just the fall. Before impact a large heavy goods vehicle struck his body. The front wheel section rolled over his head and upper torso."

"Jesus."

"It's all in the report, Detective. The initial impact fractured the skull and broke his spine in three places. The asphalt successfully removed most of his face due to being dragged 150 yards down the motorway. Then the pressure of the tires compressed his body to a point where he suffered internal haemorrhaging." Teller tendered a forced smile, and added, "Road kill."

Gallows humor, delivered with a formality inherited from too many visits to the mortuary, Nolan assumed. He leaned over and opened the folder. Inside was Teller's précis of the death and his findings. Following this was the pathology report detailing toxicology results, circumstances of death, evidence of medical intervention, as well as external and internal examinations. Nolan scanned the forensic pathologists' opinion on the cause of death, which was stated as a cranial BFT hinge fracture caused when the head was compressed under the vehicle's tires. Identification of the decedent revealed that Slade had part of the index finger missing on his right hand, severed at the proximal phalanx. Soft tissue damage could not be determined if it was a result of the fall, or that the finger had yet to heal. Last known clothing was positively ID'd by mother at the morgue (blue jeans, black trainers, biker-style faux leather jacket and a Beatles t-shirt given to him by Gram for his twenty-ninth birthday). A wallet containing a bank card, which would later transpire to hold only £3.32p, a Starbucks loyalty card and driver's license, was also found in the jacket. No birthmarks. No scars. Nolan noticed an entry detailing a partial tattoo on the upper right arm. The sanguineous crust formed over the ink suggested it was only a day or two old. The lettering was incomplete due to severe abrasion caused when the body was dragged, and as a result only two words survived: *Hell's Gateway*. Nolan remembered the pig that had been found at Stormer Hill Primary and made a mental note. Zerelda Slade confirmed that Layton had shown her the tattoo the day after having it done.

"You noticed it yet?" asked Teller, his body perched over the desk like some gargoyle over a church's ledge.

Nolan tried to scan the rest of the document but Teller didn't have the patience to wait.

"No dental records," he interjected.

Nolan remembered the conversation with Sally Anderson, and Zerelda's reticence toward visiting anyone wearing a white coat.

Picking lint from the sleeve of a navy blue jacket, Teller continued, "Apparently the mother preferred home remedy over professional help. This is why the medical history for Layton is limited. We gained school medical history from NHS records, as well as immunizations. Birth records and a midwife assessment at the time

Layton was born were documented appropriately. We also found a hospital record when Layton was admitted for an intestinal obstruction following persistent vomiting and signs of distension, from which we were able to determine his blood group, O-positive. Other than that, no other operations or A&E records could be found."

Nolan knew that O-positive was the most popular blood type and was about to mention this when Teller readjusted his gaze back to him.

"You got to hand it to the woman," Teller said. "She kept those kids in good health all their lives, feeding fevers, pulling teeth."

Nolan refused to get caught up in the ethical debate about duty of care and continued browsing the folder's contents. The pathologist reports was lengthy and filled with technical jargon that read like Morse code to Nolan. Toxicology had returned showing small quantities of alcohol but no drugs. Tests included showed no HIV or hepatitis, and gross autopsy findings of organs in situ revealed high levels of trauma to cardiovascular, respiratory, hepatobiliary, endocrine, digestive, genitourinary, reticuloendothelial and musculoskeletal areas. Nolan's eyes lingered for a while at a section where traces of calcium sulfate dihydrate, chlorine, sodium hypochlorite and thymolsulphonethanlein were found on the skin. Nolan didn't attempt to try and pronounce the last word so rotated the folder and pressed his finger against it.

"What's this?" he asked.

Teller leaned over the desk, eyes squinting.

"A chemical compound."

"Do you know what's it used for?"

"Calcium sulfate dihydrate is a main ingredient of Plaster-of-Paris. You'll also note horsehair was found on the body too, which is sometimes added to lime plasters. That's an old practice used from the turn of the twentieth century. We assumed the horsehair came from his exposure to abattoirs considering his occupation was a butcher."

Teller reclined back into his seat, pleased with himself.

"Could Layton have picked it up from an old building?" Nolan countered.

Teller's eyes narrowed.

"Possible, but unlikely."

"Why do you say that?"

"You'll see from my report that transportation vehicles often spill their loads on motorways. Slade probably picked up the plaster compounds when he was dragged, and as said, the horsehair more than likely came from the abattoir. Unless you think differently, Detective?"

Nolan shook his head.

"No, no. You're right. It makes sense."

Nolan reached for his pocket notebook and quickly scribbled down the different chemicals found on Layton's skin, making sure he spelt them right. He returned to the final pages of the report and found a section that slowed him to a halt. Handwritten on lined paper and photocopied was Layton Slade's suicide note. It was concise and barely legible, but when Nolan read through it he adapted his inner monologue to reflect the same regional twang he heard in Gram Slade:

There is no pill. There is no intervention that can help me. I did a bad thing. I hurt someone. Now I'm scared. I don't one anyone to hurt my family. It's easier to die than live. This is all bullshit. Life is bullshit. I don't care anymore. Layton.

Nolan asked, "The suicide note intimates Layton's family was in danger."

"A copy of the note was passed to CID. A formal investigation highlighted local youths harassing the family over a twelve month period, but from what I heard the mother and her other son moved out of the borough shortly thereafter." His face puckered. "Is everything okay, Detective? I saw you write the chemicals down. Are you suggesting we missed something?"

Nolan closed the folder and passed it back to Teller.

"Not at all. I just want to run them passed our CSI. If similar compounds are found at our scene, it might mean Gram and Layton frequented the same building. It's a line of enquiry that might help us track Gram's whereabouts."

Nolan could tell Teller wasn't buying that.

"I won't take any more of your time, Mr. Teller. I'll tell the DI you were asking about him."

Nolan stood to leave the room but Teller stopped him.

"What exactly has the brother done?"

"I'm sure you'll appreciate that in the interests of all parties involved, I can't discuss it presently."

Teller's cadaver skin finally gained color. He shifted his gaunt frame purposely in his chair.

"From what I understand," Teller said, his words thinned out and harsh, "Gram Slade had learning difficulties and was tormented for it. I'm no expert on psychology, but someone who's probably been a victim all their life would know the difference between right and wrong."

Nolan feigned a smile and said, "You'd be surprised at how many people we meet appear to be one thing on the outside, but something else under the skin."

He then offered his hand. A symptom of Teller's frustration caused him to stall before accepting the parting gesture. Nolan noted the grip was weak, half-hearted, suggesting the officer had neither the will nor desire to be generous even with vigour. Nolan didn't give a shit and lumbered toward the door. Before leaving he gave a cursory glance around the room. It was a nice office, clean and clinical, if not a little impersonal. It suited Teller perfectly.

CHAPTER 32

FRIDAY

A small trestle table stood in the middle of what was once the pump house of the Blackthorn Hill Water Works. Clear plastic bottles containing acetone and bleach sat beside a HDPE bucket and glass stick for stirring the two liquids together. The Ragman and Slade sat opposite each other staring blankly at the objects. A surgical mask hung from the Ragman's neck, blue latex gloves stretched tight over large hands revealing the outline of veins and fingernails. He produced a strip of linen from a tan leather satchel on the floor and proceeded to fold into a neat square. Slade observed him as though watching the creation of an origami bird from a sheet of paper. Both men rarely spoke anymore, choosing to communicate in gestures and subtle facial movements that either would translate as emotion or instruction. It was as if they were now connected spiritually and cerebrally. Ragman was the twin he had hoped for, someone with power, strength, knowledge, control, and a shared interest in death. Instead, he got Gram. The Ragman placed the mask over his face and gave Layton a look to suggest he do the same. A small cut parted the fine blond hairs on the Ragman's brow, the upper lid and skin around his eye shimmering in shades of periwinkle. Whenever the Ragman blinked, the wound bulged and skin gathered in pleats causing him to twitch in the aftermath. The injury was fresh. There was no talk of how it happened. No enquiry to if it hurt or needed medical attention. There was no sympathy shown. It was a simple cut, a mark, and they were both used to blood and scars that by now it seemed a waste of energy to apply curiosity or concern. Placing his mask over his mouth, Layton watched the Ragman pour acetone into the bucket.

"The cops are all over the Thompson place," Layton said avoiding eye contact.

The Ragman remained focused on the task of mixing. He placed the bottle of acetone down and picked up the bleach. Before pouring it in, he looked up to Layton and asked, "You went there?"

"No point in worrying. It's done."

The Ragman placed the bottle down. His stare was intense and lingered until it made Layton uncomfortable. Layton had been careful when he returned to Sycamore Drive. He had taken the small ginnel at the end of the road that allowed him anonymity before turning toward the bungalow. When he saw the cordon tape and the police vehicles, he paused to fasten his shoelace. He counted over half a dozen uniformed officers. A white tent had been erected leading into the property. Figures dressed in white coveralls moved with purpose. Lowering the peak of a baseball cap over his eyes, Layton had turned and made his way back through the ginnel to a small convenience store on the edge of the estate.

"I *was* careful," Layton said, returning back to the task of making chloroform.

"No one is ever that careful. It's time we tie up all the loose ends."

The two men walked down the poorly lit corridors of the water works with the pace of prisoners heading to the electric chair, stopping finally at the room holding Amy Taylor. This room stored an irrigation tank for the purposes of filtering water, but due to its lack of windows and solid door, had since been converted into a makeshift holding cell for many of their victims. Slade walked in, accidentally kicking a small brown bottle that smashed into tiny pieces against the nearest wall. There was no sound made from Amy Taylor. No gasp of shock or fright. Slade assumed she must have been cowering behind the door, but when he checked he found she wasn't there. The Ragman stopped below the hatch in the ceiling. The cover had been removed. Slade joined him and looked up.

"I secured it with nails only last month."

"No well enough," the Ragman replied.

"But how?" asked Slade.

The Ragman looked around the room. An outflow pipe running the length of the wall had been snapped from the brackets closest to the hatch. A section had been removed causing bilge water to leak onto the pale dusty floors.

"There," he pointed to the missing piece of piping. "She must have used that. Where does this duct lead?"

"Outside," replied Slade, his voice failing to hide his frustration. "I swear though, I nailed it shut good."

"I told you, no one is ever that careful."

The Ragman pulled the handgun from his belt. Without saying another word, he left the room and headed out of the building to the surrounding moorland.

CHAPTER 33

FRIDAY

Thick chains hung down from rolled steel joists. On the end were heavy hooks that at one time ferried large pieces of machinery from one end of the engine room to the other. Now they served to as a crook from which dead bodies hung in many forms and sizes. Palmer had been in there for almost an hour and still couldn't condition his mind to accept the horror before him. He tried to avert his gaze from all the bodies, but found that wherever his eyes fell, many others lay supine and masked in muslin and cheesecloth.

"Come on, Alex," he said to himself. "You need to get out of here."

With enough force the wooden chair he was tied to would probably break, but he'd have to really slam it into the ground. The only way to do that would be to fall back. So Palmer leaned into the backrest, and putting his weight on the balls of his feet, lifted up the front set of legs. He counterbalanced, and while lingering there a thought quickly came to him. His hands were tied to the backrest. They would hit the ground first and get trapped under the chair and his weight. He needed his hands to fight his way out of this place, or turn handles to doors. He couldn't do that with a fractured bone or broken finger. He revised his plan. Leaning forward with knees bent, and taking the weight of the chair on his back, Palmer began to move clumsily like a beetle toward the open door, shuffling in tiny steps while circumnavigating corpses on the floor, and those suspended by hooks. The chair was heavy and restrictive, but at least he was moving. Stopping at the door's divide, Palmer turned his body parallel to the inner wall, and bracing himself, threw his body and the chair into the brickwork. Pain shot through his arm, the rope tightened around his wrist, cutting into the skin. The second attempt was just as painful and made no lasting damage to the chair. Palmer moved ten steps to his right, cantered his body as quickly as he could and slammed once again into the wall. He screamed as his shoulder dislocated. The snapping of the chair frame was lost in the noise, but when Palmer adjusted his grip he felt a slackening around the rope. He fell to his knees as if praying, strings of salvia dripping from his mouth. It would take another attempt to snap the frame completely. Using the wall for leverage, Palmer rose up to his feet again and swung his body one final time at the wall. The chair splintered and cracked. He made a noise, something that began in his stomach and worked its way up like a fist through his throat. He let it out and it stirred the resting pigeons perching upon girders; their voices sounding like a heart beat the dead so desperately yearned for. A feather drifted down like a whirlybird, landing beside Palmer's foot. By now he sounded like a man speaking in tongues, possessed by a demon, muttering expletives and words that made no sense. He finally freed himself from the wreckage. His hands were still tied but he could move. Before he left the engine room, he slammed his shoulder into the wall, forcing the bone back into the socket. The click was muffled under the flesh, but he felt it settle back into place as a new wave of pain enveloped him.

Palmer entered the corridor lined with tiny lanterns and hurried back toward the room he had awoke in. A steel door capped the end of the corridor. He tried to remember if this had been the route Slade had taken him down, but in this dungeon, all doors looked alike. He couldn't go back, not into that other room where all those bodies were. He had to keep going forward and find Amy. He had to get out otherwise he and Amy will be the ones on the hooks. With bound hands, he turned his back to the door and blindly reached for the handle. After a little fumbling, the door opened. He entered cautiously, feet knocking the ends of machine parts as he moved through the flotsam. Pain burrowed into his arm like a hungry rabbit. In the darkness his breathing was amplified. It wasn’t until he heard gunshot, and saw the blast light up the room for a split second, that he realized he was not alone. The room shifted as if perched on stilts during high winds, then, Palmer received a reprieve from all that pain as a second gunshot lit up a face. It was fleeting but a dominant vision of a man exploiting his soul.

CHAPTER 34

FRIDAY

Nolan's car wailed as he came off the slip road at junction 17 of the M60 at 70 mph. By the time he passed Whitefield, he was nearing 100 mph. The sound of the asphalt under the tires sounded like the ocean during a storm. Cars sounded their horns as he weaved in out of lanes to gain pole position. The mobile phone rattled in its holder. Nolan leaned over and punched in Coonan's number. Flitting his eyes from the road to the phone's display, he activated the call and put it on speaker. It rang out.

"Fuck!" he shouted, palming the dash.

A Volkswagen Beetle in lime green pulled into the outside lane slowing Nolan to a steady 50mph. He flashed his main beam erratically, swiping his hands in front of his windscreen as if performing a carriage return on an archaic typewriter. A young woman's eyes glanced in the rear view, saw him gesturing, and indicated to the middle lane. As he passed her window, she shaped her hand into an open fist and jerked it up and down.

"And fuck you too," Nolan mouthed.

The matrix informed him there was an estimated travelling time of twenty-five minutes to junction 22. He pressed hard on the accelerator again and tried Coonan one more time. It was getting more difficult to hear the phone over the engine noise. He considered stopping on the hard shoulder when he heard Coonan's voice squeezing through the tiny speakers.

"Boss, it's Tom!" Nolan said, raising his voice to compensate for the external sounds.

"I'm about to go into a press briefing to update everyone on Amy Taylor," said Coonan. "You've got five minutes."

"I went to see Ken Teller. I think I know where Amy Taylor is!"

There was no reply and Nolan wondered if he had entered a black spot and lost the signal.

"Boss! Can you hear me?!"

Coonan replied, "I needed to move out the office so no press could hear me. Tell me that again."

"I'm traveling back to Stormer Hill. I should be there in half an hour," he said.

He struck his horn as another car blocked his route.

"I can hardly hear you," said Coonan. "What's happening?"

Nolan swerved, narrowly missing the backend of a BMW. Indicating, he slowed and veered across the lanes until he was safely on the hard shoulder. Cars roared past beeping in consternation. He pulled the phone off the holder and held it to mouth.

"I saw the Coroner's and pathologist report for Layton Slade," he said, breathless. "Based on the evidence presented to them when they found the body, I can see why they arrived at the conclusion it was Layton. The corpse had the same finger removed, ID, clothes and a recent tattoo that was confirmed by Zerelda Slade."

"I've got twenty members of the press out here baying for my blood. If you don't tell me something fucking positive right now, I'll feed you to them."

"When the body hit the motorway, it was dragged about a hundred yards across asphalt," Nolan replied, the gap between words getting shorter. "This is why Zerelda couldn't give a positive ID. The skull was crushed, most of the bones too. No DNA matches. Even the blood was the most popular type. Layton must have found someone the same height and weight as him and removed the index finger. He purposively had a tattoo done and showed it his mother so she would later corroborate. The tattoo was a phrase, Boss, the same one that had been inked on the pig at the school, Hell's Gateway."

Coonan had enough time to shoehorn a reply, "You've got one minute left."

"Traces of three chemical compounds were found on the skin. I did some research on the names. One is used as a PH indicator, the other two most commonly help disinfect untreated water before it's safe for human consumption. If I'm right, and Layton Slade staged his death so he could abduct the children, he's doing it from one location. Probably an old water treatment works, maybe one that's been abandoned for some time. You mentioned powder found in the Thompson car. I bet it contains trace elements of the same chemicals found on the body buried in Layton's grave."

Coonan jumped in, "I won't be able to confirm that as a full contact trace is going to take up to three weeks."

"And getting a warrant to exhume the body is going to take time too. So I guess we're going on faith here, Boss."

Nolan heard a man's voice in the distance. He was telling Coonan the press was ready for him.

"How many water treatment buildings do you know in the West Riding area?" Coonan asked.

"Not in use? I don't know any. A call to Yorkshire Water should give us an idea."

"I feel like I'm chasing my fucking tail," Coonan replied."Get back as soon as. I've got Woodentops searching every back yard, shed and attic for Amy Taylor. So far no one has found anything yet. Bob Wood is doing a second search of Hanging Lee and we've got regular media statements airing on local and national radio. You know as well as I that the further we are from finding that girl, the nearer she is to turning up dead."

"How's Kristen?" asked Nolan, wondering if it was appropriate to make inquiries at this stage.

"She's still at the Moffet place. I've got an FLO paying regular visits. From what I understand she's crumbling. So far we've been able to keep her from the press, but they're camped out outside the farmhouse. Someone in the village must have told them that's where she was staying."

Another voice presented itself, reminding Coonan of the time.

"I'll stick that fucking watch up your arse if you point at it again!" he snapped. "I've got to go," he said returning back to the conversation. "The cops at the MET say they tried Palmer's apartment but there was no answer. Officers and CSI are looking through the Moffet's rental cottage for evidence to where he may be, but I'm not holding much hope. My main priority is the girl. But based on what you've told me, and the evidence I've gleaned so far, I think if we can find her, we'll find Palmer."

Coonan shouted something derogatory to the person who had been clock watching. Nolan could hear the tension in his throat. The weight was building on his shoulders and he wondered how long it would be before he collapsed under the pressure again. Teller would love to hear that news.

Nolan wished his Boss good luck before turning the car back onto the motorway. He'd lost a little over five minutes of travel time making the call to Coonan, and where time is a commodity traded to the desperate for hope, he crossed the boundary into Yorkshire feeling like he had lost several hours.

CHAPTER 35

FRIDAY

Amy Taylor observed the darkness as if it held secrets. Shadows of light moved arbitrarily before her, swirling like stars and albino snakes. In their abstract form she tried to understand. She tried to read them as if they were words. But there was no reason for them being there. They were not messages. They did not guide her, or provide her with the answer to why she had been taken. They were the afterimage of the world from where she had been. In the belly of the tanker, Amy sympathized with the blind, vowing never to ignore a blue sky again, if she was lucky enough to see another blue sky.

The tanker smelt of toolboxes and pond water. Its walls softened the men’s voice much like a womb protects a baby's ears from the chaos of daily life. Amy shivered, but not because she was cold, but because the nightmare was not over yet. She had heard the tension in the men's voices when they assumed she had escaped through the ceiling hatch. They will search the air duct, and when they discover she's not there, they will hunt her down. And when they don't find her outside, they'll return again to the room where their eyes will rest upon the tanker once more. They will realize Amy Taylor, that weak little girl, had deceived them. Then she will join the other children; Lucy Guffey, George Levy and Sarah Cook. Prayers will be said for her. School children will fashion hearts from felt and embroider her name in threads of blue and yellow. Votive candles will be lit in the church, and posters bearing her face will be pinned in shop windows and to lampposts.

Amy robed her body with skinny arms to stop the shivering. Night and hunger tainted her breath. Her stomach groaned. Drawn to every sound around her, she had heard the men leave the room but had still not gathered the strength to move. Paralyzed by indecision, she waited for an answer to present itself. The answer came in two loud bangs. Gunshot. One followed quickly by the other. The sound resonated within the labyrinth of her ears. Amy bit down on her lip, muzzling a scream. Then came more silence. More waiting.

"Move," she said quietly to herself. "Move."

She inched forward through the dark, water collecting on her knees and palms. Her foot sent the pipe she had used to break the hatch rolling toward the opposite end of the vessel. She held her breath fearing one of the men may return to the room sooner if they heard the noise. Maybe it would be Gram. He was so different now. Not let like the sweet person she talked to at school. He had changed. He was cold and evil. But no footsteps announced his arrival. No tapping of curious fingers on the side of the tanker's shell. She breathed again and moved forward, searching desperately for the little door she entered through.

The drainage door had been wide enough to accommodate her frame. On the outside, a lever disengaged a bolt allowing it to open. On the inside, the mechanics of the lever could be easily manipulated to either close the door in place, like Amy had done once she was inside, or be turned to again disengage the bolt. Amy now clasped the bolt between her fingers, twisted and pushed on it until it gave way, opening the drainage on its hinges and allowing in light. She lowered her legs gently to the ground so not to land with a thump. The room was empty. She slid from under the tanker and walked towards the now open door. Peering from beyond its frame, she saw no one on the corridor. She followed the narrow passage to where another door presented itself. Inside, sunlight fell between broken roof tiles revealing various machine parts like drive belts, asbestos lagged pipes and old electric pumps. A set of footprints led from a pool of oil toward a door on the opposite side. As she stared more closely, she noticed the oil wasn't black, but a deep red instead. Blood. She tried to suppress a scream as she ran back down the corridor, past the room with the tanker. She continued to another maze of corridors, more doors. Behind every one she assumed Gram Slade would be waiting. Amy reached a dead end. There was only one door left. It was large, much larger than the others. She pressed down on the handle and walked through. Sunlight struck her eyes. Wind kissed her cheeks. Somehow, she had made it outside. Amy's eyes adjusted. A gravel road flanked by cotton grass and purple heather snaked down a low pass leading to the main road. There were no trees to shelter her. No places to hide. She was out in the open for anyone to see. But that couldn't stop her from trying to escape. She had to try and get to the main road. Amy walked slowly to begin with. She looked back. The building appeared smaller from the outside. Ivy consumed the walls. When the wind blew, small leaves shivered, bringing the structure to life. Amy didn't like that. She thought it looked like a monster, one that contained monsters, just like Gram Slade. Stones crunched under her feet, debris scattered in her wake. Her walk turned into trot, then a run. She was close to the gravel road when the Ragman lurched from an open door. Amy did not see him until he had both her arms wrapped locked in his. She kicked and screamed. As she struggled to free herself, Amy noticed him wince, as if one arm had been hurt or compromised. She tried to use this to her advantage, but the Ragman was strong, even with the injury. His hand then covered her mouth, and the familiar scent of chloroform filled her nose. The last thing she saw was a car approaching on the road, its tires kicking up dust like the tail of the Devil.

CHAPTER 36

FRIDAY

The number of people Coonan had spoken to at the West Riding Water Company had reached five before he was redirected to a Safety Engineering Manager called Richard Spiegel. There were three main pump houses in the West Riding area; Blackwood Common Pump House was a small stone built building that filtered and treated water taken from Hill House reservoir in the nearby Rush Bed Valley to the east margin of Stormer Hill. The second was named Schole Carr, which fed most of Soyland and Barkisland. Both were still in use and were regularly visited by engineers. The last was a Grade II building that had been abandoned for over ten years. Blackthorn Hill Water Works sat on Ringstone Edge Moor. Spiegel told Coonan it was built in 1949, and comprised of an engine house, boiler house, coal shed and store room within two buildings. Two cooling ponds sat at the rear along with stables and an engine attendant's house.

"It was fully modernized in the 1970s," Spiegel added with a tone that suggested to Coonan the man took his job way too seriously. "The station proved unsuccessful in providing the thousands of gallons needed per day to meet the increased demand from Stormer Hill's growing populace. It was closed down in the early millennium, but due to its Grade II listing, the building couldn't be demolished, making it undesirable as a property opportunity and real headache for the water board."

Coonan absorbed all at Richard Spiegel had to offer on the building before asking, "Has any of your engineers been there lately?"

"A structural evaluation deemed the place unsafe about seven years ago," replied Spiegel. "We've instructed our engineers not to enter without permission from their supervisors, but to be honest there's no need for them to visit. It's wasteland now."

"So no one has been there in years?"

"A third party security firm keep an eye on the place for us. We'd be liable for claims should any ramblers get inside and the injure themselves."

Coonan knew the Ringstone area. He'd trekked over its rough grasses many times in an attempt to fill his days away from work. But during all his visits he had never seen the building. Spiegel assured him it existed, and was accessible off the main arterial route leading out of Stormer Hill.

Perfect for anyone wanting a remote but easily reachable building for hiding children in, Coonan thought.

"Do you have any information on the security firm?" asked Coonan.

The sound of papers being rustled preceded his answered.

"They're called Soteria Security. They're very efficient and provide us with regular updates on the condition of the building following bad weather."

Spiegel checked the most recent reports and confirmed there had been no issues in the past six months.

"Any names attached to those updates?"

"The only name I have is an Erik Raine, the managing director. I've spoken with him, I don't know, maybe a half dozen times since they took over. Purely administration issues. The reports are all generated electronically and sent to us in PDF. There are no names attached to those, but I'm assuming the information comes from the security guards. To be honest, we've never had any reason to question it before. Should we be doing?"

Coonan reassured him, "Not at the moment, but one of my officers may get back in touch should we wish to find out more about Soteria. I'm more interested in the surrounding area at the moment. You said the road leading to Blackthorn is off the main A road?"

Spiegel instructed Coonan to search for the Water Company's signboard set back about three miles east of Stormer. He offered to meet him there, but Coonan declined, playing his enquiry down enough to not raise too much suspicion. It was one of many lines of enquiry that may prove unfruitful. What he didn't tell Spiegel was that he had provided a venue dovetailing with Tom Nolan's hypothesis perfectly. The contact trace samples taken from the Thompson car were going to take three weeks to be analyzed. This meant the crime lab's chemical and physical analysis tests would come too late to give Healey and his team a geographical location of where the murder had taken place. SOCO couldn't lift any latent prints from the soda cans, and they didn't hold any hope of lips prints or DNA either. Lip prints found on the cup in the sink matched those of Peter Thompson. The only thing they had gleaned so far from the Thompson murder was that whoever did it was careful and skilled with a knife, which fitted with Layton Slade's profile outlined by Nolan. All other main line enquires were ongoing, and officers searching Stormer Hill had found no new evidence, either physical or through witness accounts. At the moment, all they had was Blackthorn Hill Water Works and Coonan wasn't going to discount it without searching the place. He thanked Spiegel for all his help and finished the call. Less than a minute later he was in his car heading toward the moorland.

It was a half hour drive to Stormer Hill from Force HQ. Coonan did it in fifteen, slowing only when he reached the main A road leading into the village. Lay-bys, normally occupied by long distance truck drivers taking a nap, or those engaged in clandestine affairs that could ill-afford a hotel room, punctuated the long winding road. Coonan used them several times to turn his car around after he feared he'd missed the turn off, and had traveled up and down the road at least twice before seeing the small dirt road that cut through the moorland. The car's back end fishtailed as he hit the breaks and spun the car into the turn. The road had been cut into sandstone, and for a while Coonan felt like he was driving through a huge canyon. It was a good quarter of a mile before he arrived at a small wooden gate. He got out and noticed the lock had been broke. He pulled back the gate and drove on until the road leveled out at the top on Ringstone Moor. Like some kind of ancient ruin designed by the Aztecs, Blackthorn Hill Water Works shimmered in shades of green and gray on the horizon. Coonan squinted to make out where the main points of entry were. Heras fencing erected to stop people entering the building had long since been pulled down and were now twisted and bent by winds. A corrugated metal door used to secure the main entrance leant drunkenly against a crumbling wall. Coonan brought the car to a standstill. A cloud of dust from the road drifted over the windscreen hindering Coonan's view for a moment. Had he been looking, he would have seen Amy Taylor running toward the road moments earlier, and the man that grabbed her, but in haste his eyes had been consumed by the grandeur of the building. The dust settled bringing the old building back into view. Coonan gave a cursory look for any vehicles but couldn't see any. Before getting out of his car to investigate, he picked up his mobile and rang Nolan. The reason for the call wasn't for backup. He knew that as soon as Nolan returned to Stormer Hill the first thing he would do is to ask where he was, and, considering this lead came as a result of his profiling and detective work, it was only fair he get some of the glory should it turn out he was right.

"Tom, it's me," said Coonan when Nolan answered. The rev counter must have been tipping into the red because Coonan could hardly hear him over the engine nose. "How close are you to Stormer Hill?"

Tom raised his voice to compensate for the noise, "Ten minutes!"

"There's a slip road off the main drag leading into Stormer. It's a bitch to see, but it'll lead to Ringstone Moor and a place called Blackthorn Hill."

"Blackthorn Hill?!" asked Nolan.

"I spoke with the water board. There are three main pump houses in the area. Two are still active, but this one has been abandoned for over ten years. If you're right about the chemical compounds found on the fake suicide, then Blackthorn Hill is the only place closest to Hanging Lee where it could have come from."

Nolan said something but Coonan struggled to hear him.

"I'm here now, Tom. The place looks deserted. If I'm not outside when you arrive, safely assume I've gone in."

The phone's reception was breaking up.

"Sorry, Boss, what was that?!" asked Nolan.

Coonan repeated, but before he finished, the phone went dead. He looked at the screen and considered ringing Nolan back, but decided to place the phone into his jacket instead. Coonan got out of his car.

The wind coming off the moors chilled his bones. He fastened the buttons on his jacket and reached into his trouser pocket. There he felt the small plastic key ring; his children, his salvation, his only contribution to this world that he never regretted. Any he many regrets. All the bad people he put away, the crimes he prevented, all those decisions weighed on him every day. Some cops can justify that. He'd heard them many times say bad people deserved the verdict of imprisonment. Fuck their families. Fuck their children. They're all rotten to the core and will end up in prison themselves! Coonan could see the logic, understand the reasoning, but seeing a child cry their eyes out when their Daddy is taken away, that resonates. At least it did with him. Some people thought him cold, but that was just a front, the scaffold he erected around himself to save from crumbling. But deep down, things mattered. Things got to him. The only light in his life was his children. Having them was his only one true gift to the world to make up for all shit he'd caused.

Coonan made his way to the building. The main door was hanging off its hinges. Lichen and moss painted it a shade of green associated with damp weather and mornings in autumn. The first room he arrived at was the filtration plant. The centre of this room had been excavated. Inside the cavity were pipes big enough to crawl inside, all submerged in pea-colored water. Metal railings edged the lagoon, and Coonan stepped over relics of machinery long since retired to stop briefly and marvel at the Atlantis. He thought about calling out for Amy but didn't want to spook the abductors, so he moved steadily around the room, examining every recess or cavity with suspicion. There were no footprints in the dusty floor. No food wrappers or scorched floors where someone may have lit a fire to keep warm. It was as if he was the first person to step foot in this building for years. Maybe Nolan was wrong. Maybe Amy wasn't here after all.

The next building began with a small reception area. An old office chair caked in white dust rested beside a table on which old docket sheets were scattered. Four doors led off to different parts of the complex. Three of them were open. Any light within the rooms had long been suffocated by darkness. He pressed his ear against the fourth and heard a distance rumbling noise on the other side, like that of an engine. The noise was too constant and industrial sounding to be the wind. He tried the handle, and with a little force was able to push the door back allowing enough room for his body to squeeze through. Nothing could have prepared him for what lay beyond. Bodies suspended on metal hooks furbished the open room like bizarre Christmas decorations. A dozen more lay on the floor, some with arms reaching out to the ceiling, others hugging their own bodies.

"Jesus Christ," he said to himself, his throat drying.

He reached for his phone to call for backup, but stopped. Encircled by the dead was a man strapped to a chair. He recognized him as Alex Palmer. Coonan dodged the supine with the skill of a rugby player heading for a try. Alex Palmer, bestselling novelist who had made a living from writing stories about killers and psychopaths, looked like he was sleeping when Coonan arrived beside him. Blood seeped from a hole in his shoulder. Coonan placed his hand just below his nose and felt the slow pace of warm air on his skin.

"Alex," he said, cradling his head and lifting it up. "Can you hear me? My name is Mark Coonan. I'm a detective working for the Yorkshire Police Force."

Palmer didn't respond. Coonan assessed his size and height. The rope binding him to the chair ran across his chest, fastening at the back frame. It had kept him upright. As soon as he untied him, Palmer would fall flat on his face. To stop that from happening, Coonan placed one hand on Palmer's chest while the other busily fumbled at the knot. It didn't help. It required both hands. Coonan went around to the back of the chair and started again. This was when he noticed the knot wasn't a knot at all, but two ends of the rope loosely crossing over each other. Either the abductor had tied it in haste, or they knew Palmer was too weak to just pull it apart. Coonan was about to release the two ends when he heard Palmer's voice, low and pained. He walked around to the front of the chair and knelt down.

"Alex?"

Palmer slowly raised his head. His nose glistened with snot as if he had been crying.

"Who did this to you, Alex?"

Palmer looked scared. Coonan tried to reassure him.

"It's okay. I'm a police officer. I'm here to get you out."

Palmer swallowed, the effort causing him to wince.

Coonan placed his hand on Palmer's arm and said, "It looks like you've been shot. Better you stay still. I'm going to ring for an ambulance, okay? Promise me you won't do anything stupid."

Coonan reached into his pocket for his phone and began to dial. He was about to connect the call when Palmer spoke. It was so quiet and forced that Coonan had to lean in to hear: one word, spoken in a whisper that lingered before the two men for only seconds but felt like hours. Coonan leaned back. He looked at Palmer and saw the whites of his eyes were more exposed, expression bent by fear. Coonan stood, and like a man unable to comprehend a foreign language, he repeated the word for no other reason than to question its meaning.

"Run?" Coonan said.

The detective had enough time to reach into his pocket and remove the key ring that held the photograph of his children before his eyes gazed. In the split second that followed, he wondered how they would remember him; if they would reflect fondly on their time together, or feel indifferent. Then that second was over. The blade from Slade's knife issued a spray of blood that showered the key ring and Alex Palmer's face equally. Coonan rocked on his heels before falling to the floor, his hand never let go of the mobile phone, or the photo of his children.

Palmer struggled in the chair, the pain in shoulder sending flashes of white light across his eyes as bright as lightening. Slade walked up to Coonan's body and kicked it twice with his with boot before prizing the phone from his hand. He checked the screen and then threw it on the floor, spider-webbing the display under his heel. Palmer looked at the body of Mark Coonan. The collar of the detective's shirt was a vibrant red. His eyelids were still open but life had long since faded from each. There were too many memories to be found in Coonan's expression, too many regrets that Palmer had tried to purge with hours of counseling. He quietly extended an apology to the detective before turning his head away. Once again Palmer proved helpless in saving another person's life, another cop. Slade was stood watching him, as if waiting for him to speak. But

Palmer could not speak. All he could do was remained upright in the chair, a reluctant patron to some bizarre and sickening theatre of the macabre, and with each new breath he took he established a new pain. Flesh turned colder. Perception drifted further from him. Alex Palmer was dying, but not before hearing a voice, unhurried and deep. It called to him, telling him to get up. *Attend to the girl. Do what you came here to do.* That voice didn't belong to Slade. Its timbre was more familiar, haunting. It was the dame voice that repeated two words in his ear every night before he slept, a sick little lullaby to encourage nightmare; *Live with it. Live with it.* It was the voice of Todd Legge.

CHAPTER 37

FRIDAY

Amy Taylor's eyes were closed, mouth parted slightly. The stainless steel table cooled her skin, turning it pale and making the mole on her neck more noticeable. To any onlooker, she may appear to be dead. But she wasn't. Amy was just sleeping. The Ragman tenderly ran gloved fingers over her cheek, a display of intimacy he rarely indulged in, but permitted it because he sensed there was something final about the girl.

You're the last of the angels, he thought.

He brought to mind Lucy Guffey. She and Amy shared the same blanched skin and slender build. He preferred that look. They were angels. All of the children he had worked on were, save for one; Sarah Cook. She was plump and suffered with eczema around her fingers and the crease of her elbow and neck. Sarah was big too, heavy for the purposes of his work. He wanted a child like Lucy, but Layton had chosen poorly with that one. The Ragman had made his frustrations known after Layton had carried her out of Hanging Lee and put her into the boot of Richard Thompson's car. Had they not been arguing at the time, they may have seen that car before it hit them. But they didn't, and now there was a witness out there probably talking to the police. Yes, Sarah Cook was a poor choice to begin with and she brought more headaches than solutions, which is why the Ragman was so happy with Amy. She was better. The only thing he didn't like was the mole on her neck, and the delicate splattering of freckles decorating the bridge of her nose, both imperfections that distracted him from the paleness of her skin. He wondered if white ink would erase them, and if that was possible, she would be perfect. From those early days practising on pig's skin, the Ragman had become more competent with inking. His hand and mind now worked in unison, instead of against each other. He was creating works with depth and realism. Though he would never consider himself an artist, what he lacked in skill he made up for in imagination. He had that in spades. It was a tool he employed to overcome many modification issues. Some adjustments were easier than others, but some, like the angel wings, had proven to monopolise a lot of his time.

He had tried many designs at the beginning; wire from coat hangers sheathed in silk, then actual wings severed from geese provided by Slade. None of them worked. The only way to make the wings look truly real was to use human parts. He found that fusing the radius and humerus bones from the sex workers and vagrants, and cloaking the bones with skin removed from their derriere, created a more realistic look. But then came the issue of weight distribution. A child's back cannot support too much counter balance. When he first sewed the earlier designs to the children's back using twine, the structure pulled at the flesh, tearing it and causing time in stitching and mending of skin. He settled on affixing the wings directly into the spine using titanium screws. It was, even by his standards, brutal, but as he drilled holes he consoled himself by remembering that even Jesus was once a carpenter, a man who once used his hands for other things than resurrecting the dead and feeding many people. The result surpassed his expectations, and upon seeing Lucy Guffey's full wingspan for the first time, Layton Slade had stared at her for over an hour, rapt and in awe of the Ragman's skill.

There would be no issues with Amy Taylor. The Ragman had honed his skills and her frame was perfect; tall for her age, slender but with good form. He gently turned her body over so she was on her stomach. He lifted up her top and traced her spine with the tip of his finger, imagining boring through the bone with his drill. He was lowering Amy's top when Layton Slade walked in. The two men stared at each other for a moment without saying anything.

"We've had a visitor," Slade finally said.

The Ragman turned and acknowledged the disclosure with a vacant, drunken stare. He noticed blood coating Slade's gloves.

"Show me," he said.

He walked with Slade to the engine room. Lay beside the wooden chair was a well dressed man, blood framing his head. The Ragman walked up to the body and checked his jacket for ID. He pulled out a warrant card and displayed it to Slade. Slade read the name on the card. Turning his attention back to the Ragman, he said, "We don't have much time left."

"No, we don't," replied the Ragman.

CHAPTER 38

FRIDAY

Nolan looked through the window of Coonan's car. When he noticed the driver's side empty, he rang the job through to Comms and asked the operator for Coonan's status. The woman on the other end checked the system and told him DI Coonan was shown on duty, but not allocated to any jobs. This meant no one but Nolan knew Coonan was here.

"Show us state six at Blackthorn Hill Water works," he told her.

"Is DI Coonan with you?"

"That's right."

At least that's what Nolan hoped. Now he just had to make sure.

He entered the filtration room but couldn't see Coonan anywhere. A door at the end of the room led outside where a larger building was flanked by two water ponds. He didn't take the same door Coonan chose earlier. Instead, he entered a different room. There the light was poor. Barely able to see where he was standing, he used his mobile phone to navigate through the machine parts scattered on the floor. He arrived at another door that led directly to a corridor illuminated by lanterns. Three rooms divided the passageway. The first was a smaller pumping station that looked as if it hadn't been used for years. The second room was monopolised by a large black tanker. Nolan noticed the ceiling hatch above the tanker was broken. He wondered if a child could hoist themselves up and crawl through such a space. It was a small enough. He shouted Amy's name. There was no sound of movement or acknowledgement. Amy wasn't up there. Before leaving the room, Nolan picked up a piece of lead pipe and continued down the lantern corridor. The final room was locked. He pressed his ear against the door. Silence. Maybe Layton Slade was hiding behind, waiting. He measured the weight of the pipe in his hand. Happy it could render a person unconscious, he announced his intentions.

"This is police!" He waited for a moment before adding, "I'm coming in. This is your final warning."

Nolan reeled back on his heels before slamming his right foot below the lock. The force shook the door in its frame but it didn't open. He took a few steps back and added momentum to the kick. A large snap followed this time and the door flew open, snapping it at the hinges. Inside, a freestanding lamp bathed light over a steel table where the body of Amy Taylor lay. He dropped the pipe; the clang as it hit the floor as loud as a church bell. He ran to the table. Her flesh was warm, chest ebbing and flowing with life. Nolan didn't leave anything to chance. He placed two fingers against her neck. Her pulse was a little slow, but she was alive.

"Amy," he said, tenderly. "You're safe now."

She was too sedated to respond. Nolan called up for an ambulance. He gave her vital signs to the operator and explained the directions to Blackthorn Hill. Once the ambulance had been secured he called Comms to request for further patrols to attend. He then turned his attention back to Amy, stroking her forehead and whispering comforting words.

"It's over," he said with a deepening sense of relief. "It's all over."

He looked down at Amy face; droplets of water collecting on her pale cheek. It was only when he began to struggle for breath that he realized he was crying.

CHAPTER 39

FRIDAY

Gaffer tape now held Palmer's eyelids open. He could see Layton Slade in the distance of the large engine room. He was cloaked in a red robe that cascaded from his shoulders like a blood waterfall. Layton was fidgeting with the small clasp that connected the two ends of the robe at his throat. The robe did not cover his body completely. Skin the same color as dust found on the floor of Blackthorn peeked from the gap, as did a nest of dark pubic hair encircling a penis that shifted like a pendulum whenever he moved.

"Let me go," Palmer pleaded. "I won't say anything."

Slade looked over and said, "You're still fighting him, aren't you?"

Palmer looked on amazed. Could Slade know about Legge, how he reminds him daily of how he couldn't save the life of Christie Purlow, the one person he ever cared for?

"You know about Todd Legge?"

Layton stopped messing with the clasp and said, "Legge? Never heard of him. I'm talking about Alex Palmer."

A sudden coldness came over Palmer.

"But I'm Alex Palmer," he announced, a tremble of uncertainty lingering at the back of his throat.

"Sometimes you are," Layton announced confidently. "And after all of this is done, you'll go back to being Alex Palmer again. He is the messenger. The apostle. Alex Palmer will be the one who writes down what it we've done so people understand. But right now, I don't need Alex. I need that other person inside of you." Layton Slade turned to the tarpaulin-covered wall and, placing his hand on the release rope, added, "Little piggy. Little piggy. Are you coming out to play?"

"I don't understand!" Palmer yelled. "I am Alex Palmer! I'm not an apostle or a fucking murderer!"

Layton Slade gripped the rope and said, "But you are. And this is your work."

He yanked on the rope. The tarp fell to the ground, kicking up dust from the floor as it landed in a heap. Pigeons flew from their roost, beating their wings frantically to escape the scene. What stood before Alex Palmer was no longer a wall. It had been covered in the bodies of the dead, creating a weird, abstract fresco of human remains that reached a height of about thirty feet. Those that had been assembled along the bottom row showed the worse signs of decomposition. The perishing of flesh and tightening of skin made each body looks unworldly, like that of a burns victim or undeveloped foetus. Those assembled higher were dehydrated but more human-like, skin waxen and sallow. Eyes had been tattooed with black ink giving their faces a demon-like appearance. To further support the look, studs had been fixed to their foreheads to resemble tiny silver horns. The landscape of the dead seemed random, but as Palmer focused on each detail he realized that they had been positioned so that each was looking upwards, like fledglings awaiting their feed, or the pious awaiting a message from above. He followed their reverent gaze to a single chair that had been affixed to the centre of the wall, similar in style to that which he was sat upon. A length of rope had been looped around the backrest. It was seeing this chair that caused bile to rise suddenly from his gut. Flanking it were three children, two on the right side and one on the left. They were all dressed in tiny white gowns that had been split at the back to allow a set of grisly wings to unfurl. A spike had been driven through their heads and one through both feet to keep them aloft. Palmer did not need to ask what their names were. He had read about them enough to recall from memory. There was one more space left. It had been left beside George Levy, and was large enough to accommodate the frame of Amy Taylor.

Slade walked to Palmer, the air pushing open the robe to expose his naked body.

Kneeling before him he said, "They'll call me a monster because it'll help them sleep at night. But what we've done here will bring people together." Slade tendered a half-smile, "We have built them fairytales. It's just a shame you won't be able to take any of the glory."

Palmer's eyes were drying. He tried to blink but the tape wouldn't budge. He was forced to remained fixed on Layton Slade and the horror behind him.

"No," Palmer said. "I'm playing no part in it. This thing you've done here, it is the work of a madman. There is no greater message to be found. It's here to shock. It means nothing."

"But it does, you're just looking at it through human eyes."

"I see clearly. You want to be the next Jack the Ripper, but you forget one thing, he never got caught. You will. You're a bully who preys on the weak. And when the police find you, and they lock you up in a cell for the rest of your pitiful life, know this; I'll never talk about this to anyone. You won't be revered. You won't be talked about over coffee, nor will papers be written about you. You'll be known as a sad little man who tried too hard to be someone and failed. Your fucking fairytale ends here."

Layton produced a small butcher's knife. Drawing the blade across the palm, he pressed his opposite finger into the blood and massaged it into Palmer's eyes.

"Now you'll see," he said.

Defenceless, Palmer unwillingly received the donation. The rubbing motion along his eyeball sent a dull ache toward his brain. His vision blurred. Slade moved away. Tainted red, the fresco appeared more sinister now, if that was possible.

"Do you see?" Slade asked.

Palmer nodded, only to appease him.

"Good. This is what we have worked for. Now let us finish our masterpiece."

Layton stood and walked to another part of the room. The sound of metal being dragged followed a grunt of exertion. He then walked back into Palmer's view holding a small step ladder. He placed it against the wall below the chair, and gathering his robe like a woman wading into the ocean, Slade took each step slowly, using his free hand to remain stable. Taking his place on the chair, he secured the rope around his waist and yanked on it once to make sure it would hold. Once happy, he raised his knife and drew it horizontally along his left wrist, quickly changing hands to do the same to the right before dropping the knife to the ground. He then lowered his arms and allowed gravity to take over.

"You're right, the police will find me," he said. "But I won't rot in any cell. I will live on in our work. I am art. I am eternal."

The wall had been channelled out in long narrow ruts, each one ending at the mouths of the dead. They were barely noticeable at first, but as Slade's fingers guided the stream of blood from his wrists into the furrows, the complex network of valleys carved into the Hellish landscape presented itself to Palmer like pointing in brickwork. Slowly Layton's eyelids began to flutter and his head began to lean toward his chest as if taking a final bow. What blood remained in him continued to pour, coating the faces below. The rope around his waist stopped his body from falling, but it did not help to keep him upright. Layton Slade slowly folded in half, head coming to rest between his legs.

It was then Palmer felt that presence behind him once again, cold, and foreboding. Its gruff, unsympathetic voice fell close to his neck, pulling tight his skin and raising the hair on his arms.

"Live with it," they said. "Live with it."

CHAPTER 40

FRIDAY

Nolan remained with Amy Taylor until the responding officers and paramedics arrived. The first officer to enter was a young man with lantern jaw that slackened on seeing him holding the girl.

"Detective Nolan?" he asked.

Nolan didn't look up. His rank, even his name was inconsequential at that moment. They were a human construct to identify him from other people. And right then, Nolan didn't feel as if he belonged to humankind. He was numb, robbed of sense and perspective. All his experience, knowledge and feelings seemed so far away. Even if he was able to think clearly, he could have never thought the past four years was leading to this moment, holding a child in this cold abandoned water works. And that child was the one who belong to Kristen Taylor, a woman he dreamt about many times, and had imagined loving until they were old and gray. And now it was here, Tom Nolan was finding it hard to embrace the relief, a relief that meant the end of that long journey had finally come.

"Detective Nolan?"

The police officer held out his hand as if offering it to a dog to sniff.

"My name is PC Kevin Hopkinson. Is this the missing girl, Amy Taylor?"

Nolan nodded.

Two paramedics then entered the room. Nolan looked up and saw them pause as if awaiting instruction from Hopkinson. The officer turned, reassured them who Nolan was.

"You need to let her go," Hopkinson said turning back. "She's safe now."

The paramedics gathered their equipment and approached cautiously. Nolan lowered his gaze to Amy, fascinated by her hair, its softness and color. The female paramedic spoke first.

"My name is Jessica Barker, Detective. Can I please take a look at Amy? I promise we won't hurt her." Barker placed her hand on Nolan's and added, "We just need to make sure she's okay."

Nolan looked up. Tears tracked his cheeks. Redness framed his eyes. He didn't smile when Barker came into his view. He didn't explain the circumstances that led him there. Nolan did what any good person would do when all their powers, all their experience was of no use; he sighed, and reluctantly abdicated to those with more strength. As the exchange took place, Nolan cleared his throat and said, "She's cold."

"I'll take care of her," Barker replied before instructing her colleague to approach.

As Nolan cuffed each eye, the sound of another police officer traveled from a distant room. It was a male voice. Nolan tuned his ears to the sound.

"I NEED HELP IN HERE!!!!"

Hopkinson reacted first, turning on his heels and making a dash toward the door. The strength needed to propel Nolan forward came from some instinct to help others, but the long wait with Amy had weakened his legs. As he jumped off the table, he stumbled a little before finally regaining momentum.

When Hopkinson and Nolan arrived at the outer door of the engine room they found the officer bent over in two, one hand on the wall for support, the other pointing warningly into the room. He had vomited and was still heaving when Hopkinson stepped up to him.

"What is it?" asked Hopkinson.

The officer wiped his mouth, and taking a deep breath said, "A fucking massacre."

Hopkinson turned to Nolan.

"Maybe we should wait for further patrols," he said, eyes wide.

Nolan didn't respond. He crossed the threshold of the door without deliberation. The smell of rotting flesh instantly crept into his nose. It'd take a week of showering, and even then, Nolan was sure he'd never truly rid himself of that stench. As his eyes adjusted, he realized what had caused the officer to be sick. That wall, that bizarre, horrific wall. At the centre a lonely chair lay suspended, occupied by a skinny man in a red robe. Blood cascaded from his wrists to the faces of the dead surrounding him, their skin and flesh atrophied, clinging to their skulls and skeletons like wet paper. Tiptoeing over the bodies scattered on the floor, Nolan edged forward to get a better look of the man on the chair. The knot that had gripped his stomach for nearly four years loosened as he realized the chase could now stop. DC Tom Nolan had found Layton Slade.

"Detective!" shouted Hopkinson. "There's one still alive!"

Hopkinson was knelt beside a man laid out on the floor. Nolan made a dash, and upon seeing Alex Palmer shouted to the other officer outside the room. The PC was lingering at the door with cuff to his nose.

"GET THE PARAMEDICS!" Nolan shouted. "NOW!"

The officer nodded and ran out of view.

Turning back to Alex Palmer, he said "Hang on, buddy."

"You know him?" Hopkinson asked.

Nolan nodded. The duct tape was still fixed to Palmer's lids, holding them open. The whites of his eyes were cerise, the edges vibrant red.

"His eyes are drying up," Nolan said. "Help me get this tape off."

The two men went to work. Hopkinson remained at the top of Palmer's head, clamping his hands like a vice around the forehead while Nolan gently pulled on the tape. The skin stretched, thinning. Palmer let out a scream and Nolan let go, the eyelids snapping back with the same quirk as a latex glove on the hand of an airport customs officer.

"Don't worry, Alex," Nolan said. "Paramedics are here. They should have something to help."

"Alex?" Hopkinson asked. "Alex Palmer?"

Nolan didn't respond.

"We were told he was missing," Hopkinson said.

"Well, as you can see, he's been found."

Nolan welcomed the intervention of Sarah Barker who came into the room on a gasp.

"What the holy fuck," her words wringed out of irony, tone grim and solemn.

"Here!" called out Nolan, gesturing her over with his hand.

Assuring she didn't touch any of the bodies, she made her way to the men. On seeing Palmer, she applied a solution to wash away the blood and assuage his eyes. Nolan observed her hand shaking as she applied pressure to the solution bottle.

"What happened?" she asked.

Nolan stood up and backed away slowly, refusing to answer, because like her, he was still processing the magnitude of the scene. As he took a step back, the heel of his shoe made contact with another body. He looked down and saw a man lay on his stomach. Unlike those suspended from steel hooks, or scattered across the engine room's floor like grains of rice after a wedding, this one wasn't covered in white muslin. Due to the mass of blood pooling around the head, this body was fresh. A flash of recognition struck Nolan about the man's clothes. The left shoe was slightly worn along the heel. He recalled the night Coonan walked away from him when they were both on Edgerton Road.

"No, please don't let it be," he said to himself, and then, as he recognized the coat as that belonging to his Inspector, Nolan's skin goosed. He knelt slowly, angled his head so he could see the face. Coonan's eyes were still open, a motionless gaze fixed on his hand. The plastic key ring was still clamped in his grip, the faces of the children blurred by their father's blood. The incision along Coonan's neck was so deep it revealed sinew, cartilage and the white of his spine. PC Hopkinson voice emerged out of the darkness.

"Is that…"

He didn't finish the sentence, maybe because it felt like he was stating the obvious, or maybe his hesitancy was because he didn't want it to be true, that the person lay out before him was DI Mark Coonan. Nolan would never know.

"Call it in to Comms," Nolan said, his tone calm, controlled. "Tell them Detective Inspector Mark Coonan is dead and that we need more officers here. After that, you and the other officer secure the scene."

He broke his stare away from Coonan's face to look directly in the eyes of Hopkinson.

"You tell them how bad this is, you hear me?"

Hopkinson nodded and began walking away, his head tilted toward the radio fixed to his lapel. Nolan turned back around and watched as Barker applied gauze to Palmer's shoulder wound.

"Can you tell me your name?" she asked him.

Nolan intervened, "His name is Alex Palmer. How is he?"

"Looks like a gunshot wound," she announced. "He's lost a lot of blood. Here…" She grabbed Nolan's hand and pressed it against the gauze. "Keep the pressure."

She turned her attention to Coonan and checked his radial pulse, counting the beats. It was evident from her expression she found none. She spoke into her radio, requesting more resources before returning back to Palmer.

"I overheard," she said, taking control again of the wound. She looked briefly to Coonan's body. "He's another cop?"

Nolan moved his hand away and nodded.

"He was searching for the girl," he replied, relapsing into a softer voice. "If it wasn't for him, well..."

Nolan reflected on Coonan's efforts over the years to trace the children, the hours spent walking Hanging Lee and following all those negative lines of enquiries. The tired eyes. Coffee breath. The wearing on his shoe. Yes, the shoe. Probably the result of the weight he carried for not finding them. Nolan wondered if Coonan had dreamt in shades of the children, if he heard their infant voices in the darkness of sleep, just as he had, and if in death their voices would finally fall silent. The burden lifted. He hoped that was case.

"He did a fine job," Barker said, pulling Nolan from his reverie. "You both did."

She then turned back to Palmer.

"Alex, we have an air ambulance on route. You've lost a lot of blood, okay, so we're going to give you a transfusion and something to manage the pain."

Palmer still looked in a permanent state of shock with his eyelids clamped open. Nolan lingered for a moment, trying to get into his eye line. When their gaze met he smiled.

"It's over, buddy," he said. "It's finally over."

Palmer did not appear to hold the same confidence. He shook his head slowly, and with a tone that sounded as it had been dragged through broken glass, said, "No. There’s one more."

CHAPTER 41

THE AFTERMATH

Detective Chief Inspector Darren Healey from the Murder Investigation Team relieved Nolan of his role as temporary SIO as soon as he arrived at Blackthorn Hill. Healey was an old sweat with a face that looked as if it was reflected in a spoon. He didn't put much effort into the way he looked, dressing in navy blue suits bought off the rack, the shirt-tie combos chosen by the shops he bought them in, not by his own sense of style. But he had a presence about him that put people at ease. Having been the SIO in fifteen murder investigations, Healey had the usual weakness for anecdote when among his peers and senior officers. Even Nolan had heard about his time as a DS during the hunt for the Crossbow Cannibal, Stephen Griffiths, and how he was one of the interviewing officers during the Anthony Arkwright case back in 1988. He was shrewd, industrious, and had seen the gruesome side of the human spirit more than many, which is why, when he walked into that engine room an hour after receiving the call from the FDO, Nolan was surprised to see a look of sheer bewilderment shadow his face.

"Go home, Tom" Healey said.

"All the same, Boss, I'd rather kept busy," replied Nolan.

"It's not a suggestion, Tom. Take some time away from this thing."

"I'd like to get Palmer's first account," Nolan said.

Healey smirked.

"Do I really need to give you a lawful order?"

"Palmer said there was someone else."

The news that there was another serial killer out there had registered in Healey's careworn eyes. He rubbed his hand over his chin, the sound like sandpaper over pine.

"I can help," Nolan said. "I've been tied to this thing for years. I've got lines of enquiries still ongoing. I'm no good to you at home. It's better I'm out there trying to find the second person."

"Did Palmer know the name of this second person? Did he even get a look of them?"

Nolan shrugged.

"He wasn't in the best place when I asked. I want to go to the hospital and speak with him."

Nolan could see Healey coming round the idea. His team were busying themselves in the engine room. SOCO were laying out footplates. The place was buzzing outside with conversation between constables, ambulance, and CSI. Soon the press would be demanding answers. The news that there is a second man on the loose, one capable of the atrocities found in Blackthorn would send the media and the public into frenzy. Healey would need as many good officers he could get hold of to help catch the bastard, and the one who had the most knowledge was stood right in front of him. Nolan hammered home that final nail.

"If we don't act soon, they'll talk about this other person the same way they talk about Peter Sutcliffe."

"I'm sure that'll happen anyway," Healey finally said. "Okay. But you're not going to the hospital. I'm giving that job to Frank Crane. Go find your breadcrumbs, Tom. If they lead you anywhere worthy of attention, ring me."

Nolan nodded.

"And Tom," Healey said before Nolan could walk away. "I'm sorry about Mark Coonan. I worked with him a few times. He was a good man."

"He was," Nolan said, and headed out of Blackthorn Hill.

Nolan returned back to the police station and began researching Hieronymus Bosch. He found himself lost in academia and pretentious rhetoric as he tried desperately to find the relevance the painter's work had on the events within Blackthorn Hill. From what he knew so far, each body had been arranged on the wall purposely, and with an exactness matching the triptych, The Last Judgement. He also discovered that the Temptation of Saint Anthony, another painting by Bosch, had been inspired by a Dutch proverb, the same one tattooed on the pig found at the school. But what Nolan couldn't understand was why. What significance or influence did Bosch have over the case? Maybe it was just the excuse, a way of tying things together. He'd seen it before; serial killers are motivated by religion, movies, books, moon cycles, even previous serial killers. It wasn't such a stretch to think Layton Slade and his accomplice were just using Bosch as a theme, recreating his art in human form. The thought of other walls like that found in Blackthorn Hill turned Nolan's skin cold. Where would it end? A whole gallery? The first time he had heard about the painter was from James Myers. Nolan revisited the police systems to check Myers history again. He had served time for GHB five years ago, details he knew already, but when Nolan checked the prison records, he found that Myers was inside Strangways at the same time as Keenan. This was never mentioned by Myers. Nolan was led to believe Myers had heard about Keenan's death through the girl he knew. He'd lied. He knew about the death because he was there when it happened. The coroner's report connected to Keenan's death revealed Keenan had been stabbed multiple times, like Myers had said. But there was no mention of his heart being removed, nor any print of Bosch's work found at the scene. It wasn't a stretch to draw the conclusion James Myers played some part in Paul Keenan's death. Nolan rang Healey and asked that they bring Myers in for questioning. The decision was ratified by Healey, but the officers tasked to get Myers were too late. Nolan got the call three hours later that Myers's body had been pulled out of the river Irwell. Preliminary examination concluded he was drunk and fell in. Another witness gone. Another jagged piece of the puzzle missing. Nolan attended Myers's flat later that same day with SOCO and two PCs. The one bed fleapit still looked as ominous as it did the first time he visited. He remembered what Myers said. *Business was doing well.* Yeah, right.

Inside the flat, Nolan found books on Bosch's paintings. Some on Aristotle too; their pages divided using Post-it notes as markers. Myers had scribbled on each one, mostly nonsensical jabbering punctuated with explicit doodles of demon-like figures. Experts back at forensics were still analysing them to see if they could lift anything, but so far had yielded nothing. Myers's computer had been seized at the same time, and due to the growing media interest, fast tracked for analysis. The Hi-Tec Crime Unit decrypted several folders containing abusive images of children, which at last count was up to over six hundred.

The biggest leap forward came from when Nolan sought a warrant to gain entry to Layton Slade's house. It was a small, modest looking terrace fashioned from limestone situated in Rochdale, equidistant from Stormer Hill and Manchester. During house to house enquiries, neighbors portrayed Slade as quiet, a private man that was rarely seen. He was never any trouble. No complaints had been made concerning noise, or antisocial behaviour. A voter's check on the address showed the house was owned by an Erik Raine since 2001. Raine was the managing director of Soteria Security, the same one who looked after Blackthorn Hill Water Works. Coincidence? Neither Nolan nor Healey thought so. Inside the house the rooms were sparse. A mattress had been abandoned in the living room, framed by candles that had reduced under their flames. Walls had been stripped to plaster the color of salmon flesh. Across the largest wall, Slade had scribed in red paint the words, *Broeders van de Vrije Geest*. Translators working for the police later confirmed it to be Dutch, which translated to, Brethren of the Free Spirit. The kitchen had no food in the refrigerator. The wall-mounted cupboards were empty. Various knives and cleavers were neatly hidden in the drawers. There were no signs of sexual activity, no recording equipment or disused condoms strewn like washed up jellyfish on the shore. Bob Wood oversaw the search team, and after a few hours found a laptop hidden in the roof space under a layer of insulation. Like with Myer's computer, the Hi-Tec Crime Unit interrogated the hard drive belonging to Slade and found images and videos of his victims in encrypted folders, some of which had been uploaded onto a private forum within the Dark Web called, The Brethren. One of the bods at Hi-Tec Crime explained to Nolan that Slade had been careful to remove all metadata from the photos he took, even going so far as to blur the surroundings and faces of some of the sex workers and homeless he had killed. He was meticulous, but not fallible. A history cache of encrypted conversations had been found between Erik Raine and Layton Slade dating back to 2002. Time had corrupted and fragmented most of them, but communications assembled from the data revealed candid exchanges between the two men. In them, they shared their interests as unceremoniously as one may the art of fishing. There had also been reference to someone known as the Ragman who Slade wanted Raine to meet. Checks on this nickname led to dead ends. There were other folders nestled within a deeper layering encryption, but Hi-Tec Crime was confident it was only a matter of time before they could gain access. Tom Nolan told them as soon as they did to call him.

The Police National Database showed no previous crimes for Raine. He had kept a low profile, and save for a report of a robbery on his home back in 1996, which he reported, there was nothing the police had on him. Nolan visited the security firm he owned later that day but was told Raine was out of the country on business. A middle manager named Scott Ambrose coughed to the fact Raine was staying at the Hôtel Regyn's in Montmartre, Paris. Nolan relayed all this to Healey. The last he heard, West Yorkshire Police was liaising directly with the Police Nationale in France to apprehend Raine, but so far they had yet to find him. Healey had also tasked officers to seize Raine's work and home computer to establish if he had a penchant for children too, and to extract any conversations between Slade and this Ragman character. With all these ongoing enquiries still taking up time, the best lead they had couldn't be found on a computer, nor any article or art's journal. It was in Ward 9 of Calderdale hospital, and his name was Alex Palmer.

It had pissed Nolan off that Healey wouldn't allow him to the hospital for that first account. He and Palmer may not have seen eye to eye at the start, but when he found him in that engine room, whatever disharmony or reservations they had toward each other paled into insignificance as soon as their eyes met. Nolan felt Palmer needed someone he trusted, someone he knew. Instead, Healey had settled for Frank Crane. Nolan had worked with Crane on a few jobs. He considered him experienced enough to understand when discretion is as much an advantage as the law, which is why he didn't protest when his name was mentioned. Crane was rake of a man with thinning hair and dour expression, but when he spoke he had a lighter, almost adolescent timbre that made him seem less formidable than other detectives. This would work in his favour when he spoke with Palmer, Nolan assumed. He arranged to meet with Crane at a local pub after he finished speaking with Palmer at the hospital. There, Crane explained that he had sat with Palmer in a small cubicle in the A&E department of Calderdale hospital shortly before he went into surgery. Behind closed curtains Crane asked about the details following Palmer's abduction, trying to get him to focus on what he knew of this second man. It turned out that Palmer hadn't seen the man. He had only heard him. Crane had pushed for an accent, or any usual pattern of speech, lisps, slurring, anything that might help them narrow their search. Palmer described the accent as Southern, but not West Country, more like a Londoner. He also used adjectives like scary and menacing to describe the man's voice. He mentioned seeing Gram Slade to at the Moffet cottage before he was drugged, and that Slade was the one who murdered Mark Coonan. An attending surgeon put an end to the interview. It wasn't even breadcrumbs. There may have been a media frenzy attached to the case, and a nationwide search for the Ragman, but like Crane explained to Nolan, and would later to DCI Healey, the police were chasing a ghost. Nolan concluded that if there was any chance of finding out whom this second person was, he would and speak to Palmer himself.

CHAPTER 42

WEDNESDAY

It had been five days since Alex Palmer was airlifted out of Blackthorn Hill Water Works and taken to Calderdale hospital. Tom Nolan arrived in his recovery room to find the bed empty. He assumed the worst, but a nurse at the reception desk explained Palmer was taking a shower and would be out shortly. Nolan thanked her and went back to the room. The room window overlooked the east-facing car park that led directly to the Families, Women and Children's Unit. Nolan had made a mental note of which departments were in this particular wing when he entered the building. Ward 9, the one Palmer had been taken to, was two floors above Maternity Services. Below that was the Physiotherapy and Rehabilitation department where Palmer would spend time having painful treatment on his shoulder. Nolan had been given all the details of this the previous day by a Dr Bhatti, the surgeon who removed the bullet lodged in Palmer's shoulder. During the telephone conversation, Bhatti had been reticent to discuss Alex Palmer's injuries, but warmed to Nolan after he explained it was a welfare check, and that he was the attending officer on the scene. Bhatti kept the conversation professional, clinical. He spoke about the subclavian artery that feeds the main artery of the arm, and the brachial plexus, a large nerve bundle that controls main arm function, which had been compromised, though not to a point where they couldn't be saved. The details were difficult to understand, and Nolan had made a point of blaming a lack of sleep for a laymen's version.

"Could he have died?" Nolan asked, cutting through the Gordian Knot.

"Possible," Bhatti said. "Had Mr. Palmer been hit in the brachial plexu we'd be dealing with blood vessel damage and loss of motor function, all on top of severe pain. I've known maybe four patients die, and another lose their arm due to an acute injury to the subclavian artery. Contrary to what television or the movies have us believe, Detective, being shot in the shoulder is very dangerous. That said, the bullet missed both the subclavian and brachial, but it did cause damage to some of the surrounding muscle and nerves. The results of this mean Mr. Palmer will experience weakness in his right hand, but we are confident that the physio will help restore this. He was very lucky. Very lucky indeed."

Lucky. It was unlikely Palmer would even comprehend the word.

Two female voices presented themselves outside Palmer's recovery room. Nolan listened. They were talking about him. One of the voices he recognized as the nurse he had spoken to earlier. He was about to go outside and explain his reasons for being there when a mobile phone began vibrating on the bedside cabinet. He read the screen and saw the name Juliet. He hazarded a guess it was Palmer's agent. Next to the mobile was a Get Well Soon card showing the iconic image of Boris Karloff playing Frankenstein's Monster. The words, YOU'RE ALIVE! written in bold red across his head. Nolan read the message inside: *You're taking your work way too serious, Alex. Come back to us soon. Love J. x*

The phone stopped ringing. Nolan checked the screen again. There had been fifteen missed calls from that same number. He considered checking to see if the phone was unlocked, but before he could the door opened. Dressed in a burgundy bath robe, Alex Palmer shuffled in, one hand pushing a long metal stand with a bag attached, the tube disappearing into a cannula on his hand. At the side of him was a nurse, face painted scarlet due to either stress or exertion, Nolan couldn't tell which. When Palmer saw Nolan he smiled. His chin was dressed in bristles, cheeks hollowed.

"I'm not intruding, am I?" asked Nolan.

"To be honest, I could do with the break," replied Palmer. "It's not easy being this melancholic alone."

The nurse helped Palmer to the bed and made sure his pillows were positioned correctly.

"You want me to remove your bathrobe?" she asked.

"I'm fine for the time being. Thank you," he said.

She offered Nolan a smile and said she would be back later with his meds. Palmer nodded and adjusted the robe to assure his body was hidden.

"Sit down, Tom," he said.

Nolan gravitated toward the only chair in the room. He felt dog-tired and spent a moment or two trying to flatter his hair that had been styled by the wind.

"You in a rush this morning?" asked Palmer.

Nolan didn't get where he going.

"Just I've never seen you without a tie," Palmer said.

Nolan couldn't remember why he hadn't put a tie on that morning. The truth was he couldn't remember the last time he took a piss. All his attention, every waking hour had been consumed by this case. Nolan relaxed into the soft backrest of the chair and ran his hands over his trousers.

"This is nice," he said.

"It's not the Four Seasons, but at least I have a window."

"How's the shoulder?"

"Fine if I don't breathe," replied Palmer.

"You're lucky, from what I heard."

"That's what they keep telling me."

There was a pregnant pause, giving Nolan time survey the room again.

"Hospitals give me the creeps," he declared. "Guess it's all those years as a beat officer and knowing that most people you brought in these places never left."

"I take it you've not come here to cheer me up?"

Nolan thinned his lips.

"What have you heard?" Nolan asked.

"Not much. They don't let me watch TV. They had officers guarding my room after I came out of surgery, but the charge nurse said they were needed back at the station. Other than DC Crane, you're the first to see me."

Nolan leaned forward and said, "I've been tasked with asking you a few more questions. Is that okay?"

Palmer nodded and Nolan produced his notepad.

"I've read over your first account taken by DC Crane. When you were drugged, back at the Moffet cottage, you mentioned seeing Gram Slade."

"Like I said to DC Crane, I thought it was Gram, to begin with."

"What made you think differently?"

"I met him at the library the previous day. The way he walked, his manner, it was completely different to this other man. He was more articulate and focused. I also saw his hands, which weren't burnt like Gram's. One of the fingers was missing too."

"Layton Slade, that's the man you saw. He was Gram's identical brother."

Barely a sound left Palmer's mouth. Ambient noises were amplified in the silence. Faint, hushed voices on the corridor. TV shows and strained applause. A deep, raspy cough foreshadowing something sinister, something fatal.

"Layton was the one taking the children," continued Nolan. "And as you saw, he was taking other people too. The important thing now is to establish who he was working with."

"I've said this already, I didn't see his face. He was stood behind me the whole time."

"I know this is difficult, Alex. Crane said you saw what happened to DI Coonan. That's hard for anyone to take in. You've been seeing the onsite psychologist?"

"Dr. Aikman. He's the one that upped my meds. The nurses keep checking on me every half hour. I'm assuming they've got me on suicide watch."

Nolan studied him for a moment before saying, "If this is still too raw, I can come back another day."

Palmer sighed, "I know you're doing your job, Tom."

"All the same."

Palmer nodded and encouraged him to continue.

"You mentioned that Layton was more articulate. Can you recall any conversations?"

Palmer looked up momentarily before answering.

"When I woke up in at the water works, he came to see me. He talked about God. I can't remember the words exactly. But he came from a position of authority, like a believer."

"A fanatic?"

"I don't know if he was a fanatic. He believed, that much I recognized. He had, I don't know, a broader awareness of God."

"In what way?"

"I don't know. I guess the Bible can limit a person's thinking. Some of those zealots refuse to accept things, you know, like Darwin's theory of evolution; the earth is round, that kind of shit. Layton? That his name?"

Nolan nodded.

"He wasn't so blinkered," Palmer said.

"You're talking to a Church of England boy here," Nolan said, offering a smile. "The last time I was before the altar was when I was baptized at the age of six months. So you're saying Layton believed in God but wasn't religious?"

"I know, it sounds paradoxical," Palmer replied. "But it was the things he said. I think he didn't see what he was doing as a bad thing."

"There are a lot of families out there that would disagree."

"I can imagine. Look, Tom, I've been playing this over since coming out of surgery, but I honestly think he justified those deaths because he didn't see murder as a sin."

"Like a misreading of the Bible?"

Palmer shook his head slowly.

"No, not really. He came across as having a false impression of who he was. Like, he wasn't human. I think he killed those people not because he thought that was what God wanted. He did it because he thought he *was* God."

Nolan wrote his notepad.

"And did he say why he chose you?" asked Nolan.

"A witness. An apostle. More likely I was destined to end up on that wall like the others. I don't know for sure."

"Would you mind talking me through what happened before you were abducted?"

"I was cutting short my trip and had gone to tell Bill and Linda."

"Why?"

"Why was cutting short my trip?"

Nolan nodded.

"Come on, Tom. You yourself warned me about Stormer Hill, and you were right. No one wanted to talk about the children. I should have listened to you that day you took me to Hanging Lee. Maybe then I wouldn't have taken a bullet."

"So you went to Bill and Linda's place."

"And when I got back to the cottage it was cold. Bill had been the previous day to sort out the boiler in the cellar, but I guess he didn't do a good enough job. So I went down to the cellar to see if I could. That's when I saw Gram. I mean, Layton Slade."

"And it was this other man that drugged you, not Layton?"

"He came up behind me. I felt the rag on my mouth. I struggled, but he was strong. The next thing I know I woke up in that room."

"Did Layton ever talk about the other man?" asked Nolan.

Palmer shook his head.

Nolan shifted his weight in the chair, firmed his grip on the pen.

"You said you never saw the man, but when the rag was placed over your mouth, did you see his hands? Tattoos? Something that we could circulate?"

"I didn't see any part of him," replied Palmer.

"Can you remember else?"

"There was another room," he said.

"In the cottage?"

"No, in the water works. They took me there. There was a table, and on it was a woman. She'd been ..."

Palmer didn't finish.

"We saw her too, Alex," Nolan said.

Palmer looked down and began speaking again.

"Layton told me what he was doing to them. Then he showed me. She was dead, but that didn't make watching him stab her over and over any less uncomfortable."

"Can't imagine it would."

"You know, he cut his wrists in front of me. You ever see a person do that, Tom?"

Nolan's moustache veiled the subtle grinding of teeth. He recalled a job where a young woman had been stabbed in a frenzied attack close to the Calderdale boarder. He was a young DC then, dealing mostly with robberies, petty crime, the occasional rape, but this was the first death. Her body was found in a culvert. She had lost so much blood it had turned the stagnant water in the channel the color of red wine. Nolan spent a long time just looking at her lay there. His natural instinct to protect, to care, led him back to his vehicle where he fetched a sheet from the boot of his car. He covered her body and waited beside her until the paramedics arrived. The sun by then had dipped behind the Pennines, bringing with it a wind that began to lift the sheet with such regularity, Nolan convinced himself she was breathing again. But she never did. Even now, whenever he's sat outside a cafe, or restaurant, and a tablecloth lifts under the influence of a gentle breeze, he is reminded of how indelible death is on the mind. The prickling of vulnerability ran over Nolan's skin, his hands began to harvest sweat.

"Tell me you've found something, Tom. DNA from the scene, fingerprints?"

"SOCO have been down there for five days, working in twenty four hour shifts. Other than bloods from the deceased, so far all other latent prints and hair samples match Layton Slade only. You understand now that any detail concerning this other man, however small, would really help."

"You're telling me you've found nothing?"

Most of the tabloids and had been digging up the Slades' past since the news hit. It was common knowledge that Gram had learning difficulties and had been the victim of false imprisonment by Paul Keenan back in Manchester. Articles relating to the fire at the Slade home had also been regurgitated and explored nationally. The suicide note had been reprinted and Layton Slade had been given the moniker of, The Butcher, due to transferable skills gained while working on Kent Road. Though Healey had not released the Ragman as a name, it had been documented that the police were investigating a second man in connection with the abductions and murders. If Palmer was so inclined, he could spend ten minutes on the Internet and learn more about the case than Nolan could articulate in an hour. That he didn't know anything right now meant Nolan had leverage in gaining Palmer's trust.

"The woman you saw was Fiona Thompson," Nolan continued. "Layton was using a curing method on all the victims to slow down the decomposition. This is making it difficult for pathology to get an accurate time of death of each one. But we think that many of the victims came from Manchester to begin with. Some have already been identified as sex workers or vagrants. We're working closely with Greater Manchester Police to establish the rest. You'll know from your years being a cop that folk don't tend to report the homeless when they go missing. And if the sex workers were working independently, well ... let's just say that even if some were reported, once initial enquiries were done, these people wouldn't have been a high priority. The children though, that was more of a risk. It doesn't quite fit with the others. Same with Fiona Thompson. You'll read about her once you're out. Her husband was also murdered."

Nolan omitted that, save for all his internal organs and face in his refrigerator, they had yet to find the rest of Peter Thompson's body. Some details a person can do without knowing, if only to help them sleep at night.

"The precision of each victim's cuts, the evisceration of each body, they were quite remarkable, and done for a reason. Not for the sport. We believe Layton Slade had gained these skills while working as a butcher's assistant."

"Don't killers tend to choose their victims based on certain criteria?" Palmer asked. Sexual, dominance, fantasy?"

"You pick that up while researching a book?" asked Nolan.

"You're forgetting, I was a cop in a previous life."

"Play out it out then," Nolan said, encouraging him to continue his theory.

"You said most of the victims were sex workers and vagrants," Palmer continued. "They were people that could go missing quite easily without drawing too much attention. In the eyes of a believer, they're also riddled with sin. Maybe Slade was judging them. It fits with the God-like complex he projected."

Nolan mulled it over, stretching out the moment so not to discount the theory and offend Palmer.

"Maybe, but it doesn't fit."

"Why's that?"

"If Layton justified his actions because he didn't see the murders as sinful, how can he judge sin in others? And, hypothetically of course, even if sin was the only reason the victims were chosen, why go to the trouble and the risk of getting caught taking innocent children, and killing an elderly couple?"

He watched as Palmer processed this, looking to see if he could connect the dots and come up with a better working hypothesis. He was watching the cop in him resurface.

"Was Layton using his brother to get to the children?" Palmer asked.

Nolan canted his head, held his breath for a moment and released it slowly.

"That's what we believe. Detectives have been at the Slade house now for the past couple of days. Trained officers have spoken to both Gram and the mother. You can imagine how difficult it must have been to hear what Layton had done. Obviously the mother broke down, started calling us liars and all sorts of names. You can't blame her. It's not easy losing your son twice."

"Twice," asked Palmer.

"Layton Slade had faked a suicide six years ago," Nolan elaborated.

"And Gram and the mother had no idea he was still alive?"

"The mother swears she didn't. It took some time but Gram told us that Layton had been visiting him on a regular basis at their home in Stormer Hill. This isn't in the public domain yet so I can get in a lot of shit for telling you this."

Palmer nodded.

"Gram assumed he was being visited by a ghost."

"The ghost of his late brother?" Nolan asked.

"I know, but you've met Gram. He's like a child. His brother took advantage of that. Gram never told his mother or anyone at work about the ghost because he assumed no one would believe him. When Layton came around, asking about the children, Gram told him what he wanted to know. Little details you know, like, if they attended the after school club, or did their father ever pick them up. He said he didn't think any harm would have come from it. Ghosts haunt houses. They walk through walls. They don't take children."

"He didn't think any harm would have come from it?"

Nolan displayed his palms.

"In the eyes of the law he's a vulnerable witness. We have to treat him foremost as a victim. There is nothing to suggest that Gram was involved, or an accomplice to these acts. When Layton spoke with Gram about the children, he couldn't anticipate the outcome, or Layton's intentions."

"So you're ruling out aiding and abetting?" Palmer asked, incredulously.

"At the moment, all we're trying to do is find this other person. And once we do, I know I'll feel a lot better about this whole thing."

"A ghost," he whispered to himself, then chuckled, low and insincere.

"I honestly don't think for a second Gram wanted any harm to come to anyone, least of all those children."

"You said something happened, an attack on the Slade home that prompted Layton's suicide."

Nolan rubbed his neck and said, "Some local gang members were hassling Gram back in Manchester. Layton heard about it, and stepped in. Things didn't go according to plan. One of the gang tried to burn down the Slade house while Gram and his mother were sleeping. I guess Layton thought that as a long as he was alive, his mother and brother would be in danger. He faked his suicide. Did a decent job too. Made it near impossible to ID the body."

"So who's in his grave?" asked Palmer.

"We gained a warrant and exhumed the coffin a couple of days ago. We're still uncertain who's buried there, but based on all the other bodies we've found at Blackthorn, we're assuming it was a male sex worker, probably chosen because he was the same height and build as Slade."

Palmer let out a sudden and unexpected yawn.

"I'm sorry," Nolan said. "I'm keeping you."

Palmer dismissed his concern with a shake of his head.

"I'm fine, honestly. I've slept so much since the surgery my body clock is all over the place. Please, I want to try and help."

"If you're sure I'm not keeping you?"

Palmer shook his head, allowing Nolan to continue.

"I was wondering, and maybe you can just clarify this for me, but when you woke up, after being drugged, was it Layton that came to see you or the other man?"

"I told you this. It was Layton. Though I didn't know that then."

"That's right. You thought it was Gram. Is that when he spoke about being God?"

Palmer fidgeted restlessly under the covers.

"He never said he was God. It was inferred."

"Ah, right, yes. But he left you with that impression, right?"

"Yes."

"Then it must have been something he said?"

"Like I say, I can't remember the words exactly."

"No, of course. Did he mention any other names? Phrases, perhaps? Maybe a passage from the Bible?"

Nolan sensed by the way Palmer was looking at him he was getting suspicious.

"Are you going to caution me, Detective?"

Nolan let out an overstated laugh.

"Not at all. This is, how did you phrase it on the way to Hanging Lee? That's right, fact finding. I'm just trying to get the story straight in my mind, that's all. So he never quoted anything, to your recollection?"

Palmer shook his head, slowly.

"And this other man, presumably he was similar to Layton? He too justified their deaths because he didn't think he had sinned?"

Palmer allowed a silence to nuzzle in between them before replying, "I never spoke with the other man."

Nolan scratched the back of his head with his pen.

"But you remembered his accent. Presumably he spoke at some point, in your presence?"

Palmer cleared his throat.

"That's right. He spoke. Well, he said something to me."

"The exact words?" asked Nolan.

Palmer looked up briefly, returned his gaze on the detective and said, "Live with it. He said to me, live with it."

Nolan wrote the line down in his notepad and, keeping his eye on the paper asked, "And this was behind you? When he said it, I mean."

"Yes, he was behind me when he said it."

Palmer missed a beat before asking, "Have you asked Amy Taylor?"

Nolan stopped writing.

"Asked Amy what?"

"She was there," added Palmer. "I spoke with her. Maybe she saw the other man."

The rapid flicking of notepaper sounded like bird wings as Nolan searched his pocket notebook for an entry made after speaking with Crane. He had written a word down during their meeting at the pub following Crane's first interview with Palmer. Crane had said Palmer had not mentioned Amy Taylor once, which he considered odd. Crane had put it down to the fact Palmer had no idea the girl was missing, but when he mentioned Amy was in the same building, on hearing her name, Palmer appear fascinated. Palmer then went on to say they had spoken with through the connecting rooms and that he had tried to help her escape. But there something in Crane's account that made Nolan pause. It was the way Crane had described Palmer when he told him she was fine and that no harm had come to her. The word he had used to describe Palmer in that moment was *detached*. Nolan looked at that word again now and closed his notepad.

"Officers have spoken with mum and Amy. From I understand, like you, Amy only saw Layton Slade, not the other person." Nolan observed Palmer closely when he added, "She mentioned you though."

Palmer's eyes narrow as if sunlight had struck him in the face.

"I failed her," he said.

"That's not how she remembered it."

Nolan reached into the inside pocket of jacket and pulled out a small white envelope. He appraised it in his hand as if it held the secrets of the universe. Leaning over, he slid it gently onto the bedside table next to the Get Well Soon card before settling back into his seat. Palmer glanced over, and then quickly averted his gaze back to the detective.

"It's from Amy," Nolan confirmed. "She asked if I would pass it on."

Nolan expected Palmer to lean in and take the envelope, but he remained under the sheet, refusing to move his body, save to twist his head briefly to acknowledge its position.

"I'll read it later," he replied, quietly. "Thank her for me."

Nolan nodded.

"So, do the police have any theories?" asked Palmer.

"We're sandbagging. Preparing for the storm."

Nolan checked his watch and stretched out his back.

"I've kept you long enough. Besides, there are things I should be checking on back at the station."

He stood and considered extending his hand, but measured the effort it might place on Palmer's shoulder. What followed was an awkward moment where neither man seemed able to assemble the words to end the conversation warmly and so remained motionless, allowing silence to ferment. As if by chance, Palmer exercised a fleeting concern.

"How's Gram doing?" he asked.

"He doesn't fully comprehend it all. Still believes Layton is a ghost and that everything he's heard is made up. The mother said that Gram always looked up to Layton, saw him as a hero, the father they never had. I guess that's why he went along with it for so long. He just wasn't capable of understanding how evil his brother was."

Nolan tapped his fingers on the bed-mounted table and smiled warmly.

"We're doing all we can, Alex. The net is closing in."

And with that Nolan turned and made his way to the door. Before leaving he paused, and slowly twisted his body to face Palmer.

"I started one of your books," he said with a hint of reserve. "I'm not much of a reader you understand, but it's good, you know. So far."

Palmer acknowledged the compliment.

"Considering you're going be around for a while, convalescing, I was thinking, well, wondering if ..."

There was so much uneasiness in Nolan's tone that Palmer interjected.

"You want me to sign it?"

Nolan rolled his shoulder and said, "If you're well enough. I don't want to put you out."

"You wouldn't be, Tom."

"Maybe I could swing by tomorrow?"

"I'll have to check my schedule, but I'm sure I could fit you in."

The two men exchanged a mutual look of appreciation before Tom Nolan dipped his glance and ushered himself out of the room, closing the door softly.

In his car, Nolan reached into the glove compartment and retrieved a pack of Benson and Hedges. He took one out and offered a flame to its end. Cranking the window, he blew the smoke away and looked wistfully toward the main doors of the Calderdale hospital where a new mother stood rubbing her swollen belly, comforting the unborn child beneath.

How little they know of this world, he thought.

A man joined her and led her to a little red car. He opened the door, supporting her bulky frame as she lowered herself in. He did not close the door until he knew she was safe, and that the belt was fastened securely. Something in Nolan ached as he observed the man safeguarding the mother and the unborn. It began in his chest and radiated along his arms and down his spine to the ends of his toes. It was a sensation he had grown accustomed to, like the warm trickle of blood that would sometimes leave his nose. It was a sensation of loneliness.

Tom Nolan took the back roads leading away from the hospital to avoid the small villages and town that adjoined Stormer Hill. He traveled along the A road from where he could take a sharp turn toward Blackthorn Hill, but didn't. He continued until he reached the top of the moorland. Stopping on a coarse patch of gravelled land, he killed the engine. In the quietness he heard his mobile vibrating in his jacket pocket. It was DCI Healey. He contemplated not answering, allowing it to ring out so he could check the message in his own time. But the weakness in his character, the need to be distracted from his loneliness, forced him to take the call.

He cleared his throat and said, "Boss?"

"We've had word back from Paris," Healey said, his voice low, as if in a room where he didn't want others to overhear. "Erik Raine is dead. He was found this morning. Reports from the French police said witnesses saw him douse himself with petrol outside the *SACRÉ-CŒUR* in Montmartre before striking a match."

Nolan canopied his eyes with his hand.

There came a labored, weighty pause before Healey asked, "Palmer; you find anything out from him?"

"He's sticking to his story," replied Nolan. "Nothing much to add. I'll be returning to the station shortly to type up my notes. Any news on the Ragman?"

"Don't get too excited, but we found a name," he said.

Nolan's back straightened.

"I spoke with the West Riding Water Company," Healey said. "The Safety Engineering Manager confirmed that Mark Coonan had been making enquiries that day about security around Blackthorn Hill. Apparently they had an outside firm keep an eye on the place. The IT department were able to track down the computer used to generate the reports. All the computers have their own unique IP address, and each employee has their own computer. Over the past three years the same name has been linked to each of those reports. Todd Legge."

Nolan trawled his memory. He felt he had spent time with that name, waltzed it around his mind, but he couldn't remember from where.

"Before you ask, we ran it through PNC and got no positive hits. A voters check brought up only two residents in the UK with the same name, both of whom we've ruled out. I also got word this morning from the Hi-Tec Crime Unit. They were able to extract more data from Slade's laptop, more conversations. The précis given by the officer in charge was that they had found correspondence between Slade and the Ragman dating back seven years. Slade had asked the Ragman for his real name, and that same name popped up."

Nolan was still trying to remember where he had heard the name Todd Legge.

"Tom? You there?"

Nolan cleared his throat.

"Sorry, Boss."

"You can stop reading all those books about Bosch too."

"You found the connection?"

"Not me. One of the DCs spent the day researching the Brethren of the Free Spirit. They were some kind of lay Christian movement from back in the day. The short and tall of it is they used to preach some bullshit about pantheistic Christianity. God is all things and a person is as much God as Jesus Christ, or some shit."

"Alex Palmer was talking about that earlier. He believed Layton didn't see what he did as wrong because he thought he was God, and God couldn't sin."

"If you ask me, it's just a bunch of fucking nutcases using a cult as an excuse to act out their fantasies."

"How does Bosch fit into all this?" Nolan asked.

"There was some talk that he was part of this movement. All that depravity and biblical shit in his paintings, there's a theory it all stemmed from the Brethren." Healey's tone softened. "You still refusing to take leave?"

"Unsure, why?"

"I need someone to assist the Paris police with enquiries. You up for it?"

Deep resignation struck like a bell peel through Nolan's chest. His throat dried as he imagined the horrific injuries presented to him by the French authorities. He may have wanted a reprieve from all the horror connected to this case, but when it came down to it, he needed the distraction. There was no way could he spend a week or two alone in the house. The wall detailing all the missing children had been taken down, statements boxed and sealed. The place looked stark and cold now. He couldn't return to that and act normal, watching TV, dinner for one, read a fucking book. No. Nolan agreed to go to anywhere Healey wanted him too, so long as it wasn't home. He ended the call shortly after getting instructions from Healey concerning contacts in the Paris police department. In the distance he saw a fire burning on the moorland, which he watched with vague curiosity. Pale smoke ascended toward the clouds, fashioning a link between earth and the heavens. As he pondered on all that had happened in the four years since Lucy Guffey went missing, Tom Nolan arrived at a simple and inconsequential observation; the heather and course grass would need to be bone dry for the moorland to burn. He looked up to the sky and saw a scattering of clouds against a wonderful blue. He then realized it had finally stopped raining in Stormer Hill.

CHAPTER 43

WEDNESDAY

Alex Palmer's phone buzzed again. He glanced over and saw Juliet's name on the display. He considered picking it up for no reason but to hear a familiar voice. He'd have to talk to her at some point and explain what had happened, maybe counter her guilt for suggesting he visit Stormer Hill by saying he got a bestseller out of the experience. The news was all over the media and his fans would want a statement. He imagined press invasions and interview requests and sighed heavily. If he could channel things through Juliet, it wouldn't be so bad. She could say he was recovering and needed his rest. Respect his privacy, all that kind of bullshit. He was about to accept the call when the door opened. A nurse with plum colored hair poked her head in and smiled.

"Your visitor gone?" she asked.

Palmer vaguely recalled her face from the previous day. She was young, probably in her early twenties. She had a wholesome look about her that a few days ago he would have taken advantage of.

"Detective Nolan," he replied, cotton-mouthed. "Yeah, he's gone."

Palmer tried to hoist himself up so he was more presentable.

"Can you help me get out of this robe?" asked her. "I'm roasting."

The nurse walked over and lifted the bed sheet. Palmer swung his legs off the side of the bed, and careful not to aggravate the wound, the nurse began to unfasten the robe. He was wearing a hospital gown underneath, split down the back and cut below the knee.

"That's impressive," she said. She was leaning over his shoulder, looking at his back. "I was thinking of getting one myself."

She moved into palmer's eye line. He smelt coffee on her breath and saw the lilac shadowing her eyes born of long hours. She pointed to her hip.

"A heart, about here."

"For your boyfriend," he asked, smiling.

She laughed, playfully.

"No, I'm not seeing anyone."

Their eyes lingered on each other for a moment before she gazed at her pumps, cheeks blushing. When she looked up, all the coyness of a child bloomed across her face.

"Does it hurt?" she asked, looking at his arms.

Palmer gazed momentarily at the inked angels on his arms, and recalled the tree baring fruit of temptation, the robed Jesus extracting Eve from Adam's side, all the biblical renders that stretched over every inch of his body, save for his neck and face.

"Not as much as love," he replied.

The nurse smiled.

"I need to get your meds. You okay for a minute?" she asked.

Palmer nodded, his eyes never breaking from her stare. The nurse turned and made her way out of the door. Her shape was long, pinched above her pelvis. Palmer could lift her quite easily, just like a little girl. He continued to measure every part of her, from her back to her legs, and inside something stirred, something evil.

ACKNOWLEDGEMENT

Bad People went through various incarnations before becoming the book you've just read. Had it not been for two people in particular, that journey through Stormer Hill would have been a more turbulent one. An early draft titled, Hell's Gateway, and penned then under the alias Richard Nolan (the surname to which I kept and tendered to the detective in the story) was given a more than favorable critique by author Nik Korpon. For Nik's patience, diligence, and ability to refrain from being brutally wounding, I am eternally grateful. The same can be said of Sandra Ruttan who read a later version, then titled, Bad Seeds. Her eye for detail and storytelling was a real tonic. In truth, without either Nik or Sandra's guidance in highlighting each narrative faux pas and grammatical speedbump, this novel would not be what it is today. I'd also like to give thanks to Rachel Edwards for being my sounding board, advisor, and providing me with the confidence to build that "wall". To Paul Carroll, I'm indebted for giving life to the detail, as well as to my wife who didn't laugh when I said I was going to write a thriller. Finally, I'd like to thank you the reader, whoever you are. Without your time and kindness, none of this is worth it.

You are the good people.

ABOUT THE AUTHOR

Craig Wallwork is the three times nominated Pushcart Prize author of the novels, The Sound of Loneliness, To Die Upon a Kiss, and the short story collections, Quintessence of Dust, and Gory Hole. His work has appeared in many magazines and journals in both the U.K. and U.S. He lives in England with his wife and two children.

Made in the USA
San Bernardino, CA
11 January 2020

63048733R00163